"Are you coming on to me, McKennon?"

"Yes." He pressed a soft kiss to her forehead.

Frankie lifted her head to reply. He kissed her lips. A soft tender kiss, the barest press of flesh to flesh.

His answer pleased her, but deepened her guilt. With her sister in danger she could afford herself no pleasure. "Bad timing."

"In more ways than you know." He pressed a finger to her chin and urged her to look at him. Feeling suddenly shy and strangely vulnerable, she resisted. "When we get your sister back, I'd like to take you to dinner."

She cracked a smile. "What if I said you're not my type?"

Chuckling, he curled his hand around the back of her head and drew her forehead-to-forehead with him. His embrace accomplished what reason could not. Hope feathered upward from deep in her belly.

"I'd like to get to know you better." He kissed her again.

She couldn't have resisted him if she'd tried. She explored the texture of his lips and tasted the sweetness of his mouth.

"Is it a date?" he asked.

She sensed in him the power to make her believe in loyalty and goodness again. "Sure," she whispered. "It's a date."

Dear Reader,

Sexy and sweet, tough and tender. These are the men of ELK RIVER, COLORADO. The men who still stand tall and know how to treat a woman. The men whom Sheryl Lynn writes about with emotion and passion in her new duet.

You may remember the legendary Duke family of Colorado, whom Sheryl first introduced in a duet called HONEYMOON HIDEAWAY a few years back. These titles—#424 *The Case of the Vanished Groom* and #425 *The Case of the Bad Luck Fiancé*—are still available. Send $3.99 ($4.50 CAN.) for each title ordered, plus $.75 shipping and handling ($1.00 CAN.) to Harlequin Reader Service: 3010 Walden Av., Buffalo, NY 144269, or P.O. Box 609, Fort Erie, Ontario L2A 5X3

And be sure to be on hand next month when ELK RIVER, COLORADO continues with *Undercover Fiancé*.

Happy Reading!

Debra Matteucci

Senior Editor & Editorial Coordinator
Harlequin Books
300 East 42nd Street
New York, NY 10017

The Bodyguard
Sheryl Lynn

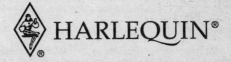

HARLEQUIN®

TORONTO • NEW YORK • LONDON
AMSTERDAM • PARIS • SYDNEY • HAMBURG
STOCKHOLM • ATHENS • TOKYO • MILAN • MADRID
PRAGUE • WARSAW • BUDAPEST • AUCKLAND

To my grandmothers, Evelyn Roberts and Alma Hawk,
gifted storytellers who inspire me to dream.
Love you, ladies.

ISBN 0-373-22514-8

THE BODYGUARD

Copyright © 1999 by Jaye W. Manus

This edition published by arrangement with Harlequin Books S.A.

® and TM are trademarks of the publisher. Trademarks indicated with
® are registered in the United States Patent and Trademark Office, the
Canadian Trade Marks Office and in other countries.

Look us up on-line at: http://www.romance.net

Printed in U.S.A.

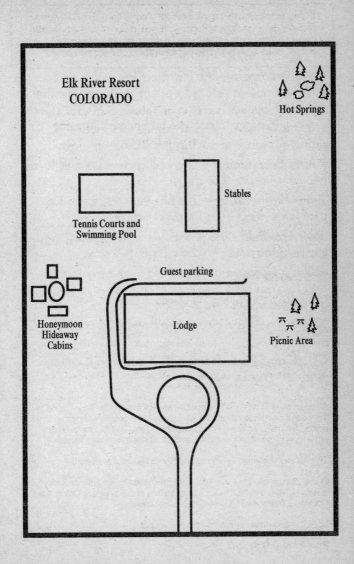

CAST OF CHARACTERS

Frankie Forrest—She'll protect her baby sister even if it means going to prison or forsaking the man she loves.

J. T. McKennon—A bodyguard torn between doing his job and saving the woman he loves.

Penny Bannerman—She's all grown up and loves her new husband to death.

Julius Bannerman—This playboy causes more problems dead than he ever did alive.

Max Caulfield—He wants his wife's money, and too bad for anyone who gets in his way.

Belinda Bannerman Caulfield—Julius is her boy, and heaven help any woman foolish enough to get between her and her son.

Bo Moran—He's about to make the score of his life.

Chuck and Paul Cashorali—Bumbling brothers who are crooks without a clue.

Chapter One

"Stop the wedding!"

Frankie Forrest's cry echoed through the thin mountain air and towering pines. A blue jay screamed in raucous reply. As Frankie slammed the car door and lunged toward the chapel, she stepped on a patch of ice. Feeling herself sliding, she shifted her weight, overcompensated, lost her balance and fell onto her right knee. Her teeth clacked, jarring her skull.

Pain jangled from kneecap to hip. Stars burst before her eyes. Arms outspread, her back at an awkward angle, she lifted her face to heaven.

A very bad sign, she thought in dour superstition. Dark forces conspired to keep her away from her sister.

Wary now, she got to her feet. She gingerly tested her right leg. Her knee throbbed, but it bent the way it should and she could walk.

A long, white limousine idled in the parking lot. The exhaust formed crawling clouds. The driver most likely kept the interior warm for the bride and groom. Frankie shivered. It had been a mild forty degrees when she left her apartment in Colorado Springs, but here, at an altitude of eight thousand feet, the temperature hovered in the low twenties. She wore a fleecy sweatshirt, but the cold pierced the thick cotton and pricked her flesh. Her blue jeans might as well have been made of nylon net—already her thighs were tingling. She glanced toward the chapel. Its roof and spire were visible through the trees. She jammed a key into the trunk lock and gave it a hard twist. The trunk snapped open. She grabbed her parka and shoved her arms into the puffy sleeves.

Her sister hated this parka and urged Frankie every year to buy a new coat. Frankie had owned it since high school and hadn't found another that felt as good. Its age showed in faded blue nylon, permanent stains and numerous small tears. She had repaired the big rips, but used whatever thread was handy, so clumsy stitches in black, white, red and green marred the ragged fabric. Penny called it the Frankenstein coat.

She noticed logos printed on the driver's-side doors of two vehicles in the parking lot. A blue circle with a bugling bull elk, its rack of antlers overlapping the circle perimeter—Elk River Resort.

"Traitors," she growled. She'd learned about the wedding only a few hours ago. A terse, anonymous voice on her answering machine had said, "Penny is marrying Julius at Elk River Resort today. Are you going to let it happen?" She'd be damned if she would let it happen.

She limped up the path to Sweet Pines Chapel. With each step her hurt and anger swelled. Penny knew exactly how Frankie felt about Julius and his family, and Penny knew why. Despite all her promises—*her lies!*—the brat had gone behind Frankie's back and married that perverted loser anyway.

As she neared the chapel, she grudgingly admitted that winter was a good time to hold a wedding. She'd been to this chapel twice before, once for her cousin Ross Duke's wedding and then again for her cousin Megan's. Those weddings had taken place in the summertime when wildflowers popped through the forest floor, and the scrub oaks and aspens were bright green with leaves. Snow, however, turned the forest into a magical place, a study in charcoal with blacks, whites and grays brushed by green and framed by a porcelain sky.

Magical, that is, if this were a wedding that should take place. Which it wasn't. If Frankie had any say in the matter, it wouldn't.

A man stood on the chapel stoop. He wore a black cashmere greatcoat over a black suit. Black wraparound sunglasses shaded his eyes. Black hair glinted in the sun. She recognized J.T. McKennon and stopped dead in her tracks.

McKennon's presence meant Max Caulfield attended the wedding. An image of her ex-fiancé's smirking face swam before her vision, and her calves itched with the urge to run. Torn between saving her sister or saving her dignity, she hunched inside the parka.

McKennon nodded. A slight gesture, noticeable only because she was so intently staring at him.

Determined that not even Max Caulfield could stop her, she continued up the path. McKennon stepped to the center of the chapel's double doors. At the base of the steps she waited for him to open the door and welcome her inside. He stood as rigidly as a solider guarding a post.

"Move over, McKennon," she ordered. "I'm stopping this charade."

Swarthy and unsmiling, McKennon looked like a mob enforcer. Two years ago, when she'd first met him, she'd dismissed him as the tall, dark and stupid type. *Tall and dark* fit, but it hadn't taken long to figure out he was in no way a stupid man. He had an engineering degree and was an expert in electronic security. He'd served with valor in the marines and for a while had operated his own martial arts studio. He was an expert marksman with firearms ranging from pistols to grenade launchers.

He possessed a dry sense of humor and an oddly appealing detachment from the world, as if he were an alien observing the natives. Frankie used to marvel over his cool head and objective world view—his mild temperament was so very different from her own hot-headed impulsiveness. Nothing rattled McKennon.

It looked as if that much hadn't changed in the past six months. "I said, move, McKennon."

"I can't do that, Miss Forrest."

She huffed. She kicked a chunk of snow. "You're guarding the door? Who do you think you are?"

His aristocratic mouth thinned. "I have my orders. Nobody goes in."

"She's my sister! I have a right—"

"Especially you." He folded his arms over his chest.

McKennon's sunglasses reflected her angry image. From far away a jay screeched a mocking note. Frankie clenched her teeth to keep them from chattering. Her jaws ached. The corners of her eyes watered, and her cheeks felt brittle. She strained to hear what was happening inside the chapel. She couldn't hear any music—another bad sign.

"Come on," she pleaded. "We're friends. You know me." As soon as the words emerged she felt stupid. Of course he knew her, since they'd worked together for almost two years, but they were not friends. He still worked for Max, and Max had dumped her like yesterday's garbage, which McKennon had witnessed in all its humiliating glory. They would never be friends.

Embarrassment settled like a lump of dough in her throat. Countless times she'd replayed The Big Dump in her head, trying to figure out what had gone wrong. She'd come to the conclusion that Max had insisted McKennon stay in the room because Max enjoyed making her crawl in front of an audience.

She climbed another step. She stood five feet, ten inches tall. Few men physically intimidated her. Unmoved, McKennon gazed down at her. She sized him up. He had five inches and at least sixty pounds advantage, plus, she'd seen him in action at the gym.

She lifted her chin in an attempt to look down her nose at him. "I want to speak with Max right now."

"Mr. Caulfield isn't here."

One of Max's biggest ego trips lay in having his very own, personal, trained ape following him wherever he went. McKennon's quietly deadly presence made Max feel like a big shot. In dark moments Frankie imagined McKennon accompanying Max to the toilet, holding the newspaper for the boss while Max did his business.

"You're lying. I know he's in there."

"No, he's not."

His calm assurance irritated her tattered nerves. "If Max isn't here, why are you here?" She paused, but received no response. "Have a heart. You know what Julius is like. Penny can't marry him. He'll ruin her life."

"I have my orders, Miss Forrest."

His smooth baritone held a faintly lyrical hint of a Southern accent. Frankie imagined she heard a note of distaste. Perhaps he despised Max's stepson, Julius, as much as she did.

Which didn't matter, since he wasn't moving. She backed off the steps and plunged her icy hands into the parka's deep pockets. She peered suspiciously at his face and wished he'd take off the sunglasses. She didn't believe him about Max not being here. Yet, it made no sense for McKennon to lie about something so obvious. "Did you screw up, and baby-sitting is your punishment?"

The taunt failed to move him.

She tossed him a glare of pure disgust and went in search of another entrance to the chapel. The tiny building, built of logs and stone, contained a native-stone apse and a double row of pine pews. She walked completely around the building, but the stained-glass windows were too high off the ground for her to see through or even to pound on. She debated throwing rocks at the windows to catch the attention of the people inside, but the windows were handcrafted antiques, and if she broke one, she'd never be able to replace it. The door was her only hope.

McKennon watched her stomp her feet to clear snow off

her boots and jeans. Goon, she thought hatefully. Nothing but a hound, following orders.

Then a solution occurred to her. She filled her lungs with winter air and let rip with her loudest, most blood-curdling scream.

McKennon jumped like a burned cat. "Stop that!"

"Help!" she hollered. "Rape! Fire! Murderers! Help! Help!"

McKennon bounded down the steps. His speed startled her. Men his size rarely moved so fast. She darted away and screeched loud enough to bring down the heavens. McKennon lunged for her left arm; she danced to the right. Too late, she recognized a feint. He snatched her right wrist in an iron grip.

"Ra-a-a-ape—"

He twisted her against his solid body and slammed a gloved hand over her mouth. His chest heaved against her back. "You're acting outrageously, Miss Forrest. Stop it."

She called him every filthy name she knew, but his hand effectively muffled the words. The leather glove tasted unpleasantly metallic. She slammed a foot down, aiming for his instep, but he anticipated the move and she struck gravel. The arm around her chest could well have been carved from oak. He practically lifted her off the ground. She fought to regulate her breathing. No easy task considering that the cold had stuffed up her nose. She snuffled desperately and hated him even more.

"I have orders. No one interrupts the wedding. Not even you. Do I need to contact the police?"

She mouthed murderous threats against the leather glove. She squirmed, attempting to slip from beneath his arm, but he held her tighter, crunching her rib cage.

A commanding voice rang from the chapel door. "What is the meaning of this?" Her uncle, Colonel Horace Duke, decked out in a black tuxedo, his silver hair shining, glared at the scene below. "Francine? Is that you? Mr. Mc-

Kennon, unhand my niece at once.'' The Colonel closed the door firmly behind him.

As soon as McKennon removed his hand from her mouth Frankie yelled, "You've got a lot of explaining to do, Colonel! But first, stop the wedding!" She managed to wriggle one arm free and rammed her elbow into McKennon's gut. His surprised *woof* gave her a small measure of satisfaction. She sprang away from him, whirled and put up her fists. "I'll get you for that, you big bully."

He tugged his lapels and used a knuckle to slide his sunglasses higher on his nose.

The Colonel marched down the steps. "What are you doing here, Francine? The latest report showed you deployed to Europe."

"Europe?" That gave her pause. The farthest she'd ever traveled had been camping trips to Arizona, Utah and New Mexico. "What would I be doing in Europe? Oh, never mind. Let me into the chapel. I've got to stop the ceremony."

The Colonel placed a hand on her arm. "They're speaking their final vows. You can't interrupt."

Taking on McKennon was one thing, but the Colonel, her late mother's brother, was another matter altogether.

"If Penny said I was in Europe, she lied. I can't believe she roped you in. Let me inside the chapel. Then I'll explain everything." She beseeched him with her eyes.

Organ music filled the still, mountain air, the bass tones rumbling through the heavy doors. Frankie groaned and covered her eyes with a hand. When the colonel took her arm and hustled her away from the steps, she made no protest.

Penny and Julius, legally wed—her worst nightmare had just come true.

The chapel doors were flung wide. Seconds later, a bride and groom appeared. Frankie took in the bridal gown, yards and yards of creamy silk encrusted with glittering crystals and gleaming pearls. A headdress rose from the bride's pale hair like a frothy crown trailed by an endless swath of pearl-dotted tulle. For a disconcerting moment Frankie felt she'd made a horrible mistake. No way could Penny have come up with a dress like that on such short notice. But no, that was Penny, looking radiant. She seemed to glow.

Frankie felt certain the top of her head was about to blow off.

Penny's smile switched off like a blown lightbulb. Next to her, slick as an oil spill, Julius Bannerman clutched his bride's elbow. He smiled greasily at Frankie.

Frankie knew McKennon always carried a sidearm, and wondered if she could get it away from him. Spending the rest of her life in prison seemed a paltry price to pay in order to rid the world of Julius Bannerman.

Behind the bride and groom, the Duke family gathered. Aunt Elise and her children, Janine, Kara and Ross and his wife, Dawn, were dressed in full finery, a further indication that this wedding had been no mere impulse. The Dukes— *traitors all!*—had helped Penny.

"I do not believe this," she said, each word clipped.

Aunt Elise hurried to the fore. Arms outstretched, she skipped down the steps toward Frankie.

"Francine, dear! I am so glad you were able to return home from Europe. Penny said—"

Frankie threw up her hands, backing away from her aunt. "I never went to Europe. I can barely afford the gas to get up here." Unable to take her eyes off her sister, she shoved her fists in her pockets.

"What diff does it make, now?" Julius said. "We're sister and brother. Isn't that peachy? Welcome to the family, Frankie darling." Full of false cheer, each note rasped across Frankie's nerves like sandpaper. Julius's Adam's apple bobbed in a convulsive swallow. "Aren't you happy for us? Now that you're here, we can all celebrate in proper good form, what hey?"

Penny snuggled closer to her new husband. Her face had lost what little color it possessed, but her eyes glinted with pure rebellion. "Go away, Frankie. I'm married and there's nothing you can do about it. Stop trying to ruin my life."

The words struck with the force of a punch. Frankie opened her mouth, but air refused to move past her throat. For the past eleven years she'd sacrificed everything for Penny. Loved her, mothered her and nurtured her. Now Penny accused her of trying to ruin her?

The Colonel reached for Frankie's arm. She twisted out of his reach. Disgusted and heartsick, she trudged toward the parking lot. She heard Penny say, "Let her go, Aunt Elise! I don't want her wrecking my wedding day." The words stung like an arrow piercing her back.

"Frankie!"

At the sound of her cousin's voice, she stopped and turned. "How could you do this to me, Ross? How could all of you do it?"

Ross Duke placed a hand on her shoulder. His brow and mouth twisted with confusion. She hadn't seen him since his sister's wedding last summer. He was the hell-raiser of the Duke clan—or had been up until the day he'd married Dawn. He'd always been her favorite cousin, but at the moment she wanted to punch out his lights.

"What's going on? Penny said you were in Europe and couldn't get back in time." He huffed, exhaling a long, white cloud. "You're opposed to the wedding, I take it."

"I can't believe that little brat sneaked around behind my back like this." In frustration, she shoved at his shoulder. "I can't believe your mom and dad went along with it! She's only nineteen."

He shrugged, showing his palms. "She's an adult. Besides, Julius seems okay. He's kind of a wimp, but he's harmless enough."

Frankie wanted to howl. "You, of all people, should be able to see right through him." She held up a hand and ticked off a finger. "One, he's forty-three years old. He's old enough to be her father." She ticked off a second finger. "Two, he's been married three, five, maybe six times already. Not one of those marriages lasted more than a year.'' She shoved at his shoulder again. ''He's a stinking drunk and probably does drugs, and God only knows what kind of diseases he's picked up from all the women he runs around with.''

Frankie clamped her mouth shut before she spilled the part about how Max had dumped her so he could marry Julius's mother. The only redeeming factor of the entire affair was that she hadn't told the Dukes about her engagement to Max. She was in no mood now to rehash the nasty details.

Ross raised an eyebrow. ''Oh.''

''Didn't it give you a clue when Penny said I couldn't make the wedding? God, Ross, I've devoted my whole life to her. I'm working my butt off to keep her in college. If I thought for one second she was making a good marriage, a herd of polar bears couldn't keep me away.''

''Oh.'' He looked as guilt-stricken as a puppy caught chewing shoes.

She idly kicked clots of snow. ''She told me, she *promised* me she wouldn't see him anymore. But she dropped out of college and didn't even tell me. She's been living with him.''

''I—we didn't know. I only learned about the wedding last week.''

She glanced at the limo, which still idled on the other side of the parking lot. ''She's been planning this a lot longer than a week.''

''What can I say?''

Unable to bear looking at him one more second, she hurried to her car. Once inside, with the door locked, she rested her face against the steering wheel.

''Damn you, Penny,'' she muttered. Their mother had wrested a deathbed promise from her eldest child: take care of Penny. She'd prevailed against the social-services bureaucrats who had stated that since she was only nineteen years old she couldn't handle the guardianship of an eight-

year-old. She'd gone to war and won, when her father's
ne'er-do-well relatives had learned Virginia Forrest had left
a sizable insurance policy for the care and education of her
daughters. She'd given up her dreams of attending medical
school. She'd given up the university and a social life in
order to mother Penny full-time.

She drew in several long, soothing breaths then fished
her car keys from her pocket. She'd given it her best shot,
tried to save Penny from making a horrible mistake, and in
gratitude received a kick in the teeth. She fumbled with the
keys, but her fingers were stiff from the cold. She dropped
the keys on her lap and slammed the heels of both hands
against the steering wheel.

Leave, she told herself. Drive away, forget this mess and
wait a few weeks until Penny came crawling in search of
forgiveness. She kept envisioning that look on Penny's
face, kept hearing the accusation that Frankie tried to ruin
her life. She rested her face against the wheel again.

Irony tweaked her. Because of Penny, she'd gone to
work for Max Caulfield. He owned the largest private security firm in the state of Colorado. He'd offered health
insurance and flexible hours—benefits her age, experience
and schooling hadn't warranted. She'd started work as a
researcher and gofer, which meant she could do some of
her work at home so she could be there when Penny got
out of school. Max had taken her under his wing, praising
her intelligence and affinity for details. When graphology
became popular as a useful tool in hiring employees, he'd
paid for Frankie's education in the field. To her delight she
discovered that handwriting analysis was something she
was good at. She'd made a lot of money for Max by helping
his clients weed out dishonest employees.

In her wildest dreams Frankie had never thought she'd
fall for her boss—or that he'd fall for her. Her worst night-
mares had failed to prepare her for the Bannermans. Belinda and Julius, mother and son, two of the most greedy,
self-serving people on earth. Max had fallen in love with

Belinda's vast wealth. Julius had taken one look at Penny and put her on his list of amusing little conquests.

Her life had been in the toilet ever since.

She opened one eye and peered at the dashboard clock. If she hurried, she'd make it to work on time.

Soft tapping on the window startled her. She jerked up her head. McKennon had removed the sunglasses.

She rolled down the window. He had unusual eyes, like emeralds shot with gold—bright and piercing against his dark face. Frankie couldn't recall ever seeing him look so concerned. Her throat choked up.

"My apologies, Miss Forrest. It wasn't my intention to get rough with you. But I had my orders."

"Stick your orders where the sun doesn't shine. I don't need your apology." She sniffed and groped through the mess on the front seat for a tissue. "Or your pity."

A hank of thick hair had fallen over his forehead, softening somewhat the hard angles of his face. His sympathy embarrassed her. She'd never been particularly nice to him. When they worked together she'd been a tad jealous of his close relationship to Max. Even more, she hadn't liked the effect he had on her. Any man who, through simple actions such as holding a door or offering a cup of coffee, could make her insides turn mushy had to have something seriously wrong with him. She hated the way he invaded her more sensuous dreams. She was a one-man woman and wasn't about to let a hulking mercenary turn her head. Sarcasm and thinly veiled insults had always kept him at bay before.

At the moment all she could do was miserably return his gaze and wish somebody, even McKennon, would hold her and assure her that everything would be all right.

"Want to talk?" he asked.

His compassion annoyed her. He had no right to feel sorry for her. He certainly had no right trying to make her feel better.

"Julius is your brother-in-law now. If you're going to

have a relationship with Penny you need to be polite to him.''

She fumbled the key into the ignition. ''Thank you very much for the advice, McKennon. Now if you'll excuse me, I need to go home.''

He laid a gloved hand on her parka sleeve. ''You'll lose her.''

Damn him to hell and back for being right. Penny was as prideful as Frankie. ''She could have at least finished college.''

''She has to make her own mistakes.''

In the rearview mirror she glimpsed approaching figures. Her cousins walked in a knot, all of them looking at Frankie's car. She loved her cousins, but at the moment she wished a spaceship would swoop down and abduct the lot of them. She shoved McKennon's hand away and exited the car. She searched the path for any sign of Penny.

Janine Duke took command, as usual. She gave Frankie a perfunctory hug, then stepped back. Garbed in a dark blue silk suit with cartouche trim, Janine looked like a fashion photographer's dream. All her cousins looked great, Kara and Ross, Dawn, too, all were dressed like movie stars. Frankie was not merely an interloper, she was an oversized, lunkish mess wearing ragged jeans and the Frankenstein coat. She must look as wild as she felt.

She glanced surreptitiously at McKennon. He'd put back on the sunglasses and his strong-as-steel facade. She guessed he was thinking Frankie was the family nut. The family loser.

''Penny won't leave the chapel as long as you're here,'' Janine said.

''Why am I not surprised?'' She turned back to the car. ''I have to go to work, anyway.''

Ross slid an arm around his wife's waist. He and Dawn exchanged knowing glances. ''If you leave now, you and Penny will have a harder time patching things up. Come to the lodge. We'll get Penny calmed down. You two can talk.''

She needed to leave. She wanted to leave so she could hide and lick her wounds in peace. She thought about how she needed to go to work, and her cat was probably starving by now, so he'd be looking for a few books to shred in order to vent his frustration. She had a video to return. Like McKennon said, Penny needed to make her own mistakes. ''None of you understands what's going on here.''

''Try us, Frankie.'' Kara, the youngest of the siblings, stepped to the fore. She took Frankie's cold hand and rubbed it briskly between hers. ''Why is Penny so angry with you?''

Startled, Frankie caught her breath. Angry? Penny had no reason in the world to be angry with anyone, much less with Frankie. Yet…she'd seen the look in Penny's eyes as she stood on the chapel stoop. There had been a strange hardness in the girl's expression, a glint of something deep and dark and hurtful.

''She has no reason to be angry,'' Frankie said hotly. ''She knows I'd do anything for her.''

Kara shrugged. ''Okay, maybe she isn't angry. Maybe she's just embarrassed. You know, about—''

''She *should* be embarrassed. Julius is old enough to be her father.'' Frankie didn't like the way her cousins shared knowing glances. ''What? You all know something. What is it?''

Silence hung heavily over the parking lot. The idling engine of the limousine began to sound very loud, like a rumble of distant thunder, and the stench of exhaust clashed with the clear mountain air. Frankie searched their faces one by one. Ross averted his gaze. Dawn stared at the toes of her pumps. Janine twirled a strand of her lustrous hair around her fingers. Kara clamped her arms over her bosom and shivered. McKennon appeared to meditate upon the distant mountains.

"Sheesh," Kara said. "Penny didn't—"

"Shut up," Janine interrupted. "Penny will tell her."

"She should have told her already." Kara reached again for Frankie's hands. "She's pregnant."

Chapter Two

Frankie wanted to leave more than ever. She wanted to go home and forget she even had a sister. She really, really wanted to snatch Penny by the throat and shake some sense into her fluffy blond head. She decided to talk to Penny. She'd be reasonable, she wouldn't yell, but she'd let the girl know exactly where she stood: Penny could have Julius or she could have Frankie, but not both. Then she would leave.

She allowed Ross to drive her to the resort lodge. He guided her to the family's private dining room and fetched a carafe of hot coffee. The coffee chased away some of the chill. She wrapped both hands around the mug to warm them. Her face felt crackly, as if it might break if she moved too fast. She lifted her gaze to Ross.

"She isn't pregnant. No way. She's too smart." Frankie knew the pregnancy had to be a lie. Penny probably used it as an excuse for a hasty wedding.

Ross sat at the table and folded his hands atop the surface. The pity in his gray eyes scratched her bones.

"She has plans," she insisted. "She's going to travel the world."

"Stuff happens, plans change. You girls need to talk."

Snorting in disgust, Frankie turned her glum gaze on the trophy wall that chronicled her uncle's long and distinguished military career. She wondered again how he and his family could have betrayed her like this. A glance at a wall clock showed that even if she left now, she'd be late for work. "Is there a phone I can use?"

He brought her a cordless telephone, then moved to the other end of the table to give her some privacy. She dialed the number of her neighbor. Sally answered with a syrupy hello.

"This is Frankie," she said. "Can I ask you a big favor?"

"Are you okay? You sound funny."

"I'm fine." Sally's concern lifted her spirits somewhat. They'd met on the day Frankie moved into her apartment and had been good friends ever since. Wait until Sally got an earful of this debacle. "I've got a…situation. I'll tell you all about it later. Can you feed Cat?"

Sally didn't answer right away. Frankie groaned inwardly. The cat, whom she called Cat, had shown up a few months ago and stayed. He was neither pretty nor sweet tempered, and he had a bad habit of shredding her books, magazines and newspapers when he lost his temper. He also attacked people on occasion. Frankie let him stay because he seemed like the one creature in the universe whose life was in worse shape than hers.

"Please," Frankie said. "I wouldn't ask if I didn't have to."

"Oh, all right. I'll take an oven mitt for protection." She sighed dramatically, then laughed. "That animal belongs in a zoo, you know. When will you be back?"

"Very late tonight. I owe you one, girlfriend."

"You owe me two."

After she finished that call, she dialed another number. She hoped anyone but Bob answered. A scratchy, petulant voice answered the phone: "Martha's Pie House, may I help you?"

"Hi, Bob," she said, "it's Frankie." She waited a beat, then added, "I can't come in to work tonight. I have an emergency."

"What do you mean you can't come in? You know I'm shorthanded."

Frankie dropped her face onto her hand. Bob ruled the pancake house as if being assistant manager made him emperor. The little twit. "It's an emergency. Call Julie."

"I know who to call. It's my job to know. I keep the schedules, you know." Papers rustled. "You're working Saturday, then."

"Fine." She noticed he didn't ask about the nature of her emergency.

"From now on I need at least twenty-four hours notice."

"I'll plan more carefully for my emergencies, Bob." She hung up and placed the telephone on the table.

"Everything okay?" Ross asked. Questions lurked in his eyes.

Frankie hadn't told the Dukes about her recent situation. Since Penny was acting so sneaky and self-absorbed, it was doubtful she had told them, either. Guilt crept through her. Ever since Max had dumped her, she'd shut out her family. Ross and Dawn lived in Colorado Springs, perhaps twenty minutes from Frankie's apartment. Embarrassment and pride had prevented her from running to them with her tales of woe.

"I don't work for Max Caulfield anymore," she said.

Ross cocked his head and assumed an expression that invited confidences. He'd always been easy to talk to.

Explanations caused a traffic jam of words in her throat. Even after six months it hurt to talk about Max. "Things got intense," she finally said. "I'm waiting tables until I can figure out how to market myself as a freelance graphologist."

"Self-employment is the best."

Grateful he didn't probe too deeply, she nodded.

"Julius is related to Caulfield."

His statement made her wince. She stared at her hands. The redness had faded, leaving them looking paper-white against the chestnut hue of the tabletop. "Max married Julius's mother. She's rich.'' She wished she'd never voiced Max's name.

''Does that have something to do with you disliking Julius?''

She winced again. Ross knew. Not everything, but he suspected something heavy lurked beneath the surface. ''Penny knows my reasons. We settled all this months ago.''

''Apparently not.'' He topped off his coffee mug and offered her the carafe. ''Maybe you kept her on too short a leash, Cuz.''

''Not short enough.'' She waved away the offer of more coffee. *''Apparently.''*

''You're a lot like the Colonel, Frankie.''

She knew Ross didn't mean the comparison as a compliment. She scowled into the steam rising from the mug. ''Contrary to what that brat says, I am not trying to ruin her life. Or run it for that matter. But she has no business getting married at her age.''

Elise Duke's high heels clicked softly on the polished wood floor. ''How are you, dear?''

Frankie shot a glare at Ross to let him know she didn't appreciate his insinuation that she was a control freak like his father. ''Where's Penny?'' She pushed away from the table, starting to rise.

Elise placed a gentle hand on Frankie's shoulder. ''It might be best if you kept your distance. She'll speak to you tomorrow.''

Somehow, Frankie felt no surprise. Her entire chest ached as if she'd been walked on by an elephant. She slumped on the chair and sipped from the coffee mug.

''Penny and Julius are spending the week in the Honeymoon Hideaway.'' Elise settled on the chair next to Frankie. Despite four grown children she looked youthful, slim and beautiful. Her serene demeanor had a calming influence. Her soft hand touching Frankie's arm chased some of the cold from Frankie's soul. ''Stay the night with us, dear. We can have a nice visit. I haven't seen you in far too long. Tomorrow, you and Penny can talk.''

She didn't want to stay. She wanted to go home to her nasty old cat and sulk in peace. ''Is she really pregnant, Aunt Elise?''

Elise shrugged delicately and flashed a wan smile at her son. ''The child shall have two parents.''

Frankie groaned. ''You don't get it. None of you gets it. If she's really pregnant then she's in big trouble.''

''Now, Francine, aren't you being a wee bit melodramatic?''

''What do you know about Julius? Did Penny tell you he's been married before?''

''Well, no. But divorce isn't exactly shameful—''

''It is in his case. He's been married several times and he has kids. He doesn't have anything to do with any of them. It's all because of his mother. She won't let anybody get between her and her baby boy.''

Ross cleared his throat. His eyebrows raised in a skeptical quirk. ''Julius is old enough to make his own decisions.''

''He's weak. His mother isn't. She's rich, spoiled and selfish. Julius always does exactly what she says. If she can't buy off his wives, she scares them off.''

''Come on.'' Ross rolled a hand as if urging her to get to the punch line. ''She can't be that bad.''

''She's worse,'' Frankie insisted. ''Julius is weak, but Belinda is twisted. She'll eat Penny alive.''

''CHUCKIE?'' Paul's voice strained in the darkness. ''I can't see nothing.''

Chuck paused with his shoulder pressed against the rough bark of a tree. He panted like a racehorse and his lungs ached. The trail where they'd parked the car was less than twenty feet away, but he felt as if he'd run a marathon. The lights of Elk River Lodge were visible through the trees. Still, on this moonless winter night, a blank world seemed to stretch away into eternity. The darkness squeezed him. An unconscious shudder rippled down his spine. What the hell was he doing?

He focused a flashlight in Paul's direction. The thin beam flashed over tree trunks and made the snow glitter like diamond dust. He found Paul's face. Eyes bulging like boiled eggs, mouth wide-open, nostrils flared, the kid looked as scared as he sounded.

"Easiest ten grand you'll ever make," Bo Moran had assured him.

The job sounded easy the way Bo explained it. That was before, in the warmth of the bar while he ate big, greasy cheeseburgers and the jukebox played old Eagles songs. Now here he was in the middle of nowhere, tromping through snow, five minutes away from possibly making the biggest mistake of his life. And he'd dragged Paul into it. He was supposed to take care of Paul, not set him up for a fall that could land him in prison for the rest of his life.

"Quit acting like a baby," he whispered.

"It's dark, Chuckie."

"Of course it's dark, you geek. We're in the mountains."

Up ahead, Bo Moran made an impatient noise. Chuck's shoulders tensed. Chuck had talked long and hard to convince Bo that his baby brother would be an asset not a liability. Paul had the mind of a six-year-old, but he was strong and quick, and he did anything Chuck told him to do, no questions. He wondered if it was too late to change his mind, get back in the car, return to the city and forget this mess. Maybe he'd even get a real job.

"I keep hearing things, Chuckie," Paul whined. "Bears."

"Ain't no bears. Come on, kid, check it out. You can see the lodge right over there. Lots of lights. Bears don't dig lights. Right, Bo?"

"Yeah, no bears. It's *wolves* that like light."

Chuck turned the light in Bo's direction. The man's deep-set eyes flared red, like an animal's. Nearly swallowed by the army fatigues he wore, his head obscured by a fur-trimmed hood, Bo looked like a kid playing soldier in the woods. Skinny, unkempt, with sunken cheeks and a pigeon chest, his mouth pulled perpetually in a sullen scowl, he appeared easy to dismiss. Chuck knew better than to dismiss Bo Moran. Around Bo Moran, Chuck's skin always itched, his spine always crawled. He doubted there was much in the world Bo wouldn't do—he doubted there was much he hadn't done already.

Chuck shifted his attention between Bo and Paul. Now that he and Paul were in, they stayed in. Life in prison would be a sweetheart deal compared to what Bo would do if crossed. "He's just messing with you, kid," he said. "Ain't no wolves. Nothing bigger than squirrels around here. We're almost there. Let's go."

"I can't see nothing. I wanna go home."

A heavy breath deflated Chuck's chest. Paul stood over six feet, four inches tall and had a body a pro wrestler would envy, but he acted like a little kid. Chuck wondered if maybe he babied his baby brother too much.

Chuck grabbed Paul's arm. "Hold on to my coat. Stick with me." He kept his voice low. "And quit your griping. You're gonna tick off Bo."

"I'm cold."

Chuck fished in his pockets for the silk ski masks Bo had provided for the job. Thin, but warm, they were guaranteed not to itch. "Put this on." He waited until Paul fumbled the black mask onto his head. He helped him get the eye holes lined up properly. "Better?"

"Yeah, but I don't like the dark," Paul whispered in reply.

He cast a worried glance in Bo's direction. "There's worse things, kid. Trust me on that." He lowered his voice to a bare whisper. "If you're really good, I'll make you a milk shake, okay? Peanut butter. Your favorite."

Paul grinned behind the mask. "Okay!"

Praying Bo hadn't heard that idiotic exchange, Chuck

focused the flashlight forward and tromped onward through the snow.

"I RESPECTFULLY TENDER my resignation…" J.T. snorted and tossed down the pen. He crumpled the sheet of paper into a ball. A hook shot dropped it neatly into the waste can. It settled atop the other crumpled papers in the can.

He shoved away from the desk. Resting his elbows on his knees, he glumly surveyed the room. On the top floor of the lodge, it was small but luxurious. Tatted doilies on the dresser and folk art on the walls gave it a homey air. The bed dominated the room, looking like a gigantic pastry beneath its European-style down comforter. A bed in which he hadn't slept well last night.

When he hadn't been brooding about how much he hated his job, he'd been brooding about his son. Spending the week baby-sitting a pair of honeymooners wasn't the dumbest job he'd ever had, but it ranked right up there in the top ten. It meant he couldn't see Jamie, and that he resented deeply.

His thoughts kept traveling back to the other day when he'd visited Jamie. Dr. Trafoya, Debbie, the head nurse, and a neurologist had triple-teamed him, seeking permission, again, to remove Jamie's feeding tube. Sweet Jamie, so shrunken and still, only half the size of a normal six-year-old, lost in a coma's black hole.

"Even if he awakens, Mr. McKennon," Dr. Trafoya had said, "his brain is permanently damaged. He'll be forever an infant. He'll never speak or walk or recognize you."

Maybe the good doctor believed that crap, but J.T. didn't. They had said Jamie would never breathe on his own, either, but when they took him off the respirator he'd breathed just fine. He responded to physical therapy to keep his limbs from atrophying. Sometimes he opened his eyes, and once he'd even made a noise which to J.T. had sounded very much like "Mama."

The doctors and nursing staff at Carson Springs hospital

gave Jamie excellent care, and he understood they feared Jamie suffered for nothing. J.T. knew better. Miracles happened every day, and he had a lifetime to wait for one.

He wanted to see Jamie now. He liked visiting in the early-morning hours when the hospital was quiet, and he could spill out his heart in peace. He checked his watch. The sun wouldn't rise for hours. No telling when the newlyweds would be up and about, but it would take two hours to drive to the hospital and two hours back. He'd be missed.

"I hate this crappy job," he muttered.

Technically, his job title was security systems engineer. After Caulfield married Belinda, J.T.'s duties had shifted. Since Caulfield now devoted the majority of his time to his wife's interests, J.T. had hoped he'd be promoted to head the corporate office. Instead, Caulfield had appointed him head of private security. He was qualified as a bodyguard and he was competent to keep thieves and vandals off the Bannerman estate, but he didn't like it.

He especially didn't like the real reason he'd been stuck with this particular duty. Julius didn't need a bodyguard. He was too much of a bug to have real enemies. Bottom line, Mrs. Caulfield needed a spy. He suspected that for the first time in her life she'd met her match. Cute little Penny Forrest held the power, as no other woman before her, to drive a solid wedge between Mrs. Caulfield and her darling boy. The old lady wasn't going down without a fight.

J.T. understood, somewhat. He'd go to the ends of the earth and back for his son. He supposed every parent was the same. Still, he resented the hell out of having to use his time to gather ammunition for the old witch to use in a war against her daughter-in-law.

Caulfield asked too much this time. J.T. turned back to the desk and snatched a fresh sheet of resort stationery. He wrote down the date and a polite greeting, then stopped. He could not quit his job.

He wandered to the wide bank of windows. He pressed his forehead against the icy glass, staring into the darkness below. Resentment deepened, blossoming with spiny petals.

Money, it always boiled down to money. "No good thing ever comes of anything done solely for money," his wife used to tell him, usually with a grin while she tried to figure out yet one more way to stretch their already-squeaking budget. Nina hadn't cared about cars or fancy houses or new clothes. All she'd cared about was loving him and loving Jamie. When she'd been alive, he hadn't cared about money, either.

Now money meant everything. Money meant more time to wait for Jamie's miracle.

Caulfield paid too well for J.T. to even consider quitting. He had no choice except to resign himself to baby-sitting newlyweds and collecting information for a paranoid woman with no life of her own.

Shaking away the dour thoughts, he showered, shaved and dressed in jeans, boots and a wool-lined flannel shirt. Despite the early hour he hoped he could rustle up a cup of coffee.

An employee ran a vacuum cleaner in the lobby's lounge. A sign on the front desk asked guests and visitors to ring a bell for service. A whiff of coffee aroma caught his attention. He followed his nose to the source. Near the doorway to the dining room a table held a large coffeepot, mugs and a plate of freshly baked muffins.

The vacuum cleaner stopped. A woman spoke softly. In the dim light he hadn't noticed the woman seated in the lounge. He recognized the red curls belonging to Frankie Forrest. He paused in the shadows, uncertain if he wanted Frankie to see him. Guilt tightened his gut.

He still carried a nasty taste in his mouth over the way Caulfield had treated her. In his opinion, Caulfield never had any intention of marrying Frankie. He had played her the way he played all women. He doubted if Frankie knew Caulfield had been seeing other women while supposedly engaged to her. She wasn't the type to suffer a philanderer.

And now this. For the second time he'd been party to her humiliation. Self-loathing mingled with hatred for his job.

Hell with Caulfield, he decided. He had an opportunity, in some small way, to make up for the past. Frankie deserved that much.

He filled two mugs with coffee. The dark, rich aroma made his belly rumble. He picked up two muffins, too.

Frankie watched him make his way through the arrangements of potted plants, sofas, club chairs and low tables. "Oh, it's you," she said dryly. She looked him up and down, her expression neutral. "I didn't recognize you without the goon suit."

Her insult took him back to the good old days. When they worked together, she used to bait him like a kid poking a stick at a caged bear. He'd liked it. She'd made him laugh.

He set a mug of coffee in front of her. "Hungry?" He offered a muffin. She shook her head. Slouched on the chair, shoulders hunched, she looked tired. He wondered if she'd slept at all. He peeled the wrapper off a muffin and inhaled the spicy scent of apples and cinnamon.

"So, how's Max doing these days?" Her tone was too carefully casual.

He wanted to make her happy by telling her Caulfield had gained weight, was losing his hair and Belinda was making him miserable. Except, that would be a lie. Caulfield was having the time of his life. "Okay."

"I guess...marriage agrees with him?"

He lifted a shoulder in a noncommittal shrug. He bit into the muffin. Rich and heavy, it tasted as good as it smelled. Head down, he watched Frankie from the corner of his eye. Slashes of eyebrows framed her strikingly pale eyes. Strong cheekbones and a square jaw gave her face interesting angles. Even seated and still she vibrated with energy. He liked her mouth. Some might say it was too wide for her face, her lips too full, but he appreciated the supple mobility and the sensual depth of color.

He bit into the muffin, savoring the texture. An idle thought clipped the back of his brain—holding Frankie, making love to her, would be as exhilarating as racing down a mountainside. Her body would be long and lean, muscular, but soft in the right places. He'd plunge both hands in that mass of fiery hair and hang on while he ravished that incredible mouth. Disturbed, he wondered about himself. He hadn't been interested in any woman since his wife died.

"So, uh, have you…talked to Penny?" Still the too-casual tone as she pulled the coffee mug to her face as if to hide her expression. She stared at the floor.

"No, sorry. I'm just the hired goon."

"Right," she muttered.

"What are you doing with yourself these days?" he asked, though he knew the answer already. Two months ago Caulfield had ordered J.T. to find out where Frankie lived and where she worked. He had assumed the boss needed her graphology skills and was conceited enough to think she might come back to work for him. After turning in his report, though, Caulfield never mentioned her again.

"Just working," she replied. "What about you?"

"Just working."

She grinned. "A couple of working grunts. Real exciting."

J.T. liked her smile. He also liked her bare face. At the office she'd worn far too much makeup for his taste. Her skin was creamy with a light dusting of coral freckles along the ridge of her cheekbones. A funny urge filled him to reach for her face, to test her skin to see if it was as soft as it looked. He broke a piece off the muffin.

"Why are you here?" she asked.

"Doing my job."

"Yeah, right. Since when does Max give a rat's behind what happens to Julius?"

"It's not my place to ask questions."

"'Ours is not to wonder why, ours is but to do or die.'"

She leveled a glower at him that struck him as both funny and sexy. Beautiful mouth. He imagined kissing her would be like riding a shooting star.

"Serious now," she said. "Is there some kind of threat? Is Penny in danger?"

Only from her nutty mother-in-law, he thought, unable to hold her gaze. Guilt raced through him again, leaving prickly trails on his nerves. "No danger."

"I don't believe you. Max doesn't do anything without a reason. Tell me the truth, why are you playing bodyguard? I have a right to know."

"I swear," he said, "no threats, no danger. My presence is nothing more than an ego trip. Julius gets to look like a big shot for his bride." The not-quite-a-lie tasted sour.

"Figures." She set down the coffee mug. "I forgot my watch. What time is it?"

He turned his left wrist. "It's 5:47 a.m."

"Penny's an early riser."

He lifted an eyebrow. He didn't doubt for a second that Frankie would go charging into the honeymoon cabin, invited or not. "Don't disturb them, Miss Forrest."

"Contrary to popular belief, I do have a life of my own. I need to talk to Penny, then get back to town. I'm wasting my time hanging around. Thanks for the coffee." She jumped to her feet and snatched up the parka that lay across another chair.

He pondered the particulars of his job description, uncertain as to whether guarding a body meant preventing the bride's agitated sister from barging in on the honeymooners. Frankie might take a swing at Julius. She'd done it before, after he'd made a crack about what kind of wedding present she ought to give Belinda. She'd given him a bloody nose. He wondered if part of the reason Julius married Penny was to get even with Frankie. Julius's capacity for spitefulness rivaled his mother's.

He watched her long-legged stride carry her across the lobby to the rear entrance. At the office she'd always worn suits with tailored jackets and short skirts that showed off a pair of world-class legs. He missed looking at her legs, though her pert backside in the tight jeans made a worthwhile show.

He grinned at his unruly thoughts and the stirring low in his groin. It occurred to him, with some discomfort, that he hadn't harbored lustful thoughts in a long time. Despite being only thirty-five years old he lived like a prissy old man. He couldn't remember the last time he'd done anything even resembling fun. Between Caulfield's demands and taking care of Jamie he didn't have much of a life at all.

He downed the remains of his coffee in one long smooth swallow and rose to follow her.

As soon as he stepped outside, icy air slapped his face. Gooseflesh rose on his arms and back, itching against his woollen shirt. Noting the speed with which Frankie traveled the gravel path to the Honeymoon Hideaway, he decided to forgo running upstairs for a coat.

The path between the hideaway and the lodge was well tended and well lit. In the predawn darkness, the trees along the path formed a black, blank wall. He caught up to Frankie at the fountain between the four honeymoon cabins. Drained for winter, the fountain glistened under a dusting of snow. Each cabin was angled so its entrance had privacy from the others. Pinkish lights glowed next to the doorways, but all the cabin interiors were dark.

Frankie tossed him a look askance. "I'm surprised they don't have you sleeping in front of the door."

He realized her dilemma: she didn't know which of the cabins housed her sister. He shoved his cold hands in his pockets. "I've thought about it, Miss Forrest. If you want to wake up your sister I won't stop you. That is, if you can assure me you aren't carrying a weapon."

The pinkish light agreed with her, turning her eyes large

and dark and softening the lines of her face. She looked like a creature stepped from the forest who would soon disappear back into the trees. "I don't have a weapon."

"I better frisk you to make sure."

She put up her fists. "Touch me and die, McKennon."

Dying might be a fair price to pay to find out what she had underneath her clothes. Cold seeped through his jeans. He shifted his weight from foot to foot, trying to muster some heat. "I'm kidding. Go ahead."

Even in the darkness, he saw her thoughtful frown. "Uh, maybe I shouldn't startle Julius. Why don't you knock for me so he knows it's okay."

She was good, he thought admiringly. "You won't startle him. He sleeps heavy. You won't even wake him up."

She threw up her hands and huffed loudly. White plumes marked her breath. "Which cabin are they in?"

"You don't know?"

She growled. He bit back a laugh.

"I don't and you do. So tell me."

He thought his natural bent toward devilment had died with Nina, but orneriness flexed its rusty wings. "Okay," he said. "I'll tell you. But, you have to kiss me first." That he said such a thing aloud shocked him. He swallowed laughter.

"That is the stupidest thing I've ever heard!"

He shrugged. "You've got a twenty-five-percent chance of choosing the right cabin on the first shot. Or, you can go back to the lodge and see if the night clerk will give you the cabin number. Or, you can wait until your sister is awake." He smiled. "Or, you can kiss me." She wouldn't, he knew, but he liked the flashing fire seeming to shoot from her every pore. Any second now she'd get the joke and laugh. Making her laugh seemed a small step toward easing some of the pain he'd inadvertently caused her.

Glaring daggers in his direction, she took a step toward the nearest cabin. Years of training had taught him to control his body language. If she hoped for a clue she wouldn't get it from him. She abruptly switched direction. He tensed instinctively, prepared for battle. She grabbed the front of his shirt in both hands, jerked him forward and kissed him fully on the mouth.

Chapter Three

Frankie meant to give McKennon a noisy smack on the lips. Then she would shove him and hope he slipped on the icy gravel and fell on his butt so he would end up looking like the big jerk he actually was. Then she'd laugh in his face and prove his idiotic kidding around had absolutely no effect on her whatsoever.

That's what she'd meant—

Electricity sparked from his lips to hers, melding her to his heat. He wrapped both arms around her shoulders and hugged her to his chest. Breath deserted her; thought deserted her. She clung to his shirtfront as if she drowned and only he could save her. Mingled aromas of soap and shaving cream and healthy male swirled through her brain like an intoxicating drug. He smelled so good. His lips were so supple, so warm. When he slid a hand through her hair and grasped the back of her head in a possessive hold, she became lost in the erotic feeling of his fingers against her scalp.

This kiss superseded all other kisses in her life. She'd kissed him a thousand times in her dreams, but this was better. McKennon touched her soul. She parted her lips and greedily accepted the thrust of his tongue. Noises slipped away one by one, the rustle of her jacket, their boots crunching gravel, the faraway whisper of a breeze through the pines, until all she could hear was her pounding heart.

She kissed and kissed him, tasting, testing, no longer present, but lost in her dreams, submersed in the solidity of his big body, entrapped and enthralled by the power of his embrace.

When he broke the kiss, a cry rose in her throat. A cry of protest, of yearning. Her eyelids flew open, and she stared into his eyes. They were black, fathomless, smoldering. His hot breath fanned her cheeks.

Dizzy now, she tried hard to muster outrage. Unable to do that, she settled for indignation, but even that wan emotion failed her.

He slid his hand from beneath her hair. Released from his hold, if not from his spell, she dropped her hands from his shirt. In her head she saw herself flinging her hair in a haughty gesture and sniffing in disgust; she swiped her mouth; she laughed in his face.

In her head.

In reality she backed a step and lowered her face. Her cheeks burned, but she shivered inside the parka. A single kiss had never set her on fire before. She'd never lost her head like that. Bemused and troubled, she peered warily at him.

"Cabin B," he said, and pointed. His voice sounded suspiciously gruff.

Oh, yeah, Penny, she thought. She took a step in the direction he indicated and paused. She half expected him to take her arm, to stop her and kiss her again. He jammed his hands in his jeans pockets and hunched his shoulders. Annoyance tweaked her.

Resisting the urge to look over her shoulder at him, she strode determinedly to Cabin B. She knocked softly on the door, then listened. She raised her hand to knock again, but hesitated. All night long she'd rehearsed conversations with her sister. Angry words, loving words, forgiving words and spiteful words. She doubted now that anything she said could change the situation.

Forget speeches and arguments, then. She would assure

Penny that no matter what happened they were still sisters, but she'd never be able to accept Julius. Then she'd say goodbye.

She knocked a rapid tatoo Penny should recognize from the countless mornings Frankie had awakened her to get ready for school. After a few seconds she knocked again. The knocks echoed behind her in a fading swirl.

"No answer?" McKennon asked.

His nearness startled her. She hadn't heard his approach.

"Something's wrong," Frankie said. She knocked harder. Her cold knuckles ached with every blow.

"She's probably been up most of the night."

She flinched. No way, no how, did she want a picture in her head of her baby sister and that creep Julius having sex. "She's a college student. Or was. She doesn't need sleep. There's something wrong."

He lifted his gaze to the star-studded sky. "Even if I could open the door, which I can't, I wouldn't. Let them sleep."

"She *has* to talk to me." She pounded on the door with her fist, ignoring McKennon's whispered warnings about disturbing the other guests. She grabbed the doorknob. It turned easily, startling her. "The door's unlocked."

McKennon glided up the steps on silent feet.

She pushed the door open. Thin pink-tinged light formed a rectangle on the floor. The rest of the interior was pitch-black. And quiet.

Too quiet. Every nerve in her body went on alert. The atmosphere stifled her with its tomblike silence.

"Penny?" she called softly. "It's me, Penny. Hello?"

"Step back," McKennon whispered in her ear. He found a switch and flipped it. A wall-mounted lamp filled the cabin interior with a golden glow.

Frankie blinked, momentarily blinded. As soon as her eyes adjusted she saw the bed. The king-size four-poster bed practically filled the room. The posters looked like Roman columns carved with twining leaves. A canopy frame made of wrought iron echoed the leafy bower theme. Julius lay squarely in the center of the bed. A thick comforter was drawn to his chin. His mouth gaped and his eyes were open. Creepy claws skittered up and down her spine.

Not right, not right, this is bad, this is very bad, intuition screamed in her head. "Penny?" Moving only her eyes, she searched for her sister. "Penny!"

"Don't move," McKennon said. "Don't touch anything." He hurried to the bed and leaned over Julius.

This is not happening, Frankie thought, watching the big man press two fingers beneath the bridegroom's jaw. A weary-sounding curse husked from McKennon's mouth, and she knew. Julius Bannerman was dead.

Frankie clamped her arms over her chest. She planted her feet at a stubborn angle and glared at her brother-in-law. She willed him to rise, to speak, to breathe. The creepy claws ran races along her spine. "What is wrong with him, McKennon?"

He dragged a hand over the back of his neck, and his eyebrows nearly touched in the middle. "Dead."

"He isn't dead," she insisted. "He's faking it. Shake him. Give him CPR. Do something."

McKennon tossed her a gee-you're-dumb look. "Raising the dead isn't in my job description."

She strode to the opposite side of the bed. Julius's face was a peculiar mottled gray color. Dried saliva crusted on the corners of his mouth. His eyes were as dull as dirty china. Stomach churning, she poked Julius's cheek. His skin felt like wax and she jerked her hand back and scrubbed it on her parka.

"Leave him alone. I told you not to touch anything. Especially him."

She held up her hands, showing empty palms. "Okay, okay. Where's my sister?" She sidled away from the corpse. "Penny? Penny!" Ignoring McKennon's orders to stop, she jerked open a closet door. Penny's bridal gown hung from the rod with the skirt and train stuffed into the

closet like a massive wad of cotton candy. But no Penny.
Fighting down panic, Frankie rushed for the bathroom.

McKennon snagged her parka hood, jerking her backward. She gagged and stumbled. He wrapped his arms
around her body and held her still. "Stop, or I will throw
you out. This is possibly a crime scene. You cannot touch
anything."

Her heart tripped painfully, making breathing a chore.
Blood rushing in her ears made thinking difficult.

"Take a deep breath," he soothed. He rocked her gently,
back and forth. "Calm down. We'll find Penny. She's okay.
Settle down."

"I am okay now," she muttered.

He maneuvered her about to face him. Like a stiff doll,
she allowed the manhandling. She knew him well enough
to know that if he said he'd throw her out of the cabin,
then he would do so.

"Stay right here. I will check the bathroom. Do not
move."

He entered the bathroom. His broad shoulders filled the
doorway. Frankie could almost see the tension vibrating
from his body. She finally found something that rattled
him—and she didn't like it one little bit.

"She isn't here," he announced. He unhooked a slim
cellular telephone from the holster affixed to his belt.

Frankie's gaze fell on an envelope propped against a
lamp on the bedside table. "Julius Bannerman" was written on the front in bold, block lettering. She snatched up
the envelope and tore off the end before he could stop her.

"I told you not to touch anything!"

She hunched protectively over the envelope. She shook
out the paper inside. She fumbled the folded paper open.
"It might tell me where Penny went."

"That does it, you're out."

It said: "Dear Mr. Bannerman, we have your wife—"

Frankie gasped. McKennon grabbed the paper from her

hand, but she had seen that first horrible sentence. "She's been kidnapped!"

"Don't jump to con—" His mouth clamped shut and his eyebrows rose. Eyes wide, he stared at the note. "Ah, hell."

Strength drained from Frankie's knees; her heart constricted in her chest. "You liar," she growled. "You said she wasn't in danger. Now she's gone."

"Be quiet." Some of the color faded from his cheeks, leaving him gray. He rattled the sheet of paper.

Thin, college-ruled notebook paper, she noticed, the same kind she used at home because it was cheap and hole-punched. It heartened her. Surely *real* kidnappers would use twenty-pound bond or newsprint covered in letters clipped from magazines, not common, loose-leaf notebook paper. Her throat felt full of cement and she swallowed hard. "What does it say?"

He cleared his throat and read:

"Dear Mr. Bannerman,
We have your wife. This is nothing personal, we have no hard feelings toward you personally. This is strictly business. We know you are a good person and your wife is a good person. We will not hurt anybody as long as you do exactly what we say. All we want is money. You and your family are very rich and will not miss the paltry amount we demand. We demand three million dollars for the return of your beautiful wife. You and your family have forty-eight hours to raise the money. We are not unreasonable people. As long as you give us the money, we will not harm your wife. Do not call the police. We will know if you do. If you call the police, we will have no choice except to kill your wife. We do not want to do that. Do not leave Elk River Resort. We will know if you do. We will contact you in forty-eight hours to instruct you about where and how to give us the money. As soon

as we have the money, we will give you your wife.
Do not act stupid in any way. We mean everything
we say.

McKennon exhaled heavily. "That's it."
She blinked stupidly at Julius's body. He looked like a
little kid tucked in snug and cozy for the night. "If they
don't want to hurt anybody why did they kill him?"
"An accident?" he offered. Head cocked, he studied Ju-
lius. "Stay," he warned her and began to prowl the room.
He searched, his eyes quick and alert as a cat's, but touched
nothing. He leaned over a small wastebasket next to the
wet bar. "Here we go."
Holding her elbows with her hands, in order to resist
touching anything, Frankie peered inside the wastebasket.
It contained several empty minibottles of scotch, foil candy
wrappers and two syringes.
"Looks like they came prepared," he said. "One for
Julius, one for Penny."
"Some preparation," she muttered. "The idiots OD'd
him." A horrifying thought occurred to her. "You don't
think they overdosed Penny, too?"
He shook his head in firm denial. "She's young and
strong. She hasn't been wrecking her health with bad living
for the past thirty years, either. I doubt very much they
meant to kill him." He held the note out to Frankie. "Are
you one hundred percent positive this isn't Penny's handwriting?"
Offended by his implication, she bristled. "Watch it."
"If she and Julius were partying with drugs and she got
scared—"
"Even if she weren't as straight-up as they come, she's
vain about her body. She doesn't eat sugar or red meat or
drink liquor. She certainly won't risk fooling around with
drugs. Besides, if Julius conked out she'd call for help. She
wouldn't write a stupid note!"
He patiently held out the paper.

To prove her point she perused the handwriting. Her analytical mind kicked in. The block printing was even and smooth, and the note contained no misspellings or cross outs. She focused on the letters *K, M* and *N*. Penny always added feminine little curlicues, even while printing. The letters were light textured, but soldiers-at-attention straight.

She noticed the writing nearly hugged the pale blue line of the right margin, indicating a personality that clung to the past and security. The left margin wavered, swooping in and out, almost hesitant in contrast to the rigidly upright lettering. A criminal who feared taking chances?

"Penny definitely did not write this." She wanted to jump on the bed, jerk Julius upright and scream in his face. She jammed her hands into her pockets. Threads snapped.

McKennon placed the note on the bed, face-up. He brought out his telephone again.

"Who are you calling?"

"The police."

"Like hell you are!"

"This is a murder, accidental or not. We can't keep it quiet."

"Oh, yes we can!" She hurried to the control panel for the heat inside the cabin. She turned the switch to Off. "It's like fifteen degrees out there. We open the windows, keep him cold. He'll be okay." She struggled with a wooden window sash.

"Frankie."

"Don't just stand there. Help me."

"Stop it, Frankie."

That he used her nickname rather than the more formal Miss Forrest gave her pause. She caught her bottom lip in her teeth and closed her eyes.

"Think about it," he urged gently. "We can't pretend nothing is wrong. Your aunt and uncle love Penny, too. And what about Mrs. Caulfield? Julius is her only child. We can't keep his death a secret from her. It's not only wrong, it's cruel."

If he'd said anything else, she'd be able to argue. But concealing a son's death from his mother was worse than cruel, it was evil. "We can't let them hurt Penny," she pleaded. "If they find out they killed Julius, they'll kill her, too."

"We have an advantage."

Eager for any tidbit of good news she lifted her eyes hopefully.

"Elk River is fairly isolated. We can manage the media and keep news of this off television and the radio. The kidnappers are bluffing. They aren't watching."

"You don't know that."

"This ransom note is straight out of Hollywood. Don't call the cops, blah-blah-blah. It's a bluff." He pointed his chin at Julius. "He hasn't been roughed up."

"You don't know that. Look under the covers. Maybe he's been shot or stabbed." She knew she argued an invalid point. Other than being dead Julius appeared perfectly fine.

"Fetch your uncle. I'll wait here."

"Don't call the police."

"I won't do anything except wait."

"Penny is my responsibility. I won't let you do anything that can harm her."

His green eyes gleamed. "You have my word, Frankie. I will do everything in my power to get Penny back safe and sound."

Inside Honeymoon Hideaway Cabin B, Colonel Horace Duke stood with his hands locked behind his back. He studied Julius's corpse. The Colonel was shaved and groomed and dressed in a dark blue sweatshirt, pressed-and-creased blue jeans and a fleece-lined denim coat. Despite having left the army years ago, the old man still rose every day at 4:30 a.m. His mind was always as sharp as his appearance.

"Might I see the note, Mr. McKennon?"

McKennon placed the paper on the bed in a position

where the Colonel could read it. "The fewer people who touch it, the better, sir."

"Understood." He scanned the note. His mouth compressed into a thin, unyielding line. "Humph. We shall assume, then, these miscreants are both serious and dangerous."

"Yes, sir."

"Have we any indications as to the identity of the miscreants? Or where they may have taken Penny?"

"Not yet." McKennon pointed at the floor in front of the door. "There's no sign of a struggle. Frankie and I stayed on the gravel, so we didn't track mud. The tracks belong to the kidnappers. They come in, they go out. No smearing. They left the door unlocked."

Frankie took a good hard look at her surroundings. The cabin was as luxurious as any five-star hotel, with plush carpeting, wallpaper, antique furnishings, flower arrangements and romantic art hanging on the walls. McKennon's observation made her realize it was quite neat as well. Julius and Penny had obviously used the wet bar, and their luggage and clothing were tossed about in untidy stacks. Still, other than a few muddy footprints—and a dead groom—the kidnappers had left no sign of themselves.

"No sign of forced entry," McKennon added.

Frankie easily imagined Julius cringing and cowering before even the mildest threat, but Penny? She looked as fragile as a fairy child, but she didn't have a timid bone in her body. She'd have fought back. Except, nothing in the room indicated a fight.

"They must have gotten in while Penny was asleep," Frankie said. "If she opened the door and saw strangers, she'd scream or something. She'd have fought back."

She crouched and laid her hand lightly atop a muddy footprint. She couldn't tell if the print was still damp or not, and feared destroying evidence by brushing the nap. "You know this country, Colonel. We can track them down." She jumped upright and clamped her hands on her hips. "You've taken part in search and rescue operations. You have equipment, right? Four-wheel drive vehicles, horses, spotlights. They couldn't have gotten far—"

"Francine, this is *not* a search and rescue mission."

"Penny needs to be rescued!"

Some unspoken communication passed between the men. Frankie wondered if she sounded as panicky as she felt. She gulped in great draughts of air in an attempt to calm herself.

You will not break down, she counseled herself. *You will not crack.*

"A heinous crime has been committed," the Colonel said. "We can't ignore Mr. Bannerman's murder and go traipsing willy-nilly into the mountains on a wild-goose chase. There are procedures."

"If the kidnappers find out they whacked Julius, they'll kill Penny, too. We have to find them first."

"Ill-advised and dangerous. I must inform the sheriff."

She resisted pacing, though she wanted to do more than merely pace. She wanted to shout, scream and throw things. "This isn't some abstract war game. If you call the law, you'll kill Penny."

McKennon grasped her arm above the elbow. He faced her impassively. His powerful fingers twitched on her elbow. She tightened her jaw and listened. "These mountains look well populated, but they aren't. Finding people who don't want to be found is nearly impossible. Especially since we don't know who they are or what they look like."

"Turn me loose," she gritted through her teeth. As soon as he relaxed his hold, she jerked her arm away and rubbed her tingling elbow. In reply to her furious look, he arched his eyebrows. The expression in his eyes said he'd do it again if she lost control.

The Colonel didn't seem to notice the way McKennon had manhandled her. He stood ramrod straight, but in his icy blue eyes she read fear. "The sheriff is a personal friend of mine and a man of discretion."

Frankie wished Julius were alive so she could kill him again.

CHUCK PICKED UP THE COFFEEPOT. Heat seared his palm. Yelping, he dropped the pot. It clattered on the rickety camp stove.

Without looking up from his magazine, Bo Moran said, "Use a pot holder, dummy. It's hot."

Chuck suckled a stinging finger and glared at the speckled blue coffeepot. His only experiences with coffee came from restaurants and automatic coffeemakers. The strange percolator gave him the creeps, along with this ramshackle old cabin. A gust of wind made the walls creak and groan. Despite a wood fire blazing in a stone hearth and the camp stove, the place felt like a refrigerator. He shivered.

"I never been camping before," he said.

Bo chuckled and turned a page. He sat on a bench seat torn from a '76 Dodge, the only furnishing in the tiny room other than a card table with a ripped vinyl top and a pair of folding stools that sat too low to be used at the table. He had his feet toward the fire and a striped blanket slung around his scrawny shoulders. A Glock 9mm pistol lay on the seat beside him. "This ain't camping, man. Camping is tents and fishing poles and eating beans out of cans."

"Sounds like it sucks." He used a pot holder to lift the coffeepot. He poured a cupful, then wrinkled his nose at the tarry brew. It smelled like coffee, but it didn't look like any coffee he'd ever drunk. He wished for some milk to cut it.

Cradling the cup to warm his hands, he circled the confines of the room. Outside, the sun glared—a fool's-gold sun, all brightness, no warmth. Wind battered the tiny cabin, and occasional gusts sliced through the unpainted, plank walls. He couldn't wait until this was over. He envisioned himself in Vegas—hot, dry, lively, lit-up Vegas, where the sunshine was warm and the air was thick enough to actually breathe.

"So what's next, Bo?"

"You'll know when I tell you. Relax."

Relax... Chuck bit back laughter. He'd robbed liquor stores, run drugs, mugged doofs in parking lots and stolen more cars than he could count. He'd never kidnapped anyone before. It surprised him how scared he felt. The caper hadn't seemed real until they'd actually entered that fancy cabin. He'd been shaking ever since.

The grab had gone down easy. Too easy. A knock on the door, the doof answered and the girl had been asleep on the bed. Shoot up the doof with dope, then pack the girl to the car. Nothing to it.

Chuck kept playing the grab over in his mind, looking for bungles and wrecks. The whole thing had gone down as sweet as candy. No witnesses, no noise, and they hadn't left behind fingerprints. It looked like Bo was right, and he was about to make the easiest ten grand of his life.

Except, he'd never done anything easy in his life. Something always went wrong.

He sipped the coffee. It burned his tongue, soured his mouth and slid down his throat like bubbling acid. It hit his gut with a thud and a jolt. He shuddered. Bo had resumed reading his magazine. A travel magazine, the only kind Bo ever read. Bo Moran's big dream was to buy a monster RV complete with toilet, shower, microwave oven and satellite TV. He wanted to travel the highways and byways.

Chuck paused at a window. Thin curtains printed with yellow flowers and teapots were held back by bits of twine from the grimy glass. He'd covered an ancient Buick, swiped from an old lady too blind to drive, with tree branches. Once they ditched the car nobody could ever trace it to him. Bo's Bronco glinted in the sun and looked misshapen with its oversized tires and steel bumpers. Trees grew right up to the house, reminding Chuck of the grisly old fairy tales he read to Paul. He half expected to see wolves slipping through the shadows.

Or FBI agents.

In and out, sweet as candy, he thought, trying hard to make himself believe it. Nobody gets hurt, nobody gets caught. In the movies the FBI always caught the kidnappers—usually by gunning them down. The Feds had helicopters, dogs and fancy electronic equipment. Bo said no way would the FBI get involved. Not a chance.

"They always call the cops," he said.

Bo turned a page.

"How long till the doof wakes up? What if he calls the FBI? They'll tap the phone. They can trace the call." He stepped away from the window, with his back to the wall.

"Sit down. You sound like a herd of elephants."

"He's gonna call the cops."

Bo rested back against the cushion and sighed. "I ever tell you a lie, man?"

Always, Chuck thought. He sipped the bitter brew.

"You ever hear the saying, If it looks good, then it is good?"

"No."

"Well, that's one of them down-home truths. As long as we look good, we do good. Get it?"

Chuck didn't get it, but he was stuck. "I'm gonna check on the girl." He turned for the doorway covered by a sheet of striped cotton. He pulled the curtain aside.

Paul sat next to the bed, hunched over, industriously filling in the designs in a coloring book with a crayon. Chuck grinned. Give Paul a coloring book and he could amuse himself for hours. The kid was a true artist. Maybe instead of a trip to Vegas when this was over, Chuck would get a bigger refrigerator for the apartment. That way he'd have more room to display Paul's pictures.

The girl appeared to be sleeping. Paul had covered her to the chin with quilts, concealing the duct tape binding her arms and feet. A black-satin sleep mask covered her eyes.

Chuck's gut tightened. He'd done a lot of crappy things in his life, but he'd never hurt a girl. Easy in and out, sweet as candy. They'd collect the money, give the doof directions, then split. No problem. But Bo hurt people—men, women, girls, even kids if it suited his purpose. Chuck let the curtain fall and wished he'd never met Bo Moran.

A brush of air tickled Paul's cheek. He stopped coloring the round table of Camelot and noticed the curtain swinging over the door. Wind hammered the thin walls, and he could feel the floor thrumming under his feet. Goosebumps itched his arms. He turned his gaze on the girl. Penny was her name—Penelope. He liked the feel of her name rolling through his brain. Penelope. It made her sound like a princess in a fairy tale, like she belonged in his King Arthur coloring book.

He eased strands of silky pale hair off her cheeks. Pretty girl, Princess Penelope.

She made a small noise. Startled and guilty, he jerked his hand off her face. She moaned and struggled weakly under the covers. She said something he couldn't understand.

"What?" he whispered. He set the book and crayons on the floor beside him. The dark corners and buckled floorboards housed mice, he felt certain. He hoped they didn't like the taste of crayons.

Penny groaned, loudly.

Little retching noises bubbled in her throat. Paul understood that sound. Chuck liked his booze even when it made him sick. When he was sick, Paul knew not to let him sleep on his back where he could swallow his own vomit. He eased an arm around her narrow shoulders and helped her upright.

Her retching stopped and he grinned at having done a good job. "It's okay, Miss Penelope," he whispered.

He glanced up to see Chuck in the doorway. His brother looked kind of sick himself. "What are you doing?"

"She's sick. I was helping."

Bo shouldered Chuck out of the way. He stopped at the foot of the bed. Paul tightened his hold on the girl. She sagged in his arms and whimpered deep in her throat. He petted her soft blond hair.

"Chuck, you better get it through that dimwit's head." Bo's eyes blazed animal fury. "If that mask comes off I'll cut her throat and his."

Chapter Four

"Yep, deader than a party at my in-laws' house." Sheriff Eldon Pitts used a thumb to cock back his cowboy hat. Staring down at Julius's body he clucked his tongue. He twisted his lips and blew a long, confused-sounding breath.

Hunched against a wall, Frankie knew that with the sheriff's arrival she'd lost what little control she had over the situation. She chewed her lower lip. Both McKennon and her uncle had warned her to keep her mouth shut and to stay out of the way. Not that she had the faintest idea about what to do, anyway. She couldn't see past being furious at Julius for getting Penny into this mess and terrified about what the kidnappers might do to the girl.

She studied the sheriff. About her height, he had a big face made bigger by a huge mustache that concealed his mouth. He appeared confused, and she wondered if he'd ever dealt with a kidnapping before. Or a murder for that matter. The county population was almost evenly divided between long-established ranchers and those who catered to tourists. Drunk drivers probably made up the bulk of local criminals.

"May I?" McKennon asked. At a nod from the sheriff, McKennon used one finger to lift the comforter high enough to see Julius's body. "No sign of violence." He then directed the sheriff's attention to the wastebasket. "I think analysis will show those syringes contained a barbiturate. Miss Forrest claims her sister doesn't drink alcohol, so Mr. Bannerman drank the scotch.''

''Booze and downers, a lethal combo.''

''But accidental. They expect him to pay the ransom.''

''Is he rich enough to pay three million?''

''His mother is.''

''Hmm, we have ourselves quite a situation.'' The sheriff clucked his tongue again. ''Might be a bad thing if those crooks find out they murdered this man.''

Brilliant deduction, Frankie thought sourly. She turned her gaze out the window. Her hope of mustering these men into organizing a search party was dying fast.

''What is your connection to all this, Mr. McKennon?''

''I'm employed by Maxwell Caulfield, Mr. Bannerman's stepfather. I was assigned as Mr. Bannerman's bodyguard.''

A twinge of sympathy tightened Frankie's throat. McKennon couldn't very well sleep in the cabin with the new-lyweds, but Max and Belinda were going to blame him, anyway.

''You didn't see anything? Hear anything?''

''I slept in the lodge last night.'' He'd assumed his mob-enforcer impassivity, but Frankie suspected it cost him dearly to admit this failure.

''I better call the coroner then. State police, too.''

''No!'' Frankie pushed away from the wall. ''We can't have cops crawling all over. The press will find out Julius is dead.''

The Colonel touched her arm. ''The sheriff has assured me that he will do everything in his power to keep the press from learning of Mr. Bannerman's demise. We will coop-erate with the kidnappers and ensure Penny's safe return.''

''Not good enough. We have to find Penny right now. We can't take any chances.''

McKennon cleared his throat, loudly. Frankie pointedly ignored him, but like a gorilla in a house, he was impossible to ignore. Before she could react, he had her by the arm and hustled out of the cabin.

"You squeeze my arm again and I'll punch you in the nose."

Shoulders hunched, he tucked his hands beneath his armpits. The wind ripped past them. A tree limb cracked, making Frankie jump. She fumbled with the zipper on her parka.

"You have got to calm down," McKennon said. "I know you're scared, but spouting off doesn't improve the situation."

"If it was your sister, I'd like to see how calm you'd be." She narrowed her eyes against the wind slicing her face. *Be warm, Penny,* she prayed. *Be safe.*

"We will get Penny back, safe and sound. I promise."

She didn't want to trust him; he worked for the man who had ruined her life. He touched her chin with a finger. His warmth startled her.

"I *promise.*"

His jungle-cat eyes snared her, entrapped her and stilled the breath in her lungs. She tried hard to remember that he worked for Max, he was loyal to Max, and he'd do whatever Max told him to do. Instead, she thought of the way he'd kissed her. He'd meant it as a joke, and so had she, but it hadn't turned out that way. Like that kiss, his promise seemed real.

Footsteps crunched gravel. Deputy Mike Downes approached the Honeymoon Hideaway. Pressing a fist to her aching chest, Frankie studied the other cabins. She wondered if the occupants noticed the commotion.

Frankie and McKennon followed the deputy into the cabin. The deputy's parka was mud splattered, and his shoes and lower trouser legs were damp and muddy. Clots of snow fell to the floor and melted into dirty little puddles. He stopped on a rug near the door. Frankie had met the deputy before. As a friend of the family he'd attended weddings of the Duke siblings. She liked his combination of shy boyishness and sharp intelligence.

"They came through the woods, sir," Downes told the

sheriff. "Three of them. Looks to be two men and either a boy or a woman. Three tracks lead away. One looked to be carrying Mrs. Bannerman."

There had been no moon last night, which meant the kidnappers had trekked blindly through the forest. Imagining such determination gave her chills. "You can tell all that from their tracks?"

He flashed a shy smile Frankie's way. "I do a lot of hunting, ma'am. They parked about a hundred yards from here on the trail above the lodge. The tracks lead straight to and from. They knew where they were going."

"Tire tracks?" the sheriff asked.

"Yes, sir. I radioed in for another deputy to guard the scene until the crime techs can get here. If we can set up lights out there we can get photographs. But we best move fast. It's fixing to snow. I can smell it coming."

The sheriff looked at the mud oozing off the deputy's shoes. "All right, everybody out. This scene is past contaminated. Mike, you wait here until the state boys arrive. Nobody else comes in."

"Wait a minute!" Frankie cried. "He knows how to track. We'll track the kidnappers. We can find Penny."

She may as well have been shouting at the wind. The Colonel grasped one arm and McKennon took the other. They bullied her out of the cabin.

"LET ME GUESS," McKennon said. "The first words out of your mouth were, 'I hate Julius Bannerman.'" Arms folded, he rested a shoulder against the doorjamb leading to Elise Duke's office.

Frankie turned an unhappy glare on McKennon's knowing expression. Of course she'd told the police how much she hated Julius, but McKennon needn't be so smug about the inevitable results. The state police investigator who'd questioned her about the kidnapping had been solicitous, to a point. He even apologized for requesting she submit fingerprints, shoe print samples and a handwriting exemplar.

When Frankie, however, launched into a diatribe about how opposed she'd been to the wedding and how Julius Bannerman had been the lowest scumball to ever prowl the earth, he'd turned hostile. It hadn't taken her long to figure out her big mouth placed her in the top ten on the suspect list.

Her insistence that the police launch a massive manhunt had gone largely ignored. The only thing her arguments accomplished was getting her banished to Elise's office. There she sat, alone, frustrated, scared and helpless.

McKennon picked up a carafe from Elise's desk, filled a mug and offered her the steaming coffee. She accepted with an ungracious grunt. "What time is it?"

"A few minutes after two."

"What are the cops doing now? Does anyone have any idea where Penny is?"

She settled on a love seat carefully, well aware she'd been wearing the same clothes for days. She felt dirty, exhausted and very much out of place in Elise Duke's feminine office. Despite it being the dead of winter, fresh flowers were arranged in vases. Elise could find fresh flowers in Antarctica if she had to. The delicate furniture, shining under coats of wax, made Frankie feel even more lost and out of place.

She blew on the steaming brew, forming concentric circles on the surface. "Did the cops call in the FBI?"

McKennon's pained exhalation told her all she needed to know. This kidnapping was going from awful to ludicrously horrible at warp speed.

"They'll get her back."

"How are they keeping this from the media? Elk River looks like it's hosting a cop convention. What if the kidnappers are watching? What then?"

"I assure you they were bluffing. No way would they hang around." He poured coffee for himself. "Did the cops ask to search your car?"

"I gave permission." Seething, she sipped the coffee.

"But I told them no way about searching my apartment. Can you believe it? They want to waste time digging around in my stuff. If they want to look that bad they can get a warrant." The coffee made her belly rumble. Hunger flared, annoying her. "What about you?"

"I gave them permission to search everything."

She wrinkled her nose in puzzlement. "Are you nuts?"

"You should let them search your place, too."

"It's a waste of time and manpower."

"It's an inside job, Frankie. The cops know it."

She almost spilled the coffee. She clutched the cup with both hands. Traces of fingerprint ink smudged the ceramic surface. "What are you talking about?"

He sat beside her and placed a hand on her arm. Bemused, she stared at his hand. An overwhelming need for comforting disturbed her. She'd always been strong and able to cope with any situation. That circumstances had forced her into helplessness alternately frightened and angered her.

She meant to jerk her arm away from his hand. She would stop staring at his long, muscular fingers, as well, and stop studying the way raised veins traced patterns under the skin. She meant to—every intention was there—but she couldn't rouse the energy to do anything except gaze unhappily at his hand upon her arm.

"For one thing, the kidnappers knew exactly where to go. The tracks led directly to the cabin."

"Meaning?"

"Meaning, a limited number of people were aware that the wedding and honeymoon were taking place at the resort."

A creepy sensation slithered through her body. Anonymous thugs were one thing. Like being struck by lightning, crime by strangers was scary, but impersonal. Being attacked by a friend, though, gnawed holes in the very idea of personal safety. "How limited?"

His brow knit. "The Dukes and the Caulfields, of course.

Whoever arranged the reservation for the chapel and honeymoon cabin. Two of Penny's friends attended the wedding and dinner along with one of Julius's. They returned yesterday to the Springs. I have no idea who Penny or Julius might have told about the wedding, but since so few were invited I imagine they kept it quiet. All in all, I suspect the number of people who knew about the wedding is small, and the number who knew the details is even smaller. Those are our suspects.''

The man who left the message on Frankie's answering machine knew. She sat straighter. Her heart thudded heavily.

''What is it?'' he asked.

She set down the coffee mug and shifted on the seat to face him. ''Who tipped me off about the wedding?''

''What?''

''Some man left a message on my machine. Why did he call?''

McKennon shook his head. ''I'm not certain what you're talking about.''

Fist pressed to her mouth, she concentrated on remembering the exact words the caller had used. ''I got back from the grocery store, and there was a message on my answering machine. A man said Penny and Julius were getting married here, and I had to stop it. I called Penny's dorm, and that's when I found out she'd dropped out of college. So I got up here as fast as I could.'' She stared fiercely into his eyes. ''Was it you?''

''No,'' he answered without hesitation. ''You didn't recognize the voice?''

''Uh-uh.'' Fear crawled through her bones. Somebody knew her well enough to know she would drop everything and race to Elk River. If that somebody was the kidnapper then he was no friend of hers. ''But you're here. There must have been some kind of threat.''

He grunted irritably and leaned forward, his elbows on

his knees and his hands laced loosely. Frankie rubbed idly at the spot where he'd been touching her.

"Well?"

He snapped his head up and she caught the tightening of his jaw and the heat in his eyes. His show of emotion comforted her. It proved he cared.

"Mrs. Caulfield needed a spy. She tried to buy off Julius and it didn't work. She couldn't scare Penny, either. My job was to discover something Mrs. Caulfield could use against Penny."

"That's disgusting."

He lowered his face. "Mrs. Caulfield could have had one of her staff call you. Maybe she thought you'd succeed where she failed."

The idea of Belinda stooping so low as to need Frankie's help seemed absurd. "She's that desperate?"

"Penny's a serious threat. I overheard several arguments where Julius took Penny's side rather than his mother's. From Mrs. Caulfield's reaction I'd say that was a first. Julius moved out about a month ago. Again, judging by how hard she took it, that was a first, too."

"Could…?" Frankie paused, loath to speak aloud her deepest fear. She swallowed hard. "Could Belinda be behind this?" Her courage failed her. She couldn't bear thinking the kidnapping might be a cover for making Penny permanently disappear.

"Not a chance," he said. "If Penny had been snatched off the street I'd consider the possibility. But Mrs. Caulfield is well aware of Julius's health. She wouldn't risk giving him drugs." He slid an arm around her shoulders and gave her a reassuring hug.

The feel of flannel against her cheek and the powerful muscle beneath soothed her somewhat. The tension in her throat eased.

Elise Duke entered the office. Her eyelids were swollen and her complexion had turned almost translucent. She dabbed delicately at her nose with a tissue. Frankie rose and embraced her aunt. Elise seemed to have shrunk in the past few hours.

"We'll get her back, Aunt Elise," she said, wishing she could mean it with all her heart.

"Yes, we will." She straightened her shoulders and lifted her chin. Despite the remnants of tears, strength glowed in her blue eyes. "We'll get her back safe and sound. My immediate concern is you, dear."

"Me?"

She hooked an arm firmly with Frankie's and tugged her toward the door.

"I'm okay. Really."

"You'll be better after a shower and a decent meal. You'll use Janine's room."

"I..." Frankie's protests died before she aired them. Elise needed someone to care for. "All right, if it'll make you happy."

"Mr. McKennon? Please join us in the kitchen. There's plenty of food."

"Thank you, ma'am."

Aunt Elise was right, as usual. A hot shower and clean clothing, courtesy of her cousins, refreshed Frankie. Despite a lack of sleep she felt strong again. Her eyes burned and her limbs were heavy, but her thoughts were clear. She'd considered and reconsidered what McKennon had said about Belinda and conceded he was right. Which meant Penny had been kidnapped for money, and they would get her back.

She joined McKennon in the kitchen where, to her guilty dismay, she couldn't seem to eat enough food. She snagged a yeast roll from a basket and slathered on butter. Across the table from her he ate heartily, as well. She noted his use of a napkin and the way he set down his utensils between bites, so she refrained from tearing at the roll with her teeth. She plucked off a ladylike piece and placed it in her mouth.

She glanced at the kitchen workers who stirred, chopped,

banged utensils and washed dishes. She wondered how much they knew about the murder in Honeymoon Hideaway Cabin B, and how much they were talking to outsiders. The only way the media couldn't know something would be if every journalist in the state of Colorado were sleeping off a massive hangover.

"Tell me more about this insider theory," she said, keeping her voice low. "Could it be Julius's friends?"

"Seems a big risk. Either Julius or Penny could recognize them. Besides, Julius's friends are pretty much like him. Party animals without much ambition."

A loud clatter nearly made Frankie jump out of her skin. A cook's assistant scrambled to retrieve the cutlery she'd spilled. McKennon folded a hand around Frankie's.

"Relax."

"How?" She dragged in air in a vain attempt to slow her pounding heart. In disgust, she pushed her plate away. "I can't believe I'm sitting here eating. I need to do something."

"There's nothing you can do." He slid her plate back in front of her. "Except stay strong for your sister."

"Thank you, O wise one."

The corners of his mouth twitched. "I'm curious. Do you dislike me because of something I did, or on general principles?"

Ashamed of the sarcasm, she concentrated on the food before her.

"Something about that note really bugs me." He leaned as close to her as the table allowed. "Did the wording seem friendly to you?"

The only wording she recalled clearly was the part about the kidnappers killing Penny. "I don't think so."

"They made a point of telling Julius he was a good person and the kidnapping was nothing personal. Remember?"

Now that he said it she did remember. "Yeah, and they used a lot of negatives. They aren't bad people, Julius isn't a bad person. It's like they were apologizing. What does it mean?"

"It fits with the insider theory."

"Or maybe a woman wrote the note. Women have a tendency to be less direct than men in their language. And Mike said one set of tracks could belong to a woman. Maybe it's one of Julius's ex-wives or girlfriends. This would be the perfect revenge, not only against him, but against Belinda, as well."

Firm footsteps announced the Colonel's arrival in the kitchen. He walked directly to the table and stopped with his hands locked behind his back. His grim expression threatened Frankie's fragile composure. He was a gruff old man, blustery and eccentric in his insistence on military order in all things, but he loved her deeply. He loved Penny, too. Strain showed around his tight-lipped mouth, and his eyes seemed to have sunk deeply into his head.

Frankie pushed slowly upright. Everything she'd eaten threatened to rise. "Is there...news?"

"Mr. Bannerman's parents have arrived. They require your presence, Mr. McKennon. They are in the lobby."

A flicker of emotion rippled over McKennon's features. Frankie guessed he'd rather face a swarm of angry bees. He wiped his mouth with a napkin and stood. "Excuse me."

Sick with sympathy over how McKennon was going to have to explain Julius's death in detail, Frankie watched him go. She sank onto the chair and lowered her face to her hands. It hit her, truly and hard: Julius was dead. She had despised him, not merely for his decadent existence and his pursuit of Penny, but for being the son of the woman who had stolen Max. Still, he hadn't deserved murder. He had people who loved him, people who would grieve his loss.

Penny would mourn. Julius may have been a lousy excuse for a mate, but Penny had loved him. When Penny loved, she loved with all her heart and soul. The kidnapping was merely the beginning of her ordeal.

A touch on her shoulder roused her.

"The authorities requested that I vacate the lodge of guests. Should anyone ask, the cover story is that we've had a break in a main gas line." He glanced at the employees laboring over the stoves. "We will evacuate the resort in an orderly fashion. The employees will remain, however."

The knots in Frankie's belly tightened unpleasantly. Elk River Resort supported the Duke clan. God only knew how much business they were about to lose.

"The FBI has set up a command post in the dining room. They finished searching the resort."

She blinked stupidly at her uncle, uncertain what he talked about. "Why would they search the resort?"

"Standard operating procedure." His facial muscles tightened as if speaking pained him. "They must eliminate the possibility that our family or any of the people under my command are involved."

"They're treating you like a suspect?"

He gazed into the distance. "They have requested polygraph examinations."

Frankie jumped to her feet. "Who the hell is in charge? Bad enough to waste manpower poking and probing into our personal lives, but now they want to use lie detectors? Did you say the dining room?"

He clamped a hand on her shoulder, his long fingers powerful and unwavering. "At ease, Francine. I suggest you remain here until your presence is required."

"Do you know something I don't?"

The skin on his neck reddened. The flush climbed, reaching his ears. His pale eyes blazed. "During questioning, not only of myself, but of others, your name continually came up."

Taken aback, she clamped her arms over her chest and

jutted her chin. "*I'm* the prime suspect? They think I murdered Julius and kidnapped my own sister?"

"That is not what I am saying. But your presence at the resort has been mentioned several times by authorities. Not to mention your disapproval of the marriage."

"Great, just great." She ducked from beneath his hand. Memories of that anonymous phone call tipping her off about the wedding sickened her. The caller, whoever he was, wanted her here to take the heat. "They're wasting time investigating me. I'm putting a stop to it."

"Calm yourself, Francine."

"Not a chance, Colonel. I'm setting those people straight right now." Ignoring his orders to cease and desist, she hurried out of the kitchen.

The scene within the private dining room astonished her. Electronic equipment covered the long dining table and the big sideboard. Frankie recognized tape recorders, but the rest was so much impressive gadgetry to her unschooled eyes. Detailed maps of the area were pinned to the walls. Two men in dark suits wore headsets. Two other men, again in dark suits, conferred with a uniformed officer. A woman wearing a blue suit sat at the table, making notes in a black binder notebook. No mistaking the suits for anything other than FBI. The room crackled with an air of efficient command.

The woman lifted her head, acknowledged Frankie's presence with a hard stare and stood. "This area is off-limits."

"I'm Frankie Forrest, Penny's sister. You seem to think I'm a criminal mastermind."

The room hushed and activity ceased. More angered than intimidated, Frankie stalked to the long table. The agent lifted her chin. She was of average height, but had square shoulders and an imposing air. She extended her hand.

"I'm Agent Pamela Patrick."

Annoyed and feeling at a disadvantage, Frankie crossed

her arms, refusing to shake hands. "You're running this show?"

"Yes, I am. And no, nobody is accusing you of being a mastermind, Miss Forrest. Please, sit down." Her voice was kind, as were her eyes.

Beginning to feel embarrassed about her belligerence, Frankie took a chair. "My uncle says you want everyone to take lie detector tests. How will that help get my sister back?"

"I don't know about lie detector tests, Miss Forrest. I assume any requests of that sort will come from the state police. They are handling the murder investigation. I assure you, my prime objective is to see your sister returned safe and sound."

Deflated, and feeling somehow robbed of strength-sustaining fury, Frankie turned her gaze to the plate-glass window. Gray skies shocked her. Weather in Colorado changed rapidly; in the mountains it often shifted with deadly speed. But low-hung clouds and winds that bent the treetops stunned her. The last time she'd noticed, there hadn't been a cloud in the sky.

"You!"

The screechy cry made Frankie jump to her feet.

In a swirl of fox fur, Belinda Bannerman Caulfield stormed into the dining room. Frankie backed up a step, striking the table. Belinda wasn't a pretty woman—she probably hadn't been pretty as a girl. She had a long, horsey face, no chin to speak of, and the outer corners of her eyes drooped, giving her a perpetually bored expression.

Tears had washed away the cosmetics from her lower face, and the skin beneath was blotchy and sallow. She looked every one of her sixty-four years, and then some. Her eyes blazed with fearsome, glittering light—focused directly on Frankie.

"Murderer," she said, harsh and low and full of hatred.

Realizing the woman meant her, Frankie pressed against the table with nowhere to run.

Unwavering, Belinda pointed at Frankie's face. Diamonds and colored gemstones sparkled on her hand and wrist. A single tear tracked her withered cheek. "You did this. You and that wretched little sister of yours. You murdered my baby, and if it takes every penny I own, if it takes the rest of my life, I will see you pay."

Chapter Five

Being suspected of murder through innuendo angered Frankie; for Belinda Caulfield to accuse her directly stunned her. Unable to form a single word she stared into the woman's tearful eyes.

"Arrest this woman," Belinda said, her voice ringing with command.

Max Caulfield loomed behind his wife. Frankie's throat went dry as awful memories collided with this present horror. To Max she'd opened her heart, mind and body, shared all her fears and joys, and offered him her trust. After so many years of battling bureaucrats and the greed of her father's family, after sacrificing her youth for Penny's care, she'd thought she found the one person with whom she could let down her guard.

She searched his face for compassion and understanding, perhaps protection from his anguished wife.

Max placed his hands on his wife's shoulders and murmured close to her ear. Belinda closed her eyes. Her swaddling of fur jiggled as if wind brushed. The woman seemed to shrink, melting, until Max was actually holding her upright.

"She murdered him," she whispered plaintively. "She killed my baby. Do something, Maxie, do something."

Max guided her to a chair where she bent over with her

face on her hands. He lifted his head and his cool, dark gaze grazed Frankie, but failed to linger.

Frankie read nothing in his coldly handsome face. The hurt of his betrayal felt fresh again. Every muscle in her body tightened and ached.

"My wife requires medical attention," Max said. Still without looking at Frankie, he added, "And it might be best if you leave, Miss Forrest. You are upsetting her."

Hot spots flared on Frankie's face. She sensed all eyes upon her. "I didn't kill Julius," she said through clenched teeth. Nobody paid her any attention. Unable to bear Belinda's sobs she slunk out of the dining room.

McKennon waited outside the door. He reached as if to stop her, but she stepped around him and threw up a hand to ward him away. "The boss needs you," she snarled. She forced herself to walk, not run.

She took refuge in Elise's office. With both hands, she quietly closed the door. Cold from the inside out, she tucked her hands beneath her armpits.

Feeling lonely and out of place she wandered the small office. She ached for Penny and she ached for Belinda, too. As much as she hated Belinda, the stark grief in the woman's eyes had touched her. She dropped onto the love seat and curled her legs beneath her. She hugged a throw pillow to her chest.

"Oh, God," she whispered, "I know I don't pray enough. I'm not good enough. But Penny is innocent, she's good. Keep her safe, please? Take me, kill me, blow me up with lightning, but let her be safe. Please, God, just let her be okay." She closed her eyes and hugged the pillow tighter, praying over and over with all her heart.

SHAKING ROCKED FRANKIE and she muttered irritably for her tormenter to leave her alone. The shaking continued while a soft voice urged her to awaken.

She opened one eye. Slowly McKennon's face came into focus. Contacts, she mused. Maybe contact lenses made his eyes so green. No, at this distance his eyes were clearly without the telltale cap of contacts. He smelled like soap in a rainstorm, heavenly. She inhaled his scent which roused a strange familiarity within her breast. He smelled exactly the way she imagined a man should smell.

"How come," she asked, and her tongue felt as thick and sticky as week-old oatmeal, "you aren't married?"

"It would be too much bother to housebreak me."

"You have a house? I figured Max just stuck you in a closet at night."

He chuckled, the corners of his eyes crinkling. "Wake up."

Realization flooded through her, snapping her wide-awake. *Penny!* She shoved frantically at the woolly weight over her side.

"Hey, hey, calm down. Everything is all right."

She blinked rapidly until Aunt Elise's pastel office came into focus. She struggled upright and rested on an elbow. Her neck creaked. Someone had covered her with a crocheted afghan. She'd fallen asleep on the love seat.

Afraid she'd missed some important development, she flung the afghan away. "Is there news? Did they find her?"

"Not yet." He rested a hand against her cheek.

Befuddled by the dimness—it couldn't be dark outside!—she peered owlishly at her surroundings. A small Tiffany-style lamp cast rosy light from the desk. His fingertips caressed her cheek. Arrested by the intensity of his expression, she leaned into the warm comfort of his touch.

A frown line deepened between his brows. He swallowed hard.

"I should have been nicer to you before." She swallowed hard herself.

"I always knew your bark was worse than your bite." He snatched his hand from her face and sat back on his heels. He turned his head, and the frown deepened.

A funny feeling lodged in her throat. McKennon acted nice because he was nice, only she'd been too stubborn to acknowledge it before. She might not be in this predicament if she'd fallen for a decent guy like him, instead of for a self-centered, cold-blooded rotter like Max Caulfield.

She rolled her stiff neck. Her feet were asleep, tingling with impending pins and needles. She rubbed her eyes. "I can't believe I fell asleep."

"You needed it." He rose and stretched. He looked weary himself.

He was a big man, with a deep chest and heavy shoulders, but his belly was flat and his hips were trim. Frankie liked him better dressed in flannel and denim than in his usual somber suits. Catching herself staring too intently at the way denim molded over his hips and thighs, she scowled at a scab on her finger. Cat had scratched her the other day.

"How's Belinda?" she asked, cautiously. She raked her fingers through her tangled hair.

"She's in bad shape. If she isn't better in a few hours she'll be airlifted to Denver. Mr. Caulfield is worried about her heart. She has angina."

"She called me a murderer." She spoke with more sadness than anger. "I can't believe she blames me."

"Don't take it personally. She's a blamer."

"Easy for you to say. She isn't blaming you." She gave up trying to order her hair. She smacked her dry lips and walked over to the ceramic watercooler in a corner. Two cups of cold water refreshed her immensely. "Is there any progress at all?"

He sat on the love seat and stretched out his legs. Arching his back, he clasped his hands and stretched, reaching for the ceiling. Sipping water, Frankie surreptitiously admired his sinuously feline grace.

"The state cops are handling the murder, and the FBI is handling the kidnapping. Exactly what any of them are doing, I have no idea."

"Do they have any leads?"

A slight grin turned his mouth crooked. "*They* ask the

questions.'' He folded his hands over his belly. ''The coroner took Julius. All the resort guests are checked out. The
state police has coordinated a manhunt, but I suspect the
FBI is calling the shots and keeping the police presence
low-key in order to protect Penny. That's all I know.''

''This is killing my aunt and uncle. The resort is their
whole life.''

''Mrs. Duke said she'll do the spring cleaning early.''

She paced aimlessly in the confines of the office. She
felt caged, helpless. ''What about the media? Anything on
the television? Radio?''

''Surprisingly enough, no.''

She passed a shaky hand over her face. Eyes closed, she
pictured Max Caulfield, so icy and calm. She realized now
he'd always been cold. He was the kind of man who knew
what he wanted and wasn't afraid to go after it. She'd admired him for it, once upon a time, and been dazzled by
his aggressive manliness and self-control. After seeing him
in the dining room, handling the situation without a trace
of emotion, she couldn't imagine why she'd ever thought
him attractive. Or capable of love.

She sat beside McKennon and crossed her arms. She
looked him straight in the eyes. ''It's Max. He murdered
Julius.''

McKennon quirked an eyebrow.

''He hates waste. Wasted time, wasted effort, wasted
money. Julius is, or was, a total waste of time. Max set this
up. Julius's death was no accident.''

''I doubt it.''

''Why? Because he signs your paycheck?'' As soon as
the words emerged, she regretted them.

As if her insulting comment failed to affect him, he fingered his chin and frowned thoughtfully. ''Caulfield is ruth-
less, but he has no motive to murder Julius. Or to hurt
Penny. Besides, this is too elaborate. It smacks of an amateur.''

''Yeah, yeah, and Max is no amateur. Which is exactly

why he'd pull something like this. No one would suspect him.''

"Julius has minimal impact on Caulfield's life. And the risk is too great. If he messes up, he loses his wife's money.''

Frankie sought holes in his argument, but couldn't find any. She didn't have firsthand knowledge of what went on in the Bannerman estate, and McKennon did. Even so, she hated letting go of Max as the villain. He fit the villainous role so perfectly.

"Maybe this isn't coming from Julius's side of the fence. Has Penny said anything to you about any threats in the past few months? Or even anything unusual? Somebody she knows might have gotten some ideas when he found out she was marrying Julius.''

Unable to face him, she pressed a fist to the base of her throat.

"What's the matter?''

Shame coursed through her and clashed with deep regrets. "Penny and I haven't talked much in the past few months.'' Her chest tightened, and a lump formed in her throat. "We had a big fight when school started. She went skiing with friends instead of coming home for Christmas.''

"What did you fight about?''

In hindsight, it seemed that ever since the Bannermans had entered their lives, she and Penny had done nothing except fight. She lifted a shoulder. "Julius. Her classes. Declaring a major. You name it.''

"I see.''

"I don't know how I screwed up so bad. I don't know what I did wrong.'' She turned to him. "Did you see her at the chapel? She hates me.''

"She doesn't hate you.''

"Then why did she get married? Why is any of this happening?''

"You can't blame yourself. I can't say I know Penny

well, but from what I've seen she's a determined young woman.''

Determined. That described Penny perfectly. For all her sweet appearance and charming smiles, Penny often shocked people with how stubborn she could be. Frankie remembered the battle over her mom's grave. In keeping with practicality and their mother's wish that her insurance money be used for her daughters, Frankie had ordered a simple brass marker. Penny had been outraged. Only a marble headstone engraved with angels and lambs would do. In a campaign lasting months, she'd pestered, pleaded and argued. When the girl began going around the neighborhood with a soup can in which to collect donations, Frankie had relented.

She realized her biggest mistake had been in forbidding Penny to see Julius. She'd lost the war as soon as she opened her mouth.

"It's been awful," she said quietly. "She wouldn't take my calls or return them. The only time I talked to her was when I went to the university and hunted her down."

"You're more like mother and daughter than sisters. Maybe it's a necessary separation thing."

She held up a hand, palm out. "Don't give me any psychobabble nonsense." Even as she snapped at him, she sensed the truth. To her dismay, tears sprang to the fore, and no amount of will could dam them. She jammed both heels of her hands against her eyes.

"Hey, hey, things will turn out all right."

All she could do was shake her head.

"This isn't your fault." His weight on the love seat caused her to roll slightly toward him. Then his arm was around her, and she pressed her face against his shoulder. He petted her hair. "None of this is your fault, Frankie. We'll get her back. I promise. You'll make things right between you."

His flannel shirt made her hot forehead itch. The sensation distracted her enough to get her emotions under control. Snuffling, she rubbed furiously at her face. She managed a nod. "Sorry...don't usually fall apart."

He kept holding her. Continued petting her. His lips brushed her forehead. Realization about what he did hit with a jolt. She lifted her gaze to his. He appeared as startled and discomfited as she felt. His biceps flexed against her shoulder. His hand made a convulsive movement against her back, sending shock waves down her spine. She hated herself for the impulses making her nerves jump, and worse, muddying her thoughts.

"Uh..." Her cheeks warmed.

His face darkened and he compressed his lips. His eyes seemed to burn, the golden flecks in the green sparking like embers. His scent, somehow luxurious, filled her head and made her dizzy.

"I need a drink of water," she whispered. She wanted him to kiss her again and take away all the pain.

"I'll get it for you." He made no move to rise.

She wanted him to stay—she desperately needed him to go. Confusion held her fast. Were this one of the dreams in which he starred she'd be jumping his bones. But it wasn't a dream, it was a nightmare, and Penny was in terrible danger and J. T. McKennon was the last man on earth she wanted, or needed.

She pressed upward, compelled by his mouth, hungry for a kiss—

"Cute."

Max Caulfield's dry voice snapped Frankie from her spell. Gasping, she shoved at McKennon's chest and scrambled to her feet. McKennon rose, as well, but gracefully, his expression now as cool as if he'd slipped on a mask.

Arms crossed, Max leaned a shoulder against the doorjamb. A faint smile tweaked the corners of his lips, but his dark eyes were as sharp and humorless as ever. She hated him with every fiber of her being.

"Still sneaking around, spying on people, huh?" she snapped.

His disdain for her came through loud and clear. He wore the same icy smirk he'd worn when he'd dumped her. The relaxed body language that said he considered her of less significance than a bug. A bug he'd squashed beneath his feet and walked away from without a second thought.

She wanted to hurt him. Slap the smugness off his face. Knock him in the head and see some emotion in his eyes. Make him pay for the past and the present.

He glanced at McKennon. Emotion flickered across his face, a slight drop of an eyebrow, a flash of annoyance perhaps.

A crazed impulse gripped her. Max hated to share, and he hated even more when the bugs he crushed got back on their feet. She wrapped an arm around McKennon's lean waist and snuggled up close to him. Forcing a smile, she said, "What do you want, Max? You're interrupting."

He scratched his chin with one manicured fingernail.

How, she wondered, had she ever thought him sexy? Wonderful? Husband material? He was slime.

"Close the door on your way out. J.T. and I don't care for an audience, thank you very much."

"Is that so?"

She rubbed a hand suggestively over McKennon's broad chest. "Yeah, that's so. I really should have sent you a thank-you card for introducing us. Mc—*J.T.* is a whole lot better in bed than you ever were."

He dropped his arms. His dark eyes blazed. "Always the classy broad." He turned on his heel, tossing over his shoulder, "McKennon, come with me. I need to talk to you."

Appalled by what she'd done, Frankie sprang away from the big man. All she could do was stare at him with her mouth hanging open and her face feeling as if it might incinerate.

McKennon passed a hand over the side of his hair. He tugged at his shirt collar, straightening it. He slid a look at the doorway then back to her. "Hope your little joke was worth it, Miss Forrest. You just got me fired."

J.T. FOLLOWED HIS BOSS down a long corridor. As he walked, in no hurry to catch up, he pondered the situation. He should be angry at Frankie for pulling such a stupid stunt. He doubted Caulfield felt any jealousy or insecurity about an affair between his chief security expert and his ex-fiancée, but he would not tolerate having the two of them in a position to exchange notes.

Except, he felt no anger. By remaining silent he'd played along. He could have pushed her away or denied an affair. Instead, he'd let her poke at Caulfield, and even enjoyed it a little bit. That flare of emotion on the boss's face had been strangely satisfying.

Watching Caulfield's rigid back and listening to the crisp crack of his shoes on the wooden flooring, J.T. decided he felt relieved. No more Caulfield and his increasingly arrogant attitude. No more sitting through long-winded bull sessions, during which Caulfield extolled his own prowess and wove fantasies about crushing his enemies. No more tolerating Belinda Caulfield's self-absorbed demands.

No more big, fat paycheck.

He mentally ran through his financial situation. Insurance for Jamie had run out long ago, so he was stuck paying the entire monthly bill of five thousand dollars. Consultations with specialists, physical therapies and occasional emergencies added to the cost. He drove a ten-year-old car, lived in a cheap apartment and eschewed credit cards and entertainment. His only real expense was his wardrobe; Caulfield insisted his security people look like top professionals. He squirreled away any extra money for Jamie's future. Someday his son would need tutors, then there would be college.

He supposed he could survive for a month or two until he found another job. But where to find a job that paid as well and didn't require extensive travel? Satisfaction drained away. He hated this job, but he needed it desperately.

Caulfield reached the end of the hallway. A door led outside. A mudroom filled with heavy coats and overshoes lay to the right. Wind battered at the door, moaning as if frustrated at being denied entry. J.T. repressed a shiver, along with the urge to shove his hands in his pockets.

Caulfield turned around and clamped his hands on his hips. He threw back his head and laughed.

Bemused and wary, J.T. stood at stiff attention.

"I should have kept that girl on the side," the boss finally said. "Nobody can make me laugh the way she can. But for a broad as smart as she is, she's got a blind spot as big as a barn door."

Now thoroughly confused, J.T. kept stupid questions to himself.

"This is good." Caulfield nodded, his eyes narrowed. "Coming on to you is her first mistake. What has she told you?"

"Nothing, sir." An impulse rose to tell Caulfield that Frankie hadn't been kidding. That would wipe that grin off his face. The impulse stuck in his throat like a wad of pulp.

"She's a sucker for charm, McKennon. Keep playing her."

He couldn't help himself. "I thought I was about to be terminated, sir."

"Over a twit like her?" He snorted derisively. Shaking a finger, he added, "But that's good. That'll be perfect. Tell her I canned you. Play on her sympathies." He laughed again. "I want you to nail her."

Usually, J.T. had little trouble following the boss's machinations. At the moment he was lost. Unless... "So you honestly believe Miss Forrest had something to do with her sister's kidnapping?"

"Kidnapping? We're talking flat-out murder and extortion. Marry Julius, knock him off, then little Miss Penny gets to play the grieving widow. The *rich* widow with my three million bucks! That won't happen.''

"Have you discussed this with the FBI, sir?''

"No, and neither will you. This is personal. Frankie isn't getting away with it, and I'm the man to make sure she doesn't. Get close to her. Hell, get her in the sack for some pillow talk.'' He winked salaciously. "Do you some good. I want evidence. I want a confession. I don't care how you get it as long as I'm the man who drags her in front of a judge. Got it?''

"Yes, sir.''

"You know what you have to do.'' Caulfield stalked back the way he'd come. As he passed, he shot J.T. a hateful glare. "Killing Julius,'' he said tightly. "Know what that means? I have to listen to that old bat moan and groan for the next ten years. For that alone, I could kill Frankie with my own hands.''

Stunned, J.T. watched the boss walk away.

ENOUGH IS ENOUGH, Frankie thought as she entered the dining room turned command post. If she were to get Penny back, she had to reclaim control of herself. No more weeping, no more panic, no more hand wringing. She paused inside the door to watch the FBI agents and state law officers. She felt immense relief McKennon wasn't present. With the relief came shame. All her life she'd prided herself on her integrity—she did not use people. But she'd used McKennon, and he'd be the one who suffered for it. Max was probably spiteful enough to not merely fire the man, but to blackball him in the security field.

She owed McKennon a huge apology.

From the far end of the long dining table, Agent Patrick lifted her head and met Frankie's eyes. "There's no news yet, Miss Forrest.''

Frankie heard pity. She sensed it in the gazes directed her way. Shoulders back, spine straight, she approached the agent in charge. "I'm a professional graphologist, Ms. Patrick," she said. "Might I look at the ransom note again? I may—"

The agent interrupted with a curt, "No." She smiled, but it appeared forced. "I appreciate the offer, but all evidence is currently being examined by our experts." She gestured with a hand, and another agent materialized at Frankie's side. "This is Agent Boswell. We have more questions we'd like you to answer."

At being dismissed so easily, Frankie bristled. "Any idiot can see this is an inside job, Ms. Patrick. I used to work for Max Caulfield. I've examined the handwriting of many of his employees. I might be able to learn something useful."

"I know all about your history with Mr. Caulfield."

Frankie heard the threat. "I didn't kill Julius. I don't care what his mother says. Or what Max says, either. I had nothing to do with any of this. So don't you dare brush me off. That's my sister out there!"

The agent's nonreaction reminded Frankie to stay in control. Her back muscles trembled with the effort it took to maintain an easy posture.

"Penny is flesh and blood. She's nineteen—a child. She's pregnant, for God's sake! What are you doing to find her?"

"Miss Forrest," the agent's voice dropped to a soothing purr, "our number-one priority is to have your sister returned alive and unharmed. We will not annoy her abductors or attempt any wild heroics. We will get her back."

"How? What are you doing?"

"I've brought in every agent in the regional field office. By tomorrow morning twenty more will arrive. We have officers from the state police and the Colorado Bureau of Investigation running down leads and interviewing potential witnesses." She glanced at the window. Sleet pattered across the glass. "At first light, if weather permits, we're sending up choppers to search from the air. We have reason to believe the kidnappers are holding your sister nearby. I can't say any more, so you must trust me."

"Why can't you say any more? Because you think I did it? Is that why I keep getting shoved into corners?"

"Boswell, please escort Miss Forrest out of this room."

Frankie stepped away from the man and glared until he lowered his hands. The kindness left Agent Patrick's eyes. Without a smile she appeared much older than Frankie had first assumed. The agent tapped a pencil against the table-top.

"I understand your concerns, Miss Forrest."

"You don't understand squat! Those bastards threatened to kill my sister." She slashed her hand through the air. "Aside from bringing in a bunch of bells and whistles and hassling my family, I don't see you doing a thing to help her."

This time no amount of growling or glaring dissuaded Agent Boswell. He clamped a hand around her upper arm in a grip one step below painful.

As he dragged her out of the dining room, she yelled, "I'm not that easy to get rid of! You'll have to deal with me one way or another!" She turned her fury on the male agent. "Let me go!"

He complied, but only when she was in the hallway and he stood between her and the door. Good sense stopped her before she punched him in the nose. Getting tossed in the pokey for assaulting an FBI agent wouldn't help Penny. She curled her hands into fists.

"Frankie!" Her cousin Janine hurried down the hallway toward her. She waved. "There you are."

Janine hooked her arm with Frankie's and tugged her in the direction of the kitchen. "I'm glad you're awake. We have work to do."

"What's going on?"

"We're raising money."

"Huh?"

"The ransom." Janine wrinkled her nose as if appalled

by Frankie's stupidity. "We've got twenty-four hours to raise three million, and we need all the help we can get."

Frankie stopped short, causing Janine to stumble. The horror of realization swelled in her breast as Frankie stared at her cousin. Her stomach churned and bile rose in her throat. *Three million dollars!* A paltry sum, the kidnappers claimed. Paltry to Belinda Bannerman Caulfield maybe— the same woman who accused Frankie of murdering her son.

Chapter Six

Frankie strode through the hallways of the sprawling lodge. Three million dollars! Three million dollars or Penny died—and probably not as peacefully as Julius had, either. Belinda Caulfield could write a check in that amount. She owned Bannerman Fine Jewelers, a chain of retail stores selling jewelry in malls across the United States. Only Max could convince Belinda to provide the ransom, and Frankie had to go and insult him. Worse, she'd insulted him through his trusted, right-hand man.

Her family could never raise the ransom money. Not in the twenty-four hours remaining, anyway. The Dukes were well-to-do, but a long way from being wealthy. Elk River Resort was worth a lot of money, but it was heavily mortgaged. As for herself, she hadn't even paid her phone bill this month.

Frankie had dropped in on the brainstorming session. The Colonel, Ross and Janine were making calls to friends and far-flung family. Frankie needed her aunt. Elise could charm the pants off a statue. Maybe she could charm Belinda Caulfield.

In the lobby, she stopped short and frowned at the activity. Men and women on ladders lowered chandeliers from the high ceiling. Others stood inside the huge round fireplace, cleaning the interior of the copper chimney hood. Still others dismantled the window coverings. Frankie's jaw tightened. The Colonel took care of his employees with the same compassion with which he'd cared for his army troops. Despite the family's current troubles the employees remained to work and collect their paychecks.

Frankie spotted her aunt seated in the lounge on the far side of the lobby. Though his back was to Frankie she recognized McKennon's broad shoulders and shiny black hair. A spasm of pain jerked tighter the ever-present knot in her belly. Having to face him after what she'd done made her want to crawl on her belly, groveling and pleading for forgiveness. She forced her feet to move.

McKennon had his wallet out. He showed Elise a photograph of a little boy.

Elise looked over her shoulder. "Oh, there you are, dear. How are you feeling? Did a nap help?"

"Yes."

McKennon closed the wallet and sat forward to slide it into his back pocket. She wondered who the child was. Unable to look at his face for fear of what she might see, she focused on her aunt. "What's going on?"

"J.T. was telling me about his son." Elise rose and patted McKennon on the shoulder in a motherly gesture. "I'm sure everything will work out," she told him.

Son? Hurt slithered through Frankie. She'd known McKennon for years, but never heard him mention having a kid. She wondered if he had a wife, too. She shoved her hands in the pockets of the borrowed sweatpants. "I need to talk to you, Aunt Elise. It's about the ransom money."

"Don't you worry, dear. The Colonel is calling in all markers, and the bank is willing to work with us on a loan."

"We're talking three million dollars. There aren't enough markers." She glanced at McKennon. He appeared interested in the conversation. Her skin itched with the effort of sensing his vibes. Did he hate her? Was he angry? She couldn't tell.

"We will raise the money." Elise nodded firmly.

"Belinda Caulfield has the money. Three million is chump change to her." She grasped Elise's slim arm. "You were the best fund-raiser in military history. You can convince her to give up the cash. I know you can."

"I don't know about that, dear. She's suffered a terrible tragedy. I doubt she can bear any more involvement."

"You have to try."

"Not possible," McKennon said.

She watched two women removing hanger clips from sheer draperies. "Why is it impossible? Because she hates me?"

"That, too, but mostly because she's ill. She's heavily sedated. I imagine Caulfield will be taking her back to the Springs first thing in the morning. She needs to see her own doctor."

She made herself look at him. His expression was grim. Lines had deepened around his eyes and mouth. Beard shadow darkened his jaw. The urge to grovel and plead for his forgiveness freshened in her heart. "What about Max?"

"He seems a reasonable man, J.T.," Elise said. "Will he help?"

"I don't know."

Elise checked her wristwatch. "Perhaps the Colonel and I can present our case to Mr. Caulfield. The poor man must be starving. He's been at his wife's side ever since she collapsed. We'll take him a nice supper. I'm certain he'll want to help." She made her farewells and hurried away.

Frankie chewed her lower lip. She kept seeing Max's cold eyes and colder smirk. "She doesn't stand a chance," she said wearily. She turned to go, but McKennon made a soft sound. She froze, chilled by embarrassment and guilt. Knowing her apology was going to have to happen eventually, she decided sooner was better than later. She sat on the couch.

Frankie fidgeted with a loose string on the sweatpants. *I'm sorry,* she practiced in her head, but that would sound weak. *I'm an idiot, I have a big mouth.* That sounded as if she made excuses.

"How are you doing?" he asked.

She shrugged. The thread snapped. She mushed it into a tiny ball between her fingers. "I didn't know you had kids."

"One. A little boy."

Her discomfort deepened. "You're divorced? He lives with his mom?"

"My wife died."

The simple statement of fact made her cringe. How could she have worked with him for two years without knowing such a huge part of his life? Maybe Max's betrayal hadn't crushed her faith in her instincts. Maybe she'd never had any instincts to begin with. Maybe she'd been a fraud from the get-go, an arrogant sham, deluding herself into thinking she could understand people. "I'm sorry. What happened?" Wishing she hadn't asked, she curled her lips between her teeth.

"A guy playing bumper tag on the highway lost control, jumped the median and struck my wife's car head-on. She was killed instantly."

Nodding, she fiddled with her fingernails. She hadn't had a real manicure in months. She'd given up professional manicures, her favorite luxury, after Max dumped and fired her. She'd given up beautiful nails for Penny. How very petty, she thought. McKennon had lost his wife. "You have a live-in nanny or something?" She pictured a cute blonde who adored her employer.

"He's in a hospital. He's been in a coma for the past four years."

She snapped up her head and gawked at him, horrified as much by his dry intonation as by the tragedy of a child in a coma. "Oh no," she whispered.

"Jamie was in a car seat strapped in the back. It saved his life, but he suffered extensive head injuries. He hasn't recovered yet."

Something hot and hurtful loosened in her chest. Instinctively she reached a hand toward him. "God, I am so sorry. I wish I'd known. I've been so mean to you."

He entwined his fingers with hers, and the corners of his mouth pulled in a gentle smile. "I like it when you're mean."

Hearing how she'd sounded—as if McKennon needed her pity and if she'd known he was so pathetic she'd have been nice to him—she hung her head in shame. She ought to plug up her big mouth with cement and be done with it. "How about when I'm stupid?" She sighed. "I really messed things up back there. I bet Max took big chunks out of your hide."

"Don't worry about it."

"He fired you, didn't he? I am so sorry. I'll talk to him. I'll eat dirt. I don't know why I did what I did, it was so dumb. All I want is Penny back, but there he was, with that smile of his and I went crazy. I'll make it right, McKennon, I swear—"

He pressed a finger to her lips. "I'd advise that you stay well away from Max Caulfield."

She shook her head in firm denial. "I can't let this happen. You can't lose your job because of me." She caught his hand in both of hers and clasped it to her breast. "You've been a real friend. I sure don't deserve it. I can't let you take the heat."

"Stay away from Caulfield. I mean it."

"I'm not scared of him."

"You should be. He thinks you're behind Julius's murder."

"So what? I don't care what he thinks."

"You better care what he *does*. He told me I can keep my job if I can gather enough evidence to convict you."

Uncertain if she'd heard him correctly she blinked rapidly. "What evidence?"

"He doesn't care what it is as long as you're convicted of murder."

Knowing he wouldn't joke about something this serious, she searched his face, anyway, for any hint that he was teasing. "That is so stupid. I didn't even know about the wedding until yesterday. How could I plan a kidnapping?"

"Do you remember the Greenhill case?"

Under any other circumstances she'd be laughing her head off. She'd never committed a criminal act in her life. The very idea that anyone would suspect of her something so awful as murder transcended ridiculous. His mentioning Greenhill stripped the situation of any shred of humor.

Greenhill, a former executive for a computer company, had been suspected of selling company R&D reports to competitors. Max had gathered enough evidence to get the man fired, but not enough to convict him in a criminal court. Then, miraculously, stolen files had turned up in the trunk of his car on the very same day the firm's security guards miraculously decided to search Greenhill's car.

"Greenhill was too smart to leave a paper trail. He did everything by computer."

"I never believed that rumor about Max planting evidence." Six months ago she hadn't believed it. Now she wondered.

"I'm not saying I believe it, either. I'm merely exploring the possibilities. Have you had any contact at all with Julius since you left the company?"

The knuckles on her right hand tingled in ghostly memory. On that last day as she'd departed Max's office after The Big Dump, Julius had been there. Smirking, knowing full well what had happened to her and why, he'd said, "Don't bother giving Mum a blender for a wedding present, darling. She has plenty." She'd decked him. She figured the FBI and the police knew all about that, too. McKennon, as well. She looked away.

The seriousness of the situation slowly sank in. If Max murdered Julius, then he murdered Penny. And he would send Frankie to prison for life. The implications were too horrible to contemplate.

"For all his faults, Max isn't a criminal." Her appalling lack of conviction made her chest hurt. "Is he?" She turned back to face him. "You wouldn't work for a criminal."

"You're right, I wouldn't. I've seen him stretch the boundaries, but never cross them." He lowered his gaze.

"How far does he stretch them?" She sat back and stubbornly crossed her arms. "Does he ask you to do… unethical things?"

"He pays well." His voice held a tinge of annoyance. "I get twice what I'd make working the same job anywhere else in the state. And yes, I need the money. Jamie's care can cost as much as ten grand in a month. But he doesn't pay enough for me to break the law. He's never asked me to do anything illegal. He knows I wouldn't do it."

Shame over getting him fired came rolling back full force. Her asinine action had lost him more than a mere job—he'd lost the means to care for his son. She passed a hand over her eyes. She knew exactly how it felt to go from a fat salary to a zero bank account balance.

"I'm not scared of him," she said. "He isn't going to start planting evidence because of me." She wished she meant it.

"This situation—" he spoke slowly, as if testing each word "—is different."

"What do you mean?"

"I told you, Mrs. Caulfield is a blamer. If her son's murderer isn't handed to her quickly, she's going to blame the person closest to her."

"So he'll hang me to get his wife off his back?" She waved both hands in the air. "That's ridiculous."

"Is it?" He arched an eyebrow. "Mrs. Caulfield's net worth is somewhere in the neighborhood of three hundred million dollars. Caulfield has a private jet, a fleet of cars, full-time servants, you name it, he's got it. Mrs. Caulfield dislikes travel so now she can send him to attend to her business concerns. You know how much he loves to travel."

Sensing more, she waited. When nothing was forthcoming, she filled in the blanks herself. Max had never made a secret of his true ambition. He wanted to be filthy rich, rolling in it, able to snap his fingers and have people falling all over themselves to fulfill his every whim.

"He has a lot to lose if Belinda turns on him," she said. He nodded in reply.

"He'll lose everything?"

"As far as he's concerned, yes. He's finalizing the sale of the corporation. If his wife cans him, he'll have to start over from scratch. He's desperate. It makes him dangerous. You have to stay away from him."

As she glared at the security expert, knowing him honest, loyal and ethical, a fierce joy rose in her belly, a fire fueled by righteous indignation. Max had gone too far when he tipped his hand to McKennon.

"We'll show him, won't we?" She placed a hand on his knee. If the lobby weren't full of people she'd have kissed him. Kissed him out of gratitude, but also because he had the most beautiful lips she'd ever seen. "You think he's dangerous? Wait until you see me in action, McKennon. If he's responsible for a single bruise on Penny, I will kill him with my bare hands."

"FRANKIE?"

Startled awake, Frankie blinked furiously until Janine's face came into view. Disconcerted, she struggled upright and looked around. Bookshelves covered one wall, and a corner desk held an impressive array of computer equipment. Framed art posters were arranged on the mauve-colored walls. Janine's room, she remembered. She rubbed her aching eyes with the pads of her fingers. She hated waking up in strange places. She wished she were home in her own narrow bed, snuggling her own pillow and listening to Cat thump around grumbling over her refusal to jump out of bed at his bidding.

"What time is it?"

"Almost eight."

Groaning, she flung off the covers. "Why did you let me sleep in?" The expression on her cousin's face finally sank in. Janine looked as if she'd been punched in the belly. "What is it? What's wrong? Did they find Penny?" Chilled, she pulled on the sweatpants and socks she'd worn yesterday. She scrubbed her bare arms.

"Nothing wrong...exactly." Janine pulled a cord. Window draperies parted.

Almost eight o'clock she'd said, but the world outside was as gray as dusk. Swathes of icy snow frosted the window glass as if applied with a cake spatula. Frankie hurried to the window and stared outside. Snow blanketed the earth. Pine trees bent under heavy loads. The low-slung stables were barely recognizable. The parking lot looked like a huge, dimpled comforter. Fat snowflakes drifted from the clouds, forming a moving curtain that turned the surrounding forest into haze.

From a distance an engine roared. A huge plume of shooting snow marked somebody operating a snowblower.

"Where the hell did this come from?"

Janine leaned back on one hip, crossed her arms over her chest and glared at the wintry scene. "Better question, when is it going away? Yesterday they said four to eight inches, but we've got two feet of snow out there and drifts up to eight feet. The windchill factor puts the temperature in the minus teens."

"What about the roads?" She stared in amazement at the all-encompassing whiteness. Normally she loved snow, relishing any chance to go skiing. Right now it terrified her.

"Chain laws are in effect, but the roads are still open. The wind died, which is good. The real problems are along the Front Range. This storm stretches from Wyoming to New Mexico. It hit Colorado Springs and Denver hard. The cities are all but shut down."

Frankie wondered if the kidnappers had a weather coningency plan. "When you say shut down you mean the banks, don't you?"

Janine nodded. "But look at it this way, if we can't get out, then the kidnappers can't get out, either."

Rapid knocking made Janine turn to the door. It opened and her brother's dark head peeked around the jamb. "Everybody decent?" Ross asked, then entered without awaiting a reply. His gray eyes gleamed with excitement, and his smile was the first Frankie had seen in days.

"We did it!"

"Did what?" Frankie and Janine asked in unison.

"We found Connie Haxman. She'll get us the cash. Every dime we need."

The name struck a familiar chord with Frankie, but she couldn't place it. She questioned her cousin.

"Dawn's friend. She's on a cruise in the Caribbean. We finally got through to her ship. It took some doing, but Dawn is a champ when it comes to working through telephone mazes."

Frankie raised her eyebrows. Now she remembered. Ross's wife, Dawn, had once been a wealthy woman, but a thieving ex-husband had left her practically penniless. Dawn's friends were the wealthy scions of Colorado society. Connie Haxman was Dawn's best friend—her extremely rich and apparently extremely generous best friend.

"She's going to give us the money? All of it?"

"She has her people working on it right now."

"I could kiss you!" She flung her arms around his neck and did just that. A big wet smack on his cheek. Laughing, he caught her around the waist and spun her in a circle. Her feet left the floor.

"All right, you guys, we still have work to do." Ever practical, Janine forcibly separated them. "I take it Dawn is handling the arrangements back in the Springs?"

He clapped his hands once. "Right. Two FBI agents are going with me to collect the money. I should be back here by six o'clock." He rolled his eyes. "Do those jerk kidnappers have any idea how much room three million bucks takes up?''

Frankie cast a worried look out the window. "Can you get through? What if they close the roads?"

"Never fear." He clamped an arm over his belly and bowed in the manner of a royal gallant. "The latest weather report says this should stop by noon. If I need a snowplow the FBI will provide one. We're a top priority. If all else fails the Colonel has friends in high places at Fort Carson. If a snowplow can't get through, a tank still can." He kept grinning. "But this storm is good news, Cuz. You know how freaked out the media gets over any change in weather. The only things you can find on any station are weather reports. Nobody knows about Julius."

Colorado weather could be a wicked thing. A blizzard one day, seventy degrees the next. Anybody with an ounce of sense realized that predicting the weather in the Rockies was an iffy proposition at best. Monkeys throwing darts at a weather map could probably do as well as the National Weather Service meteorologists. For some odd reason Colorado newscasters got excited about storms. Having never lived anywhere else, Frankie didn't know if this was common amongst media types, or peculiar to the area. In any case, Ross was right. World war breaking out or the assassination of the president might override storm news coverage, but the kidnapping of a local girl would not.

For the first time since her sister's disappearance Frankie felt real hope. The lightness clung to her while she showered. Janine had left Frankie's own clothing, clean and pressed. She never ironed her blue jeans and the creases amused her. Her belly rumbled with honest hunger.

She hoped to find McKennon in the kitchen.

She met him in the hallway outside the room. Flattered he'd sought her out, she smiled. He wore a dark red cable-knit sweater. The color complemented his eyes, making them jewel-like. Her insides did a funny little dance.

"Good morning." She fluttered her eyelashes. "What brings you all the way up here?"

He jerked a thumb over his shoulder. "Mrs. Duke is power cleaning the guest wing. She moved me to this floor."

She stopped fluttering. "Oh."

"Did you sleep well?"

"Just fine," she muttered. When would she learn? She'd never had any luck in the romance department. Even if McKennon were remotely interested in her as a desirable woman, now was not the time or place.

He touched her shoulder. "What's wrong?"

"Nothing is wrong. Everything is going right for a change. Did you hear? We're getting the money." To answer his questioning look, she told him what Ross and his wife had been able to accomplish.

"That's great."

His smile was so genuine and warm Frankie feared she might melt into a puddle on the carpet runner. She scowled at the ridiculous yearnings piling up within her heart. He hadn't meant anything when he kissed her, and if he was kind, it was because he was a kind man. He probably fed stray animals and helped old ladies across the street.

"So what's wrong?"

"Nothing." Her irritability made her wince. It wasn't his fault he didn't like her. Passing a hall mirror, she glimpsed wet hair already springing into unmanageable corkscrews. A man like McKennon need only look at a woman and she'd be his. Why should he bother with a too-tall, graceless, big-mouthed, bad-tempered carrot-top?

"Hmm," he murmured. "Nothing. That can only mean you're angry with me."

At the top of the stairs she turned to him. "I'm not mad."

"You look angry. You sound angry." He cocked his head, a gesture appealing in its boyishness. "I thought we were starting to become friends."

"Yeah," she said, unable to hide her self-disgust. "That's us, best buds." Uncomfortable with the conversation and uncomfortable with him, she took the stairs down two at a time.

In the kitchen, Kara stood next to a table, looking as quivery as a hunting dog who'd just flushed a covey of quail. Elise and Janine were seated, but they stared wide-eyed at an FBI agent.

"What is it?" Frankie asked. She sensed danger.

The FBI agent answered. "The kidnappers called, Miss Forrest. They've made their demands."

"They said forty-eight hours," Frankie protested. She turned on McKennon as if he held some power over the course of events. "It hasn't been forty-eight hours."

Everyone hurried to the dining room turned command post. Frankie imagined that with the blizzard the kidnappers' plans had changed. She prayed they'd changed for the better.

The Colonel awaited them in the dining room. Arms behind his stiff back, he presented a sterner countenance than usual. Agent Patrick didn't look as crisp as she had before. There were bags under her eyes, and her face, devoid of makeup, appeared haggard. She'd probably catnapped on one of the cots set up against a wall. Used coffee cups littered the table.

"How do we get Penny back?" Frankie asked.

Agent Patrick nodded at a man who sat in front of a large reel-to-reel tape player. He had a pair of headphones hanging around his neck. The agent pressed a button and the reels began to turn.

"Julius Bannerman here," a man said, his voice edged with appropriate tension. "Do you have my wife?"

"Mr. Bannerman," a stiffly mechanical voice said, "take notes. I will not repeat myself—"

"Do you have my wife? I want proof she's still alive."

"—you will leave Elk River Resort at exactly 6:00 a.m. tomorrow. You will drive directly to Eleven Mile reservoir on Road 247. You will drive at twenty miles per hour until you reach Road 59. You will continue on that road at twenty miles per hour until we contact you. You will be entirely exposed, Mr. Bannerman. If there are any signs of any cops in the area, if there is a plane or helicopter flying overhead, we will kill your wife. Once you hand over the money you will receive instructions on how to find your wife. Thank you.''

A soft clack, then the agent posing as Julius said, ''Wait a minute, I want proof my wife is alive. Let me speak to her. I didn't understand. What…damn it.'' He spoke to a dead connection.

The agent shut off the machine.

Nobody spoke. Frankie scowled at the tape player. She'd never heard such a weird voice in her life. It swooped up and down, each word clipped. Emotional inflection ranged from deadpan to a shout. ''That's it?'' she asked no one in particular. She turned her disbelieving gaze on the agent in charge. She supposed she'd seen too many movies where the kidnappers put the man paying the ransom through hoops. ''Nothing else? That was a recording, wasn't it?''

''In reality,'' Agent Patrick said, ''it's effective. The area surrounding the reservoir is fairly flat and open. The mountains around the reservoir are full of roads and trails. The unsubs are picking the time and place for the exchange.''

''Where did the call come from? Did you trace it?''

''It's a cellular phone. The signal didn't last long enough for us to fix the position. We did get a lock on the number, though, and will trace the owner shortly. The phone unit is probably stolen.''

''Modern technology,'' Frankie muttered. ''Don't you love it.'' She glanced at McKennon, taking strength from his rock-solid presence. ''I'll do it. I'll deliver the ransom.''

''No,'' Agent Patrick replied. ''That's an unacceptable risk. We have a trained agent who resembles Mr. Bannerman. He'll make the drop. We will do absolutely nothing to endanger your sister. Her safety is our number-one priority. Apprehending the suspects takes a distant second."

"Oh, please! The kidnappers know who Julius is and what he looks like. They tucked him into bed, for God's sake. If you send in a ringer they'll know he's a cop."

"Miss For—"

"You know I'm right! So let me go. I'll tell them Julius chickened out. I'll explain who I am. They won't be threatened by me."

"No."

She held out her hands, beseeching her uncle. "Tell her, Colonel. She has to let me go."

"Impossible, Francine. We cannot risk your life."

"What about Penny's life?"

"You will have to trust us, Miss Forrest. We know what we're doing. We've done this before."

Turning a slow circle, Frankie searched every face, seeking any sign of insurrection amongst the law officers or support from her family. Nobody met her eyes. Penny's fate was entirely out of her hands.

Chapter Seven

Frankie hated waiting. In bank lines, she fidgeted; put on hold on the telephone she often lost her patience and hung up; traffic tie-ups made her seethe in frustration. On this snowy day while trapped inside the lodge, she had no choice except to wait. Wait for Ross to return with the ransom money, while praying the snow and ice on the roads didn't block his way, and wait for tomorrow when Penny was returned.

She tried hanging out in the dining room, but Agent Patrick made it clear that Frankie would have absolutely no input about delivering the ransom and recovering Penny. Consistently rebuffed and made to feel unwelcome, she withdrew. She offered to help her uncle in snow removal, but he had employees to operate snowblowers and plows. The Colonel gave her a shovel to clear snow off the lodge's front porch and steps. That didn't take long, even with pausing every few seconds to look for Ross's return. She attempted to help Elise, but her aunt merely gave her a distracted look and said, "It's so sweet of you to offer, dear, but unnecessary. Kara and I are taking care of everything." Frankie sought out Janine. Her cousin buried her worries in piles of bookkeeping. After enduring murmurs and vague replies to her attempts at conversation, Frankie gave up.

Unable to bear the worst-case scenarios her restless mind

kept conjuring, she sought out McKennon. She found him in the kitchen. Seated at the table he held a cup of coffee in one hand. He frowned at a yellow legal pad. The soft tap, tap, tapping of his pencil against the table top formed an underlying rhythm to the noise of two young men in the process of dismantling the huge stove.

McKennon noticed her as soon as she entered the room. Still tapping the pencil, he watched her approach. She noted a list of names on the legal paper, written in his spare engineering-style printing.

"How are you holding up?" he asked.

"Other than being as useless as a fireplace in a pickup truck, okay." She sat on a chair next to him. "What are you doing?"

"Trying to remember everyone who visited Julius in the past six months. He had an interesting little hobby, and one of his visitors might have gotten an idea from it."

She scanned the list of names, but recognized none of them. "What hobby?"

"He'd come up with a theme like Summer Sounds or How Much I Love You, then record songs and commentary off the radio. Splice it all together. Mix and match." He grinned as if amazed. "Kind of like storytelling. Some of his tapes were actually interesting."

Frankie found it disturbing to imagine Julius with a hobby. The picture she held in her mind was of a debauched alcoholic who seduced and discarded naive young women. Knowing he had a creative side made him all too human. She wondered if McKennon had a hobby. His hands were large and muscular, but supple-fingered and graceful. She envisioned him carving intricate sculptures or playing a piano. "What does his hobby have to do with anything?"

"The FBI identified the owner of the cell phone and the voice on the recording."

She gasped, partially rising. How dare Agent Patrick keep such a vital clue from her!

He placed a hand on her arm. "It isn't time to celebrate. Sorry. The kidnappers used Julius's telephone."

She sagged on the chair. "They stole his cellular phone."

"Nice touch, eh?"

"But the FBI identified the caller. That's a lead."

"It's David Sams."

"I know that name," she said. She racked her memory cells.

"David Sams is a radio talk show host."

She cocked her head first one way then the other, unable to fathom why a radio personality would get involved in a kidnapping. "Isn't he the guy who's always spouting off about crooked government and liberals? I've never listened to him, but I've read about him in the newspaper. My God, why would he kidnap Penny?"

Lowering his eyelids to half-mast McKennon slowly shook his head. "Stay with the program, Frankie. David Sams didn't kidnap your sister. The kidnappers recorded his voice off the radio."

"Oh, like Julius's hobby."

"Exactly. Tape the commentary, extract individual words, then splice them together to make the tape."

The cleverness sickened her. "We're dealing with really smart people." She closed her eyes and prayed they weren't smart enough to realize Penny was a potential witness.

"Smart people don't become criminals," McKennon said. "These guys are slick, but they'll get caught."

"Before or after they kill Penny?"

He caught her hands, enfolding them within his own. His strength warmed her. "Don't go there," he said.

"I can't help it. A million things can go wrong. Ross could get snowed in. The kidnappers can realize the FBI guy isn't Julius."

"Ross will get through. The FBI knows what they're doing."

"What if Max is behind all this? Is he still here?"

McKennon nodded and lifted his gaze to the ceiling to indicate that the Caulfields still resided upstairs. "He wants to make sure his wife doesn't have a heart attack on the way back to the city. I think he's arranged for an ambulance."

Max was making sure of other things, she mused darkly, such as ensuring he'd covered his tracks.

"Okay," he said, "worst-case scenario, Julius was deliberately murdered and the kidnapping is a cover-up. There's still no reason to hurt Penny."

"She's a witness."

"No sign of a struggle, remember? They're probably keeping her drugged. All they want is money." He stuck the pencil in his shirt pocket and picked up the legal pad. "I can't think of any more names. Let's drop in on the command center and see if they've learned anything new."

"Agent Patrick hates me."

He chuckled as if she'd made a joke. "Come on."

"Why are you being so nice to me?"

"I like you."

Her heart did a funny little hop-skip. Fearing if she opened her mouth she'd say something stupid, she fiddled with the hem of her sweatshirt.

"Besides, I'm a sucker for a pretty lady."

"I'm no lady." She meant it as a joke, a feeble attempt to distract herself from the horror of the situation, but it fell flat. It sounded like dead-on truth. A real lady, such as Aunt Elise or her cousin Janine, never would have pushed Penny into sneaking around with a jerk like Julius. A lady wouldn't have fallen for Max Caulfield's sleazy charm. A lady wouldn't be feeling like death warmed over and looking far worse, while wishing McKennon would take pity and kiss her again.

In silence, she followed him to the dining room.

Agents and law officers, grounded from searching by the storm, gathered in the dining room. They drank coffee and busied themselves with maps and paperwork. McKennon guided Frankie to Agent Patrick.

McKennon handed over the list he'd made. The agent perused it and twisted her lips. "Short list," she said. "Visitors with business concerns signed in and out, but personal friends weren't noted. Mr. Bannerman had a private entrance."

"Mr. Caulfield claims his wife is a stickler about security."

Frankie tapped an impatient foot on the floor. With every word out of the agent's mouth Frankie disliked the woman more.

"She is," he said, "to a point. I discussed with her on numerous occasions that guarding the front gate made little sense if the back gate stood wide-open. Julius continuously forgot to set the alarm system and often left the driveway gate standing open. She made it clear that I was not to interfere in her son's life." He indicated the list of names with a lift of his chin. "Those are people I've witnessed visiting Mr. Bannerman."

"Maybe I can help, Ms. Patrick," Frankie said.

The woman smiled, but it looked forced. "How so?"

"Let me study the ransom note. McKennon can give me details about Julius's friends. Age, sex, occupation, general temperament." She actually wanted to study the writing to see if anything indicated Max was the author, but she managed to keep that tidbit to herself. "I'm a professional graphologist. If nothing else I might be able to narrow your list of suspects. Or even come up with a profile of the author."

"Thank you for the offer, but it isn't possible. The note is in the hands of our experts."

"You must have a copy. I can work from a copy."

"We don't have a copy."

"Liar."

McKennon took her arm. "Frankie," he warned.

She wrenched away and held up her hands, palms out-

ward. "Yeah, yeah, fine. I'm just a piece of dirt in the
bureaucratic gears."

"Miss Forrest—"

"Don't bother. I'm leaving." She stomped out of the
dining room. Her anger faded quickly into dismay and self-
loathing. She knew the FBI agents were doing exactly what
they should be doing. She knew her requests to examine
crucial evidence were out of line. She walked quickly, but
aimlessly, uncaring where she went. She was trapped and
helpless and unable to accomplish the one thing that mattered—protect Penny.

She ended up in the rear of the lodge at the employee's
entrance. A small window in the mudroom gave her a view
of the outdoors. The snow had stopped and the wind had
died. A thermometer mounted on a pole outside showed the
temperature holding at sixteen degrees Fahrenheit. A thin
beam of pallid sunshine illuminated the edge of the forest.
She wondered if the sun would ever come out for her again.

"Frankie?"

The sound of McKennon's voice made her back muscles
tense. *I like you,* he'd said. She couldn't imagine why.
Holding on to the windowsill she continued staring at the
landscape. Misty sunlight pierced the thinning cloud cover.

"Are you all right?"

No, she wasn't all right. She was scared. "Agent Patrick
is one cold fish. I could set her toes on fire, and the only
thing she'd say would be ouch."

"She's a pro. She'll get Penny back."

Sarcasm climbed her throat. Except, McKennon didn't
deserve it. He deserved a whole lot better than anything
she had to offer.

"I know this is hard for you. I know what it's like to
have somebody…lost."

He spoke of his child. A coma, surely, was akin to being
lost. She turned from the window. "How do you stand it?
The waiting. The not knowing. Not having any control.
How do you keep from going crazy?"

"Sometimes I do go crazy."

"I've never seen you lose control."

He shrugged a shoulder. "You don't know me that well."

She wished she knew him better. As if sensing her deepest desire, he held his arms open. She walked into his embrace and rested her cheek against his shoulder.

"As long as there is life, there's hope. As long as I can hope, I have faith. That's what keeps me going." He rubbed her back in slow circles, easing away the tension. He pressed a soft kiss to her forehead.

She lifted her head to reply. He kissed her lips. A soft and tender kiss, the barest press of flesh to flesh. It touched her deeply. She wanted to weep. She lowered her head quickly and squeezed her burning eyes shut.

"Are you coming on to me, McKennon?"

He stroked her hair, his fingers separating thick curls. "Yes."

His answer pleased her, but deepened her guilt. With Penny in danger she could afford herself no pleasure. "Bad timing."

"In more ways than you know." He pressed a finger to her chin and urged her to look at him. Feeling suddenly shy and strangely vulnerable, she resisted. "When we get Penny back, I'd like to take you to dinner."

She stiffened in his arms, stunned by the invitation and again pleased. Ensuing guiltiness made her belly ache. "Serious?"

"Yes."

"You're not my type." She cracked a weak smile. "My men tend to be the fickle, cheating, low-down, dirty-dog type."

Chuckling, he curled his hand around the back of her head and drew her forehead-to-forehead with him. His embrace accomplished what reason could not—some of the tension drained away. Her thoughts stopped roiling and cleared. Hope feathered upward from deep in her belly.

"I'd like to get to know you better." He kissed her again.

She couldn't have resisted him if she'd tried. She explored the texture of his lips and tasted the sweetness of his mouth. Sweet oblivion. Sweet yearning. She touched her fingertips to his face, feeling the faint rasp of beard bristles and the strong bone underlying firm skin.

Then, ashamed of herself for kissing him when Penny was in danger, she pulled back and stepped away from his arms. She studied the toes of her boots. Old boots, as comfortable and ratty as the Frankenstein coat.

"Is it a date?" he asked.

She peeked, finding his eyes warm with kindness. She sensed in him the power to make her believe in faith and loyalty and goodness for the sake of goodness again. "Sure," she whispered. "It's a date."

FRANKIE FINALLY FOUND A JOB. She guessed Aunt Elise finally realized her niece was ready to crawl out of her skin so took pity on her. On her knees behind the front desk, she cleared shelves and drawers one at a time, being careful not to disorder the contents. She used a rag and polish to clean away dust and debris.

She watched a nearby doorway for McKennon. He'd promised to help her after he made some telephone calls. He hadn't said who he was going to call, but she gathered by his eagerness to achieve some privacy that it had to do with his son.

The front door opening caught her attention. Ross, she prayed, returned with the ransom money. She peered over the top of the counter.

Two uniformed men wheeled a gurney into the lobby. Max Caulfield met them. Knowing they'd come for Belinda, Frankie resumed her task. The sound of Max's voice distracted her. She peeked over the counter again and watched until the men were out of sight.

After several minutes they returned. The uniformed men

carried Belinda, bundled as if for a sleigh ride, on the gurney. An FBI agent and the Colonel accompanied Max.

At the sight of the older woman strapped down and staring blankly at the ceiling, Frankie felt pity. The few encounters she'd had with Belinda had always left her on edge and feeling outclassed. An intimidating woman, she moved through life like an elephant queen, confident that no one dared mess with her. Frankie saw nothing intimidating about the shrunken woman on the gurney. Max rested a hand on his wife's shoulder. His lips moved.

Along with pity, Frankie experienced an anger so deep and hurtful it left her light-headed and heavyhearted. Belinda had more wealth than she could spend in a lifetime. Yet, what did she have to show for it? Comfort, ease, more possessions than any one person could possibly use, and a son who was causing as many problems dead as he ever had alive. Where was the charity, altruism and great good that could come from such great wealth? Belinda could pay the ransom. It would barely make a ripple in her bank accounts. She could save the life of her daughter-in-law and the life of her soon-to-be grandchild.

The Colonel spoke briefly to the FBI agent before he headed for the guest quarters. The remaining men maneuvered Belinda out the door.

Anxiety prickled in Frankie's chest. Unpleasant wetness filled her mouth. Could Max plant evidence implicating her in Julius's murder? She didn't see how. She'd moved into a cheaper apartment, so he no longer had a key to her place. She no longer associated with any of their mutual friends. He didn't know she worked at Martha's Pie House. Or did work, she thought. Bob had probably already replaced her.

Troubled, she resumed dusting. She eyed a nearby telephone. She should call Sally and find out if anything unusual had been going on in their apartment complex.

The front door shut. She peeked. Max had a cellular telephone pressed to his ear. His dark face was angry and intense. She hoped the ambulance carrying Belinda hadn't gotten stuck in the snow. She strained to hear what he said. He slammed the telephone unit shut. He stalked toward the doorway leading to the private quarters. Frankie ducked behind the counter and cringed, praying he didn't catch her spying. He strode past without a glance her way.

Curious, she hurried to a window. The Colonel's crew had efficiently cleared the road leading to the highway. The late-day sun was stronger now, and snow melted where it had been plowed thin, revealing reddish patches on the gravel road. The vehicle carrying Belinda was long gone.

"What are you up to, Max?" she muttered.

She wished the FBI would let her examine the kidnapper's note. Max knew exactly how traceable typewritten and computer-generated printing could be. Every typewriter had its own signature, its own unique typeface. Computer technology and the hundreds of fonts available on bubblejet and laser printers made tracing a particular print-out to a specific machine difficult, but not impossible.

Frankie didn't believe Max understood exactly how handwriting analysis worked. No one, not even the most highly skilled forger, could completely disguise his handwriting. Writing didn't originate in the hand, but in the brain. An untrained eye saw penmanship, but she saw the workings of a person's mind.

"Graphology is voodoo," he'd told her when the subject first came up. "But it might be profitable voodoo." Her training, study and experience had proved to her it wasn't voodoo or pop psychology, but was indeed a valid tool. If Max had written the note, then he'd made a fatal error.

Irony pinged her. She'd analyzed Max's handwriting many times for practice and for fun. His handwriting was large, heavy, dark and closed, a trait called pastosity. It indicated overindulgence in sensual gratification. His word spacing indicated selfishness with little openness toward others. He left the bottoms open on the letters *O* and *A*, indicating dishonesty. Once madly in love, she'd dismissed the negative traits she'd discovered. Graphology had applied to everyone, but not to him.

If she'd listened to what common sense told her about Max, she'd have quit working for him long before the Bannermans ever entered their lives. Penny never would have met Julius. No wedding. No kidnapping.

No threat to Penny from a cold-blooded megalomaniac who used people as if they were paper towels.

Wondering how to prove Max was behind the murder she resumed dusting. A flashing red light caught her attention. She sat back on her heels and watched the telephone. It didn't ring, but the light indicated an incoming call. The light turned steady. Max adored gadgets. A week didn't pass without him buying a new computer program or some high-tech toy. He could have easily made the tape from the so-called kidnappers. He knew all about voice identification. Leave it to him to figure out a way to circumvent it. He'd probably figured out a way to reroute the call through Julius's telephone, and had made the call from right here inside the lodge.

Agent Patrick had to listen to her. *Be cool, be professional,* she counseled herself. She straightened her shoulders and assumed a serene expression. She would present her argument as if she outlined a case for a client. Here are the facts, here are the conclusions.

Forcing herself to walk calmly, to breathe deeply and slowly, she made her way to the dining room. She sorted her points in her head: why Max would handwrite the original note as opposed to using a computer; why and how Max would create the kidnapper's tape; how Max never went anywhere without a telephone, sometimes two of them, and kept abreast of all the latest technological advances such as Call Forwarding and diverting phones through various numbers.

When she reached the dining room the first person she saw was Max. She ducked out of the doorway, then carefully peeked around the jamb.

Max leaned over Agent Patrick. One hand on the table, the other on his hip, he spoke with his mouth very close to her ear. The woman smiled. All traces of the ice-for-blood bureaucrat who so easily tossed Frankie out of the command post were gone.

A touch on her back nearly made Frankie scream. She whirled about. McKennon lifted a questioning brow. She sagged against the wall and clutched the fabric over her pounding heart.

"Don't sneak up on me like that," she whispered.

"What are you doing?"

She spotted an open door down the hall. She hustled McKennon into a storeroom. She checked behind her to see if anyone emerged from the dining room before she shut the door. The storeroom was ringed by floor-to-ceiling shelving containing staple goods and paper supplies for the kitchen.

McKennon smiled indulgently. "If you want to be alone with me I can think of better places. Flour sacks and bulk spices aren't my idea of romance."

She snorted a laugh before clapping her hand over her mouth. She glared at him. "This is serious," she said. "I was watching Max."

"Any reason in particular?"

He maintained that cool, detached air, but she caught a glimmer of humor. Annoyed, she poked his chest with a finger. "You know my reasons. And do you know what I just saw? He's flirting with Agent Patrick."

His lack of reaction dismayed her.

"I think they know each other. From the way he was hanging all over her, they know each other real well."

"Don't jump to conclusions."

She clamped her arms over her chest. "What other conclusion can I reach? He's whispering in her ear and she's lapping it up. He was practically nibbling on her ear."

"That's the way he is."

"No, it isn't."

He stared past her as if the lineup of dried onion, garlic powder, oregano, basil, marjoram and thyme were fascinating.

She bristled with suspicion. "What are you saying? He makes a habit of hitting on women?"

"That, too."

His meaning was crystal clear. Her mouth dropped open. "He cheats on Belinda?"

"Discreetly."

"That is disgusting!" She stomped a tight circle. "How could you work for a philanderer?"

His cheeks darkened. She drew back in amazement. He was actually embarrassed.

"The money is good, and it's none of my business."

"Unbelievable. He'd risk losing Belinda's money for an afternoon quickie?"

"She's aware," he said.

"That's even more disgusting. If Max had ever cheated on me I'd have killed him." She paused uncertainly. "Did he cheat on me?"

McKennon's silence filled volumes.

She backed up a step, striking the shelf. The dusty smell of flour heightened the oppressive sense of closeness. "He *did* cheat on me. And you knew. Why didn't you tell me?"

"Tell you what?"

"That he was seeing another woman."

"You would have believed me?"

He had her there. She'd been so madly in love, Oliver Stone could have presented her with videotaped evidence and she'd have laughed in his face. Old hurts rose in her breast, aching as if fresh. Adding to it was the humiliation of knowing McKennon knew she'd been an utter fool.

He grasped her shoulders. She tried to shake him off, but he held her firmly and forced her to look at him. "I don't like what he did to you."

"Yeah, well, that sure didn't stop you from sitting back and watching it happen."

He winced. "I deserve that."

She craved details. She wanted to demand the name of the other woman—or women! The impulse sickened her. *Get over it,* she told herself. It no longer mattered.

"I compromised too many principles working for him," McKennon said.

She peeked, finding him serious and perhaps a little bit sad. "I know what it's like to really need a job."

He made a disgruntled sound deep in his throat. "It's finally sinking in. When Jamie wakes up he's going to care less that I got the money and more about *how* I got it. I'm sorry for standing by and saying nothing." He exhaled heavily. "I'm sorry for not asking you out first."

Her eyes widened. "You wanted to ask me out?"

"You're an interesting woman." He cupped her chin in his palm. "Beautiful, too."

The hurt faded fast. She couldn't blame him for turning a blind eye to Max's shenanigans when she'd done the very same thing herself. And for much the same reasons. Max had dazzled her with a juicy paycheck and a juicier benefits package long before he dazzled her with his romantic attention.

"So what are we going to do about Max? He isn't merely flirting with Agent Patrick. He's convincing her that I'm the prime suspect. He sent Belinda home. That leaves him free and clear to go after me."

Chapter Eight

"Ross!" Frankie flung her arms around her cousin's neck and hugged him until he grunted.

Alerted as if by telepathy, the Dukes gathered in the lobby. Elise kissed her son. Kara clapped her hands and bounced around like a puppy. Even the normally reserved Janine gave Ross an enthusiastic hug. The Colonel clapped Ross on the back.

"A hero's welcome." Ross grinned. "It's about time you all started showing some appreciation." With one arm around his mother and the other around Kara, he nodded at the pair of FBI agents who'd accompanied him to Colorado Springs. "We're all set."

Frankie turned her attention to the suitcases the FBI agents lugged. Four large suitcases, which were heavy, too, judging by the way the men strained.

"How are the roads?" Frankie asked.

"Colorado Springs is a slush pool, but the highways are clear. The weather forecast tomorrow is for clear skies and warmer temperatures. There shouldn't be any problems at all with the ransom drop."

Frankie wanted to believe it. She tried her best to believe it.

"According to my new best friends here," Ross said, "we still have a lot to do. Right, fellows?"

An agent said, deadpan, "Right, Mr. Duke." The other

agent cracked a smile. The men loaded the bulky suitcases on a luggage cart. Everyone headed for the dining room.

McKennon fell in beside Frankie. He brushed her hand. Knowing the action deliberate she smiled.

The smile disappeared when she saw Max. He stood to the side, out of the way of the FBI agents, who cleared papers, maps, coffee cups and dishes off the long table. Frankie made a point of ignoring her ex-fiancé.

Agent Patrick supervised laying out the suitcases and opening them. As the three million dollars were revealed, a hush settled over the room. Even Frankie, who'd never set much store by the accumulation of wealth, sucked in her breath. Neat bundles of twenties, fifties and hundreds bound in paper bands had a strangely hypnotic quality.

"Sheesh, makes you want to roll around in it," Kara said. Heads turned. A few people chuckled. The young woman blushed and ducked.

"Let's get to work, boys," Agent Patrick said.

"What are you going to do?" Frankie asked. "You promised, no hotdogging, no heroics. Right?"

The agent smiled indulgently. "For your benefit, let me explain exactly how this will work." She nodded graciously at Elise and the Colonel. "Mr. and Mrs. Bannerman arrived at the resort in a stretch limousine. We can't use it for the drop. Mr. Duke has provided a Jeep Cherokee equipped with snow tires and chains. The vehicle is equipped with a tracking device in the event that the kidnappers hijack it."

Frankie looked around at the gathering of agents and state police officers. None of them resembled Julius. "Who's making the drop?"

With a wave, the agent indicated a slender man with a long face and droopy eyes. The man approximated Julius's height and weight, but other than that didn't resemble the man in the least. Frankie didn't like it.

"He'll be wearing a parka with a hood and sunglasses. The unsubs will be interested in the money, not his face.

He, too, will be wearing a tracking device. The Jeep's radio has been modified into a transmitter. It looks like a car radio, but he'll be able to use it for one-way communication. If the vehicle is hijacked we'll hear everything the unsubs say.''

"Slick," Frankie muttered. She still didn't like it.

"We'll rig the suitcases with tracking devices," Agent Patrick said. She picked up a bundle of hundred-dollar bills. "We'll also rig several money bundles. The devices have a limited range, but the units are small enough to hide beneath the paper bands. Should the unsubs switch the suitcases we can still track the money."

Frankie glanced at a map pinned to the wall. Red circles along the route the FBI ringer was supposed to drive made her suspicious. "How many cops will be posted out there for the kidnappers to see?"

"The official presence will be one hundred percent covert, Miss Forrest. No air traffic. No official vehicles. No radio communications for the unsubs to intercept. We will take no overt action of any kind until your sister is safely in our custody."

"Everything is covered," McKennon whispered in Frankie's ear.

Grudgingly, she conceded the point. With one exception: Max Caulfield. She'd learned earlier that the FBI monitored every call going in or out of the resort. Max had his own telephone, though. With a single call he could tip off his accomplices about the bugs and tracking devices along with the location of surveillance teams.

"Now if you'll excuse us," Agent Patrick said. "We need room to work. We'll rendezvous in the lobby at 5:30 a.m. Thank you."

All civilians, except for Elise and Max, left the dining room. Frankie guessed Elise made arrangements for feeding the law officers, but as to why Max was allowed to remain she hadn't a clue.

A hearty meal awaited them in the kitchen. Savory stew

redolent of onions and celery, baskets of fresh bread and corn muffins, bowls of fresh fruit and cinnamon-spiced apple pies. Elise joined them, but appeared unable to stay seated. She flitted about freshening drinks and fetching jams and jellies.

Seated between Ross and McKennon, Frankie picked at her food, her appetite diminished as much by the late hour as by her ragged nerves. Chatter swirled around her. She noticed nobody mentioned Penny or the ransom drop.

She couldn't get Max out of mind. If he'd murdered Julius, would there be any kidnappers at all to collect the ransom? He must be surprised the Dukes were able to raise the money.

She leaned close to McKennon. "I need some fresh air," she whispered.

"Are you okay?" he whispered back.

His concern touched her. She managed a wan smile. "I just…I need to move. I'm ready to climb the walls. Want to take a walk outside?"

He wiped his mouth with a napkin, complimented Elise on the dinner and excused himself. Too nerved up to make a reasonable excuse, Frankie merely left the kitchen. She didn't have the heart to share her fears with her relatives. The Dukes suffered enough over Penny's loss without having to worry about Max, too.

She and McKennon fetched hats, gloves and coats before heading outside. As soon as she stepped into the night her breath seemed to freeze in her chest. She gasped, instantly chilled. Icy air latched on to her cheeks as if with claws. She shivered inside her parka.

McKennon made a soft exhalation of wonder. The night was perfectly still and perfectly silent. With only a sliver of new moon to obscure their glory, billions of stars blanketed the sky. The surrounding trees looked like silhouettes brushed with silver snow.

"I never see a sky like this in the city," he said.

"Yeah," she said, "it's gorgeous." She hurried along a

pathway cut between five-foot-tall drifts. "I'm freezing!" She aimed for the stables. Every footfall crackled and squeaked on the icy snow. She tried the big sliding door, but couldn't budge it. Whether locked or iced over she didn't know. A smaller door opened easily. She entered the stables.

A lone low-watt lightbulb filled a supply room with soft, shadowy light. Slapping her arms and stomping her feet she loosed a long breath. "Whew!"

McKennon looked around. "Not much warmer in here."

"A little bit warmer." She made sure the outside door was securely shut before entering the stables proper. She found a light switch on the wall near the door. Horses shuffled on straw and whickered greetings. The smell of sawdust, horses and sweet feed wafted into her frozen nose. A dark horse thrust his head over a stall door and snuffled. His thick winter coat made him look bearded and as fluffy as a toy. She petted his nose. Hot horse breath seeped through her knit glove.

"I have a confession to make," McKennon said. He strolled the aisle, patting the noses of curious horses. "It's been a long time since I've made love to a woman, and you're beautiful." He grinned crookedly. "But damn, Frankie, it's cold."

Her mouth dropped open.

He lifted an eyebrow. "That's not why you want privacy?"

"You are such a jerk!"

He laughed. The rare sound enchanted her. She could listen to his laughter all day. All night. To her left was an empty stall with a bed of straw laid thick and inviting on the floor. A striped horse blanket draped over the stall wall. Tempting.

"I'm kidding," he said.

Disappointment pinged her. She hadn't brought him here for a tryst—not that she had the time, energy or inclination, anyway. Still…

"You don't want me to be kidding?"

She swiped the air impatiently with both hands. The dark horse snorted and pulled back into the stall. "I didn't bring you out here for sex."

"Good. We ought to at least have a first date."

The promise in his words unnerved her. She glanced at the empty stall, and her cheeks warmed. In spite of the circumstances, McKennon turned her on. She felt a connection with him she'd never felt with another human being. He seemed to understand her, but more than that, he approved. He saw the real Frankie and liked her, anyway. He was an exciting man, and ever since he'd kissed her, she'd wanted more. She crammed her hands deep into the pockets of the Frankenstein coat.

"I want to talk about Max. But I don't want to worry my family."

He stroked the snowy blaze of a sorrel horse. "I knew that."

"Why is he here? Why didn't he go home with Belinda?"

"He has a vested interest in Penny's safe return. She's Mrs. Caulfield's daughter-in-law, and a witness to Julius's murder. Knowing Mrs. Caulfield as I do, I'd guess he'd better not go home unless he's carrying news of an arrest."

"He's surprised we came up with the ransom money. But I don't think anybody is going to pick it up. It's not part of Max's plan."

"I'm in no way agreeing with you, but for the sake of argument, even if Caulfield is involved, three other people are involved, too. We know for a fact they have Penny."

She got his point. Accomplices needed to be paid.

"And, if he's involved, why harm Penny? Without Julius she offers no threat."

"Unless she really is pregnant. That gives her a solid claim against Julius's estate."

"He has no estate. Any money his mother gave him he spent."

"Oh." The horse was leaving wet streaks on her coat. She gave him a final pat and moved out of reach before he began chewing her hair. "Then who's the insider?"

"If it's only money and they didn't mean to hurt Julius, then it could be anybody. If it's murder..." He turned his hands palms upward. "Like you said, ex-wives, ex-girlfriends. Maybe he caused some trouble with one of Mrs. Caulfield's employees."

"Is there any way we can find out? Records or something?"

He pondered the question. "Maybe."

Hope leaped in her heart like a joyous animal. "There is?"

"Mrs. Caulfield insists on meticulous records keeping. I can check the computer."

"Now?"

His eyes sparkled with humor. "Not right here."

She huffed in exasperation. Frozen breath clouded in front of her face.

"I should be able to access the records over the phone. Caulfield backs up everything onto his mainframe. But, you have to kiss me first."

"I never realized you were such a sexist, chauvinistic pig." She sashayed down the sawdust-strewn aisle. She glanced at the empty stall, tempted yet again. Straw trapped body heat...

He pressed a hand over his heart. "You wound me."

"You'll know when I wound you, buddy." She kissed him. His lips were cold, but her thoughts were not. Touching him, smelling him, made all her dreams pale by comparison. Fabric crackled and crunched as he hugged her tightly. She wanted to do a whole lot more than merely kiss.

"JANINE." Frankie gestured from the kitchen doorway. Her cousin excused herself from the table.

"Are you okay?" Janine asked. She flashed a cursory smile at McKennon.

Frankie bristled. She suspected she looked like hell at the moment. Her face was probably bright red from the cold and her hair was its usual mess. She sniffed. Despite the stress Janine looked stunning. With a word she could have McKennon falling at her dainty feet.

Realizing she felt jealousy appalled Frankie. She prided herself on the ability to rise above petty games—like Who has prettier hair? Who has a better figure? She'd never once indulged in nasty gossip or made catty remarks. She'd never competed for a man's attention or tried to make herself look better at another woman's expense. Even with Max she'd passed off his attention toward other women as merely being the way he did business.

Now, visions rose of shoving Janine into a snowdrift until her perfect complexion mottled purple and her luxurious hair hung in icy strings. A sly crack about a stain on Janine's shirt struggled for release. She managed not to say anything, but couldn't resist sliding over a step to put herself squarely between McKennon and her cousin. Arms clamped over her chest, she towered over the smaller woman.

"Frankie?" Janine peered at her. "What is wrong? You have the funniest look on your face."

"I was wondering if you have a laptop computer with a modem we could borrow."

Janine twirled a strand of chestnut hair around her finger. "Yes, but why?"

McKennon glanced toward the dining room. The sound of voices drifted through the doorway. "I want to check some files."

"Maybe we can get a lead on the kidnappers," Frankie added.

"Is that legal? Isn't that what the FBI is doing?"

No, it wasn't legal. Since he'd been fired, McKennon's snooping around was akin to theft. Still, greater good pre-

vailed. "The FBI don't know these people the way Mc-
Kennon and I do. We might spot something they can't
see."

"You can always use the computer in my office."

"We need to go someplace where no one will interrupt.
Or object to what we're doing." She meant Max, but let it
sound as if they hid out from the FBI.

"I don't know if you should be interfering." Janine
shrugged. "But anything to help." She walked down the
hall to her office.

Armed with a laptop computer and a telephone cord
McKennon and Frankie went upstairs to his room. While
he set up the computer she wandered the room. It had a
bath, a bed and a desk, no frills.

Now hot, she peeled off her coat. The room felt stuffy
and too small. Only distance from McKennon's compelling
charm could save her from herself. She sat on the end of
the bed and fingered the faded floral pattern on the bedspread. She caught herself sniffing, seeking his scent.

"Will this work?" she asked.

As if in reply the signature squeal of a modem making
a connection to an answering computer blared out of the
laptop's tiny speaker. He typed rapidly. A menu filled the
computer's flat screen.

"Max keeps all of Belinda's records on his computers?"

"I hope so. Here we go."

Warmth encircled her heart. McKennon took a huge risk.
She knew Max routinely audited his computerized files and
examined them for access. He liked to know who was
snooping around where and for what reason. He'd know,
eventually, that McKennon had looked at the files despite
having lost authorization.

"Is my file still in there?" She scooted across the bed
so she could see the screen better.

He typed in commands. Despite the size of his hands,
his fingers were agile and swift on the compact keyboard.

The screen changed. "Here you are." He whistled softly. "Graphology pays well."

"Hmph. I think he was paying me to sleep with the boss." Wishing she hadn't said that, she clamped her mouth shut. To his credit, McKennon declined comment. "What does he say about my leaving?"

He scrolled through the lengthy file. "It says here you gave two weeks' notice, received severance pay, and your health insurance remained active for three months." He arched an eyebrow. "There's a letter of recommendation attached. According to the log it's been sent out to three companies."

She rose to read over his shoulder. The letter of recommendation practically glowed with her praises. Words like, "best in her field" and "conscientious" leaped off the screen.

Not a single word about how she'd stormed out after Max had dumped her. Or how two security guards had overseen her clearing her desk. Or how she'd given Julius a punch in the nose and ended up being escorted out of the building with a security guard on each arm. She recognized the names of the companies to whom letters of recommendation had been sent. It astonished her. She'd been honest on her résumé, but she'd always assumed Max had done nothing more than confirm her employment.

"I wonder how many other employees he's lied about."

McKennon laughed. "You're a cynic."

"I've got plenty to be cynical about." She returned to the bed. The file troubled her. She'd assumed Max hated her. The file said otherwise. Perhaps he'd put a good spin on it to prevent her from suing him for wrongful discharge or sexual harassment.

He typed new commands. The screen changed again. "Remember Robert Marshall?"

"Bobby? Sure. He couldn't stay awake."

"Which is exactly what it says here. No letter of rec-

ommendation. Just a memo saying he worked for Max."
He scrolled up and down through the file.

"So who else is Max sleeping with? Other than his wife,
that is?"

"Not relevant," he said dryly.

"How do you know? Maybe some woman is tired of
him jerking her around."

"I doubt it very much."

"Why not? Deputy Downes said one set of tracks belonged to a woman."

"He said *maybe*. Besides, women don't mastermind kidnappings."

"They aren't smart enough? Evil enough? You're saying
a woman has never kidnapped anybody, ever?"

"Historically men are the force behind kidnappings.
Women may be involved as accomplices, but rarely insti-
gate the crime."

Having read much of the same research and trade jour-
nals as he, she sniffed. "Kidnapping for ransom isn't entirely a crime of greed. It can also be revenge."

"True. But why a revenge that doesn't hurt Caulfield?
It isn't his son who's dead, his daughter-in-law who's missing, or his money paying the ransom." He turned on the
chair so he could see her. "Besides, this is not a crime of
passion."

She remembered too well how she'd felt after Max
dumped her. She'd been so hurt and so angry she'd obsessed about getting even. Dark, nasty fantasies had
plagued her—vandalize Max's car or house; confront Belinda with every detail of their love affair; fake a pregnancy
just to see him sweat. No matter how wild or twisted the
fantasy, all of them involved somehow seeing his reaction
to whatever she'd done. She'd wanted to hit him where it
hurt the most.

"You absolutely will not consider Max the prime suspect?"

"Not until we find evidence that says otherwise." He returned his attention to the screen.

Muttering about his stubbornness—and receiving no reaction—she watched him scroll through files. On occasion he jotted notes on a sheet of Elk River stationery. His dogged work took her back to the good old days. Max's corporation office had an open floor plan, with private conference rooms for meeting with clients, but all the employee desks had been in one large room. McKennon's desk hadn't been far from hers. What fun it had been to fantasize about the real man beneath the dark, formal suits.

"Hmm."

Frankie perked up. "What did you find?"

"Mrs. Caulfield's driver was hired eleven months ago. I can't find a file on the person he replaced."

"Really? Do you have access to archived files?"

The keyboard clicking softly with the speed of his typed commands. "Let me check under another directory."

"Do you know the other driver?"

"Before my time." He loosed a frustrated noise.

"What's the matter?"

"Not on file. The only former employees in the database are those fired or replaced since Mr. Caulfield came on board. Which is two."

Frankie chewed her lower lip. "Is Belinda hard on employees? I bet she's hell to work for."

"She's neurotic and demanding, but she doesn't keep what she wants a secret. No head games or inconsistencies. Most of her people have been with her for years."

"What about the two employees who quit?"

"No leads there. One was the cook's nephew who worked the summer until he left for college. Another was a groundskeeper who retired. The only way to research her former employees would be to get into her hard-copy files."

She flopped back with her arms outspread, staring at the ceiling. "I bet Belinda did it," she muttered.

J.T. pushed away from the desk and swiveled on the chair to face her. Stretched out, with those long legs dangling over the bed, her sweatshirt hiked to reveal a few inches of creamy, smooth belly, she looked impossibly tall and incredibly beautiful. He scowled at the direction of his thoughts. Getting involved with her could only hurt both of them—in more ways than one.

Except, damn it, he wanted involvement. Her presence shook up his world. He felt his loneliness. He ached for a woman's touch—for Frankie's touch.

"First rule for a sleuth," he said. "Settle on a lead and follow it. When that fizzles then go on to the next. Don't keep bouncing around."

She lifted her head enough to glare at him. She hooked her hands behind her neck in an I'm-not-listening-to-you-and-you-can't-make-me posture. Stubborn. His hands itched to hold her.

"Then, who do you think is behind it?"

"I don't have enough information." He lifted a shoulder. "But I haven't eliminated anybody, either."

"You're trying to drive me crazy."

"Why would I do that?" He wished she'd stop looking so beautiful, so fiery yet vulnerable. Kissing her was an act of madness. Holding her flayed his reserve and tattered the edges of his self-control. He wanted more than a mere kiss.

Her eyes narrowed and now burned with a speculative light. "You think it's Max, too, don't you? Only you won't tell me because you think I'll do something stupid. Is that it?"

He noticed her eyes were different colors. Her right eye was bluer than the left. A subtle difference, but intriguing.

She propped herself on her elbows. The sweatshirt molded around her breasts. "You're protecting me from myself."

At the moment she needed protection from him. An ache formed in his hands and spread to his wrists and forearms and shoulders. Her knees were inches from his. He could touch them if he chose. Touch those long legs. Lift her sweatshirt and examine her soft belly.

Her glare faded. Her mouth softened. "Why are you staring at me?"

Years of martial arts training had taught him discipline and self-control. He could count on one hand the number of times in the past twenty years in which he'd lost his temper. He controlled his appetite, his body language and his speech. He took great pride in his high tolerance for cold, heat and pain. He had little respect for men who couldn't control their impulses and animal desires. His mind was the master, and his body was the tool.

Frankie's warmth carried the scent of soap and female to his nose. A stirring in his groin pulsated echoes throughout his entire body.

She pushed upright and drew her head aside. Thick eyelashes lowered, and he was undone. "Say something," she whispered.

Her throaty words rippled through his soul. He struggled for control, but felt himself losing. "You better leave."

She picked idly at the bedspread. She peeked from the corner of her eyes. His chest filled with hot wax, and blood pulsed against his ears. She shifted on the bed. Her knee brushed his and electric sparks leaped up his leg.

"Why?" she asked.

"I'm about to do something stupid."

She walked her fingers over his kneecap. "How stupid?"

He captured her hand within his own and felt the fineness of her bones. A great, aching tenderness filled him. The tip of her tongue appeared and she licked her lips, catlike and alluring. Compelled by forces more powerful than himself, he leaned closer to her beautiful mouth, her fascinating mouth, the mouth he'd been fantasizing about ever since he met her. She canted her head ever so slightly and met him halfway.

He was lost.

She broke the kiss abruptly and placed both hands against his chest. "You and I together are pretty stupid."

His back muscles tensed and bunched. It took every ounce of self-control he possessed to keep from pouncing on her and squashing her into the mattress beneath him. "Probably."

"I mean…" She lifted a hand as hesitantly as a shy bird and touched one finger to his cheek. "A guy like you can have any woman you want. A *nice* woman. Cute. Cuddly. Sweet." She looked away. "Pretty."

"You're beautiful."

Her eyelids quivered, and her lips parted. A breathy sigh escaped her exquisite lips.

"You're driving me crazy. I want you too much." He shifted on the hard chair, but his jeans seemed to have shrunk a few sizes. "Now is not the right time."

She swallowed hard. "You're right. This is crazy. I—I better go." She lunged to her feet.

A roar of protest built in his chest, and he jumped off the chair. The chair tipped and struck the desk with a clunk. He wrapped an arm around her waist and hugged her close. He was hard and wanting, burning for her. "Don't go."

"But you said—"

"We aren't stupid together. You're perfect, wonderful. The timing is bad right now, that's all." *Let her go,* his rational mind commanded, but it was a weak and faraway command.

"You said—"

"I don't know what I'm saying. I look at you and…" At a loss for words, he kissed her instead. Soft lips, warm and moist and when they parted, offering entry for his questing tongue, he groaned deep in his chest. He wanted to ravish her mouth; restraint pained him. He kissed her slowly, deeply, treasuring the silky thrusts of her tongue and the freshness of her taste and her sensuous scent swirling through his brain.

When they broke the kiss, he stood rigidly, holding her,

aching for her. Eyes closed he slid his tongue over his lips and savored the sweet lingering taste of her.

"McKennon?"

He opened his eyes.

"I...need you. Even if it is crazy. Or stupid."

Logic made one final grasp at control. "We better not. I don't have any protection."

"I've got that covered. Honest." Frankie hurt as if something inside had broken. It hurt to breathe. The glorious sight of him pained her eyes. Only he could repair her. She curled her fingers into his soft flannel shirt. This was crazy, and it was stupid, and the timing was awful, but she couldn't leave. An earthquake rending the room asunder and lightning strikes and a howling tornado could not have torn her from his arms.

"Are you sure?" he asked.

His deep voice, the Southern accent now pronounced and incredibly sexy, was sweet agony against her ears. "Positive."

He guided her down onto the bed. The soft mattress embraced her, enfolded her. She felt his heart pounding against her breast. His kisses against her mouth, chin, cheeks and eyelids inflamed her. She kissed him feverishly in return.

He nibbled her earlobe. "I'm going nuts."

So was she. She tugged his shirt free and roamed her hands freely over his back. Taut muscles delighted her. She explored his ribs and shoulder blades and spine. He lifted his head enough for her to see his eyes. Those smoky green depths shone with desire and heat and glorious madness.

"The room is too hot," she gasped.

He needed no other invitation. With excruciating deliberation he tugged off her boots and socks then touched the button on her jeans. He paused, watching her face. His knuckles seared her belly. She began unbuttoning his shirt. His smile melted her joints, and she fumbled with the buttons as if she'd never accomplished such a simple action before. He showed far more expertise in unbuttoning and unzipping her jeans. He pushed and pulled the heavy denim off her hips and legs.

"You have incredible legs." He lifted her right leg and kissed her behind the knee.

A firestorm of sensation shot up her leg. She gasped and wriggled.

"Like? Don't like?" he asked politely.

A moan bubbled in her throat. She liked it very much. He kissed her inner thigh. And again. He kissed her leg thoroughly, taking his time, rendering her incoherent with desire. When he touched his mouth to her silk panties, she cried out and grabbed his hair with both hands.

Drowning in joyous sensuality, she squirmed as his kisses traveled her belly then up and around the arch of her rib cage. Impatiently she jerked her sweatshirt over her head. He deftly slipped a hand beneath her back and unhooked her bra.

"You've been practicing," she said.

"Uh-uh. It's like riding a bike. Never forget." His pupils had swelled so only a thin ring of green showed. On his knees, straddling her belly, he cupped her breasts in his hands.

"You're killing me." She was so wet and hot and turgid she knew she was going to explode. "Get naked."

He grinned wickedly. "Say please."

She cupped her hand boldly over his crotch and squeezed his erection. He jerked.

"You say please."

He disrobed in record time. She couldn't look enough to satisfy her greedy soul. The chiseled lines of his shoulders and chest. The dark patches of hair on his chest and the way it narrowed down his belly and widened in his groin. Hungry and needy and in no mood for teasing games, she pulled him to her, frantic in her efforts to touch him everywhere at once.

And his hands. Those big hands so clever and tender and strong, aroused nerves she didn't know she possessed. She entwined her legs with his, thrusting against him, wanting him within. When he did come within, the fire was so intense it stole her breath.

She didn't need air. She didn't need anything except him, moving faster, lost in the rhythm, lost in the fire.

"Got…to…slow…"

"No!" she cried, holding him tighter, wanting to draw him in deeper, harder. She bucked against him, urging him to greater speed.

Release came in shattering waves. She cried out, but barely recognized herself. She caught his hair in both hands, riding the crest.

"Frankie." He thrust so deeply he moved her across the mattress and he trembled and every muscle in his body went taut against her body. A long, shuddering sigh whispered against her ear and aftershocks gripped her limbs, stripping her of strength and any desire or ability to move.

She stroked both hands down his back, feeling his sweat and filled with a fierce, prideful pleasure in knowing what she'd done to him. He breathed hard.

He shifted as if to leave her, but she held him tighter, loath to release him. She wanted him close. She wanted this feeling of being cherished and safe and warm.

To hell with the world.

Chapter Nine

Cradled in McKennon's arms, Frankie stared into the darkness. She didn't worry that she'd overslept because at some time in the night he'd shut off the computer and set the alarm clock. Pleasant achiness suffused her limbs. Her thighs tingled with sexy soreness.

McKennon put off tremendous body heat. Sweat prickled her breasts where his arm lay. His even breathing soothed her. She wanted to awaken him for another bout, but laziness held her still.

The man sure knew how to make love.

Love... She frowned, uncomfortable with the notion of falling in love. She thought she'd loved Max, but look where that had landed her. It's lust, she told herself. A culmination of all the fantasies she'd woven.

Actually being with him was better than any fantasy. For all his size and strength he was so tender he'd nearly reduced her to tears. When he touched her and kissed her, he showed no sign of cool reserve or detachment. She'd never in her life felt so completely present in the moment. So completely merged with another human being. With him she found peace.

He shifted and kneaded the flesh of her shoulder. He made a sleepy sound.

He slipped a hand across her belly. Though hardened from martial arts calluses, his hand was smooth, rousing carnal memories. A slow melt left her shivering inside. Emotion rose in her throat and filled her chest. Her lower lids burned with trembling tears.

"You awake, baby?"

No one had ever called her baby before. She'd never realized she wanted anyone to call her such a silly pet name. A tear slipped hotly down her cheek. She dashed it away.

"What's the matter?"

Her neck and facial muscles ached from suppressing tears. She didn't know what was wrong. Except, for the first time in her life she felt thoroughly cherished. Their bodies meshed as if they'd been custom-made for each other. The sound of his heartbeat compelled her to snuggle, to listen and dream and envision a future with this man.

This was more than sex. More than desire. McKennon gave her hope in a way nothing and nobody had ever before. His lovemaking left her soothed, relaxed and content. She thought about being thirty years old and how maybe it was time to settle down, have a family, to love…allow herself to be loved.

Knowing he awaited an answer, she said, "I'm worried about Penny."

He petted her hair, separating the tangles with his fingers. "I know. Do you want to get up?"

She did, but not for the reasons he assumed. She'd given McKennon more than her body last night. Natural caution had deserted her. Body, mind and soul, she'd held nothing back. She felt as if she'd been in a cage and now the door stood open. She hated the cage, but she feared freedom. Ambiguity tore her up inside.

He shifted on the bed and turned on the bedside light. The brightness wounded her eyes, and she squinted. He maneuvered until he rested on an elbow and looked down at her. With a thumb he stroked first one lower lid than the other. The tenderness of his action made her want to cry again.

"Regrets?" he asked.

Odd word, that. It sounded stiff, somehow formal, and far away from describing her roiling, tumbled, jangled emotions. "No."

"Me, neither." He stroked the ball of his thumb down her nose. "You're incredible."

She turned her face away. Life had been ever so much simpler when she'd thought him a jerk.

"What's the problem, baby?"

"It's Penny. I'm having a good time and God only knows what kind of hell she's going through."

"Feel guilty?"

She feared looking directly into his eyes. She hadn't the strength. "I guess."

"I can relate. I can't even go to fast-food joints. Every time I think about cheeseburgers, fries and shakes I know what Jamie is missing. Doesn't seem right to enjoy myself when he can't."

She looked at him then. Oh, but his face was so beautiful. The hard jaw, the even features, the way his jungle-cat eyes seemed to glow. A softening occurred in her chest. "I used to think you didn't have any feelings at all."

"I have loads." He chuckled. "But I'm a manly man."

"That you are." A wan smile tugged at her mouth. "You're kind of scaring me."

"Why is that?"

She moved a hand over his shoulder. Even in repose, his muscles were rock solid. In the old days, when she accompanied Max to the gym, she used to watch McKennon while he worked the bag or practiced his karate moves. She and every other female within viewing distance. "I have a bad habit of losing people I care about. My dad walked out after Penny was born. I don't even know if he's dead or alive. Mom died. My friends got married and had kids and we lost touch. Now Penny is missing." She stopped before she began griping about Max.

"I'm not that easy to get rid of." He kissed her. His

mouth tasted sleep-sour which she found delicious. Desire built, languid and hot, rippling through her body. When he touched her breast, an electric jolt made her jerk. "Nice rack," he murmured, grinning wickedly.

"Crude."

"Nice bosom, then?"

In response to the way he rolled an erect nipple between his fingers, a low purr rumbled in her throat. "Bosom. Too prissy."

"Picky, picky. Okay, how about…great honkin' hooters."

She'd never dreamed he possessed such a bawdy sense of humor. She laughed. He lowered his mouth to her breast and laughter died.

A knock on the door startled a gasp from her. McKennon sat upright. She snatched covers over her nakedness. Annoyance tightened her forehead. She was thirty years old, for pity's sake. If she wanted to make love with McKennon then who was to say she couldn't?

"Are you expecting someone?" She wondered where her clothing might be.

"Not at this hour." Renewed knocking made him grumble. He flipped back covers and swung his feet to the floor.

Horrible scenarios filled Frankie's head. Maybe it had snowed again last night and ten-foot drifts blocked the lodge doors. Or the kidnappers called to up the ransom amount. Or they'd found Penny and she was dead—she shook that thought away. "Where are my clothes?"

He scooped clothing off the floor, tossing jeans and an inside-out sweatshirt to her. Clutching the clothes to her chest she scrambled off the bed. "I'll wait in the bathroom."

"It's all right," he whispered. "It's probably your aunt looking for you."

Frankie rolled her eyes. She felt like a little kid about to receive a lecture for being naughty. "Put on a shirt then." She scooted into the bathroom and closed the door.

She pawed through the clothing and found her panties, but not her bra. She imagined it laying on the floor in plain view of whomever visited. Muttering curses, she dressed.

"She's been chewing my ass since 3:00 a.m. I need something I can use, and I need it right now."

Max? Frankie pressed her ear to the door and strained to hear. What in the world was Max doing in this room?

"What have you got for me? Tell me everything Frankie has said."

McKennon spoke too softly for her to hear, but Max had said enough to rouse ugly suspicions. She opened the door. McKennon wore his goon face, blank and hard. Max's eyebrows reached for the ceiling. He raked his gaze over her body, and she knew what he saw. Tousled hair, a well-kissed face and bare feet. A woman who for one, brief, shining moment had imagined herself falling in love. He saw a total idiot.

Dismissing him, she focused her glare on McKennon. "What *have* you got for him?" Say something, she thought at him. Anything, something—*tell me last night wasn't a lie!* "You're still working for him, aren't you? You're setting me up."

Head down, he answered, "It isn't what you think."

She knew what Max was capable of. Lying, sneaking, manipulating, distracting—apparently, she'd fallen for his tricks again. Apparently McKennon had learned much from the boss.

Head high she stalked into the room. With all the dignity she could fake she gathered her remaining clothing. She pushed past McKennon and Max. Being so near to her ex-fiancé made her flesh crawl. Brushing McKennon's arm broke her heart.

"Frankie, wait."

Her back muscles went rigid. She kept walking. *Get thee to a nunnery, girl,* she thought. Men were scum.

"OKAY, GEEK-AZOID," Chuck said to Paul, "you keep her nice and warm. Right?" He tucked a blanket around the girl's feet. He and Paul had wrapped her up in two flannel shirts, three pairs of socks and two blankets. Still she shivered. She hadn't made a peep since they'd moved her from the cabin to the back seat of the Bronco. He suspected she was scared out of her wits. He didn't blame her; he was shaking himself.

Paul tugged a corner of blanket over the girl's head. "Can't let the hot leak out." He grinned happily. "Snug as a bug, Miss Penelope?"

The girl replied with a timid mewling sound.

Chuck looked around for Bo, who had returned to the cabin to tote out the rest of their belongings. He leaned close to the girl. "Hey, it's okay. You don't need to be scared. You're going home this morning. Everything's cool. Just be quiet and don't let him hear you talking."

"She says I can come visit," Paul said. "She's gonna make me hot chocolate with marshmallows. And cookies!"

"Shh, don't let Bo hear you talking." Chuck couldn't help a smile. Paul hadn't a clue as to what was really going on. "Remember now, you two, not a word."

He backed out of the Bronco and closed the door. He slapped his upper arms and stamped his feet on the icy snow. The sun had yet to make an appearance. The black morning sky bursting with stars and a sliver of moon made him feel small and out of place. Vegas—hot, dry, and alive with neon—kept sounding better and better. Especially now that his luck had gone into the upswing. Everything was still tooling along as sweet as candy. He couldn't lose. By noon, he, Paul and a bag full of money would be zooming in the air toward Vegas.

Bo brought an armload of sleeping bags to the back of the Bronco and shoved them inside. He closed the hatch.

"That everything?" Chuck held out a hand. "Toss me the keys, man, and let's get this monkey house rocking."

"Take the Buick. You're making the pickup."

Chuck cocked his head one way then the other. He and

Bo had gone over the maps until Chuck had memorized every road and trail in the area. The plan was simple. Pick up the cash, hand off the girl, and split, rich and happy. "Why are you changing the plan?"

"Ain't changed nothing. This is the plan." Bo's smile looked ghastly in the wan yellow illumination from the Bronco's interior light. "Don't worry about your brother. I'll keep him safe."

A sick sensation weighted Chuck's gut. He should have known. Bo hadn't let Chuck convince him to bring along Paul. Bo had known all along that Paul made the perfect hostage. Now, if by chance, the doof had called the cops, Chuck would get popped, not Bo. Torture with rubber hoses and hot irons couldn't make Chuck drop a dime on his own brother. A perfect plan. For Bo.

"That's a hot car, man. I don't want to be cruising in a hot car."

"The old lady hasn't opened her garage in ten years. Nobody knows it's hot." He fished in a deep coat pocket and brought out a tiny cellular telephone. He handed it over.

Chuck stared at the black unit the size of a cigarette pack. He tried not to stare at the bulge the nine-millimeter formed in Bo's coat pocket. Bo also carried a shiv with an eight-inch, razor-sharp blade. He was notorious for his skill with a knife.

"Soon as you get the cash punch in star one-two. That'll hook you up with me."

Heat climbed the back of his neck and over his scalp. He stiffened against his temper. In a fight Bo would either cut him to pieces or shoot him dead. Then he'd kill Paul. If Chuck got popped by the cops, Bo would kill Paul. If Chuck ran with the money, Bo would kill Paul.

He glanced at his baby brother. The big goofball grinned like a hound dog eager for a car ride.

"If I smell a cop," he said, "I ain't doing it."

"If you smell a cop, buddy, call me. We'll send our boy his wife's right hand in a box. Now go."

Chuck cleared snow, ice, tree branches and debris off the old Buick. Despite being over twenty years old it was in great shape. Driven by a little old lady to and from church, he thought with a grim smile. He wrestled the door open. The bench seat felt like a block of ice. He turned the key. The engine roared to life. He glanced at the Bronco. Paul waved happily. Chuck tossed the telephone on the seat beside him and opened the map. A big red *X* marked the pickup site.

With the headlights on high he maneuvered the big car toward the road. Snowdrifts bogged the wheels. Both hands on the wheel, cussing Bo Moran, he slipped, slid and plowed through the snow. He couldn't even see the driveway so he steered between the trees. Gravity aided the car in the downhill trek, but the big engine groaned as the car fought through drifts. Rooster tails of snow flared behind the spinning wheels.

By the time he reached the asphalt he was shaking and sweating, but so cold his teeth chattered. He turned the heater on full blast.

Snowplows had cleared a single lane. Asphalt gleamed wetly under the headlights. Chuck touched the accelerator, and the car heaved forward, but the rear end skidded. "Slow," he muttered, heart pounding. "Steer into the skids, keep the wheel straight. Okay, old Buick, old friend, nice and easy." He'd spent most of his life in Nevada and California. Neither state offered much opportunity for practicing winter weather or mountain driving. Uncaring if he reached the rendezvous point late, as long as he reached it, he puttered along at twenty miles an hour.

With every mile his confidence grew. The old Buick lacked four-wheel drive or even front-wheel drive, but it hugged the road like a boat on water. By the time he reached the forest service road he took one hand off the wheel and turned on the radio. It took some fiddling, but he finally found a country and western station with minimal static.

The road climbed into the forest. Thickly growing trees blotted out the faint light from the rising sun. He whistled along with a Garth Brooks heartbreaker. Up ahead the headlights shone into open space, which meant a sharp turn. He took his foot off the accelerator and allowed the incline to slow the car. He made the turn at a scant fifteen miles an hour. The old Buick handled like a dream. He patted the dashboard.

"Hey, old girl, want a trip to Vegas?" He laughed out loud. For the first time in his life his luck was holding.

Still laughing, he braked lightly on the downhill.

The Buick skidded. He pumped the brake and felt the brakes catching, but the car didn't slow. Sweat beaded on his forehead. He didn't dare take a hand off the steering wheel to turn off the heater. Forest and mountain climbed to his right. Nothing but treetops lay to the left. He tried the brake again and felt the car sailing on ice. He turned the wheel hard, uncaring if he crashed into the mountain.

The big Buick sailed into nothingness.

Chuck watched the headlights skim trees and sky. Tree branches cracked and crashed. The Buick's nose aimed for the ground. It tipped, throwing Chuck against the driver's door. He heard impact.

Then nothing.

Chuck's eyelids fluttered. He knew he'd been unconscious, but not for how long. Utter blackness surrounded him, and for a moment he feared he'd gone blind. He grew aware of a pale green light emanating from the radio. A commercial announcer cheerfully hawked a vacuum cleaner. The Buick's headlights glowed as if underwater.

I'm alive, he thought, and laughed. Blades of pain rocketed through his skull. The laughter trailed into a groan. He made as if to reach for his forehead, but his arm refused to move. He struggled, but the steering wheel trapped his right arm against his thigh. Every movement made his head throb and scream.

The damned engine continued to purr along at a soothing idle. Heat from a vent blew onto his face. His legs ached, with his knees feeling as if they'd been hammered. When his eyes adjusted to the gloom, he looked around. The bench seat had jammed forward at a skewed angle and trapped him beneath the steering wheel. He could see his right arm, but he couldn't feel it.

"Thanks a lot, Bo," he grumbled. Grunting, wincing, he finally managed to reach the interior dome light. The Buick was buried in tree limbs and snow. Snow piled halfway up the cracked windshield. It completely covered the driver's window.

He struggled to free himself from the steering wheel, but he was crunched up at an awkward angle. He couldn't work up enough leverage to push against the floorboards and shove the seat back. His legs tingled with impending numbness.

He tried the door. The latch worked, but no amount of pushing budged the door. He began rolling down the window. An avalanche of loose snow poured onto his lap. He quickly rolled the window back up.

"Telephone!" he exclaimed. He searched for the cellular unit. There it was on the passenger-side floor. Its microdot indicator light showed it was activated and ready to call for rescue.

He couldn't reach it.

A rumbling noise caught his attention. A vehicle on the road above! He tried to reach the radio to turn it off, but missed by a scant few inches. He blared the horn until the piercing noise brought tears of pain.

"Help!" he yelled. "I'm down here! Help me! Help!"

When he stopped holding the horn he heard only the radio. Alan Jackson sang a love song to a Mercury. He honked the horn again and again and again and again.

Somebody had to come. His life depended on it.
Paul's life depended on it.

FRANKIE STOOD as close to the agent monitoring the radio
as he would allow. The faux Julius had left the resort at
exactly 6:00 a.m. As per instructions he'd driven directly
to the reservoir and picked up Forest Road 247. He'd
reached Forest Road 59 ten minutes ago. He kept up a
running commentary about everything and every person he
saw.

Nobody in the dining room spoke. Elise and the Colonel
held hands. Ross sat between Kara and Janine. FBI agents
monitored radio links to the men and women staking out
the mountain roads.

"...passing a logging truck with our guys. No signal
from them. No sign of civilian traffic. Damn it! This is like
driving on a skating rink. Lots of ice up here, people.
Nasty."

Feeling she was being watched, Frankie glanced toward
the doorway. McKennon stood there. Sorrow filled her
chest and left her aching. She'd been a fool. An utter, naive,
trusting, idiotic fool. He'd told her exactly what Max
wanted and how he meant to get it. She'd filled in the
blanks with foolish imaginings.

Countless women before her had survived one-night
stands with manipulative jerks. She could, too. She dragged
her attention off him.

"Mile seven," the Julius stand-in said, "nothing. I
haven't seen anybody except our guys."

Frankie shifted her glare to Agent Patrick. "Maybe the
kidnappers see our guys, too."

"My people are doing nothing to raise alarm. Relax,
Miss Forrest."

Easier said than done. The minutes ticked past with excruciating slowness. Radio transmissions and the increasingly annoyed voice of the drop-off man were the only
sounds. The sky beyond the big window slowly changed
from black velvet to pearl to turquoise. Elise left the room,

but returned shortly with a cart containing coffee. Kara helped her mother serve. *Thank-yous* rippled through the dining room like an echo.

"I'm at the county line," the agent said. "Still nothing, and I'm past the surveillance posts." The transmission broke and crackled with static. "I'm going five more miles before I turn around and try another sweep."

"Something is wrong," Frankie said.

"Please be quiet, Miss Forrest."

A man hurried into the dining room and whispered in Agent Patrick's ear. Her eyes widened momentarily before narrowing and her entire expression tightened. "Where?" she asked.

"Everywhere," the man replied.

"What?" Frankie cried. "What is it? What's the matter?"

Waving for silence, Agent Patrick turned on a small television atop the sideboard. A snowy picture showed Belinda Bannerman Caulfield garbed in black and wearing sunglasses.

"...offering a million-dollar reward for the arrest and conviction of my son's killer."

A disembodied voice asked: "Do the police have any leads at all, Mrs. Caulfield?"

"The police are doing nothing! My son was murdered and the police have done absolutely nothing to bring his killers to justice. I will have justice. I will not rest until those vicious brutes are convicted and sentenced to death."

Frankie felt certain this had to be some kind of macabre joke. Or maybe she still slept and everything that had happened this morning was part of an elaborate nightmare.

The camera switched from Belinda to a news anchor. "In case you're just tuning in, folks, that was Belinda Bannerman Caulfield, the empress of retail-mall jewelry stores. Two days ago her son Julius Bannerman was brutally murdered in his sleep. Thus far, the police have no leads as to the identity of the butchers who committed this heinous crime.''

The camera switched again, this time to a close-up of the Colorado Springs police chief. The reporter asked for his take on the situation. The man looked somewhat befuddled and extremely annoyed as he muttered a terse, ''No comment.''

The FBI agent who'd brought the news to Agent Patrick's attention switched the channel. Another morning-news show depicted a pan shot of a Bannerman Fine Jewelers store. The camera zoomed in on a young man wearing a suit and a gold name tag. Off-camera, a reporter said, ''Julius Bannerman's murder must be a horrible shock for you.''

''Uh, well, I've been working for Bannerman's for the past three years. Everyone knows Julius was really close to his mother.''

The agent changed the channel again. Belinda was featured, her voice hoarse but firm as she told the world about the million-dollar bounty she offered for the arrest of her son's killers.

The agent flipped through channels. Every station carried the story about Belinda and Julius. Nobody mentioned Penny, the wedding or the kidnapping. Somebody turned on a radio. The story was all over the radio airwaves, too, with sound clips from the press conference and commentary from talk-show hosts. The spin on all the stories was that a leading scion of Colorado society had lost her son in a brutal murder and the authorities were doing nothing to find the killer. Commentators challenged listeners to answer why private citizens could not depend on law enforcement to protect them.

Frankie turned her disbelieving gaze on Max. He appeared as shocked as everyone else in the room, but she knew it was an act. He'd put Belinda up to this. With malice aforethought and complete indifference toward Penny's life he'd convinced his wife to broadcast details of the murder. Stiff-legged, fearing if she relaxed her muscles she'd collapse, she stalked across the dining room.

"You did this. You killed Julius and now you're killing Penny to cover your tracks."

"That doesn't even merit a response," he said coolly.

She swung at him. McKennon slipped between them and blocked the blow. She struck his forearm with her forearm. It was like striking a two-by-four, and the shock waves numbed her arm to the shoulder. Her uncle and Ross grabbed her arms and dragged her away from Max.

"He's the killer! Make him tell me where Penny is!"

Chapter Ten

"Where's your gear, McKennon?" Max Caulfield dropped a gym bag on the floor. His stiff shoulders radiated tension. He turned a slow circle as if checking out escape routes or the location of enemies.

The lobby was empty. The FBI had requested that all resort employees remain in their quarters. Not that it did any good, J.T. mused. The big mystery was a mystery no more, and all secrets were out on the table. Belinda's press conference was making national news.

J.T. observed the boss. The crisply starched shirt and closely shaven face. The glossy shine on his shoes. In his forties, Caulfield kept himself fit and trim, as meticulous about his personal appearance as a cat. Appearances meant everything. It drove him crazy if any person failed to recognize him for what he was: successful, attractive and in charge. A rottweiler in a dog-eat-dog world.

"By the way, if I haven't said thanks, then thanks," Caulfield said. "Frankie has a wicked right hook."

J.T. hadn't blocked Frankie's punch for Caulfield's sake. He'd blocked it because if she'd hit him he'd have had her arrested and charged. If not for a roomful of law enforcement officials Caulfield would be now nursing a busted nose.

"What the hell is wrong with you? Get the car." Caulfield tossed a set of keys.

J.T. quelled his reflexes. The keys struck his forearm. They clattered to the floor. He wondered if perhaps Frankie was correct and Caulfield had staged the kidnapping. He didn't see why Caulfield would do it. He was a man who never did anything without a damn good reason. Perhaps something had happened between Julius and the boss, something sufficiently threatening to Caulfield's position.

"Pick up those keys." His voice quavered with rage. His dark eyes blazed.

"Did you put Mrs. Caulfield up to the press conference?"

"Is that what your problem is? Don't be an ass."

"Do you care at all what happens to Penny?"

"Pick up the keys and get the car. We're leaving. Do you have any idea what kind of mess we'll find at home? Do you? Every reporter in the state will converge on the house. In the country!" His cheek muscles twitched. "I always wanted to see myself on the cover of *People,* but not this way."

Caulfield had lost his temper before, but never like this. An angry flush crept over his neck. His ears had turned bright red. A vein pulsed in his temple. He appeared on the verge of a stroke.

"I quit." J.T. spoke before he'd fully decided, but once said, it felt strangely satisfying.

"You can't quit."

J.T. lifted an eyebrow.

"This is all about Frankie, isn't it?" He swiped a hand angrily through the air. "I screwed up. Blew your cover. I'm sorry. Feel better now?"

"Have a nice drive." J.T. turned his back on the boss— former boss.

"Don't cross me, McKennon. She isn't worth it. No woman is worth it."

She was worth it. Frankie Forrest was worth fifty Caulfields. He'd find another job. Or two jobs, or even three. He and Jamie would do just fine. When his son awakened,

J.T. would feel right about how he'd earned the money to pay for Jamie's care. And now he had a chance to make up for what he'd done to Frankie. A chance to feel alive again.

"Damn you, McKennon! The evidence says Frankie is going down. Stick with her and you're going down, too! I'll bury you."

Not if I bury you first, J.T. thought darkly.

"J.T., come on, man. We're a team. I need you. You're the best there is."

Bristling at Caulfield's familiarity, J.T. turned around. Anger tightened his scalp. "We are not a team. Never were."

"I thought we were friends, J.T."

He resented this ploy. "You thought wrong. I thought wrong. You're wrong about Frankie, too. I won't let you turn her into the scapegoat for Julius's murder. You know as well as I do that she had nothing to do with it."

"Do you honestly think Penny could have pulled this off by herself? Cute girl, but dumb as a box of rocks. Nobody would buy it." He shook a finger like a schoolteacher making a point. "I know for a fact Frankie is behind this. If you'd pull your head out of your crotch, you'd see it, too."

He knew something, J.T. realized with a start. Evidence? What evidence? Caulfield never made wild guesses or wasted his time on unprovable theories. He didn't make lame accusations, either. If he set his sights on a target he had a good reason for doing so. J.T. suddenly realized his own mistake. He'd let himself believe Caulfield was merely blowing smoke. Frankie was in a hell of a lot of trouble.

Caulfield extended the car keys, politely. "Forget this crap about quitting. This conversation never happened."

"No. It's over." He turned on his heel and walked away.

He reached the dining room, and from the doorway he observed Frankie. Heaviness settled in the pit of his belly. Making love to her had transcended sex. With her he'd felt fully alive, fully human again. A hard shell around his emotions he hadn't even been aware of had cracked and opened his soul. It was as if he'd been asleep and now he was awake. It hurt.

It hurt to see Frankie now. Flanked by cousins, she sat rigidly on a chair. Her big, haunted eyes and drawn face wore an expression of somebody who'd stepped to the gates of Hell and peeked inside.

She's going down, Caulfield had promised. Evidence. How far would he go? How far could he go? Caulfield had the smarts and the resources to do almost anything he set his mind to. Somebody had lured Frankie to the resort. To stop the wedding? Or to get her out of the way so he could plant evidence.

He entered the room. Frankie didn't even glance his way, and that hurt more than anything. Steeling his emotions he approached Agent Patrick. "Any word, ma'am?"

She indicated the television set and radios with a weary sweep of her hand. "Other than being in the midst of the story of the year, nothing. I'm bringing my man in. There's no sign of the unsubs anywhere. Where is Mr. Caulfield?"

"Headed back to the city."

"Did he know his wife was going to pull this stunt?"

"He said no, ma'am." He had his doubts.

"Civilians," she muttered.

"May I speak to you privately?"

She stepped outside the dining room with him. Arms crossed, scowling, she didn't appear receptive to anything he might say. He had to say it anyway.

"I've quit Mr. Caulfield's employ. Some of the things he's said to me lead me to believe he might possibly be involved. He may be withholding evidence."

She made a little hissy noise through her nose.

"He informed me that he's going to make sure Frankie Forrest takes the heat for the murder."

"If she didn't do it, then she has nothing to worry about. In any case why tell me? Murder is the state's problem, not mine."

That wasn't the answer he expected. Nor did he expect her open hostility. No doubt she had her own problems with a kidnapping gone bad. This wouldn't look good in her next progress report.

"I don't have time for this, Mr. McKennon. I know Max's reputation. It's solid."

Oh boy, he thought. Frankie was right. The agent was firmly in Caulfield's court. "A few months ago Mr. Caulfield asked me to find out where Frankie was living and working. I didn't think much of it at the time, but now it seems peculiar. He gave me no reason why he wanted the information."

"Maybe he was lonesome."

"Somebody tipped off Frankie to the wedding. Anonymously."

"I'll take it under advisement."

"Agent Patrick," a uniformed state officer said. "We have a situation." He gestured for her to pick up a telephone.

Activity ceased and voices hushed as all attention centered on the agent in charge. Her end of the conversation consisted mostly of "Uh-huh," and "Right." She sank onto a chair and hunched over, with a hand across the side of her face to muffle her words. After she hung up she looked to the colonel.

"They found her?" he asked.

"We may have taken a kidnapper into custody."

"Penny?"

The agent shook her head. "Police are at the scene of a car accident. The driver is en route to the hospital in the Springs. There was a map in the car with a site marked on Forest Road 59. And he was carrying Julius Bannerman's cellular telephone."

The Colonel's face turned red. "What about Penny?"

"The driver is unconscious. Hypothermia and carbon monoxide poisoning. We think the car he was driving is stolen. We won't know anything else until he's awake and talking." She pointed at a pair of agents. "You and you, come with me. The rest of you continue monitoring communications."

Pandemonium broke out with the Dukes swarming around Agent Patrick. They shouted questions and demanded answers. J.T. took the opportunity to slip in next to Frankie. She cringed away from him. Her eyes blared hatred.

"I have to talk to you."

She clamped her arms over her chest and hunched her shoulders into a solid, unyielding block. "Get away from me."

He lowered his voice. "I promised to get Penny back. I meant it."

"I know exactly what your promises mean. Zip. Now get away from me." Her chin quivered and tears hovered on her lower lids. "You used me."

"I was protecting you."

"Like I believe that."

Feeling squeezed by the cacophony of anxious voices rising and falling around him, he offered his hand. "Five minutes. Give me five minutes. Please."

"Why should I?"

"Because I'm the only thing standing between you and Caulfield. Now come with me."

As if it hurt to move, she rose creakily and shied away from his proffered hand. Arms still crossed, she sidled past him toward the door. Once in the hallway he caught her elbow and hustled her toward the stairs.

"Where are you taking me?"

"My room."

She twisted violently away. "Like hell!"

"You need to get out of here." Realizing he did this all wrong, he stepped back. He slid a hand over the back of his neck. Tension ached in his scalp and spine. "I was wrong."

"No kidding." Her voice quavered. Her knuckles were white from clutching her elbows.

"I should have explained what I was up to. I thought I was protecting you."

"Nice recovery attempt, but I'm not buying."

"I quit this morning. For real. I no longer work for Caulfield."

"Now where have I heard that before?" She pulled a thoughtful face. "Oh yeah, from you. Silly, silly me, I felt sorry for you."

"When he ordered me before to gather evidence, I knew there was no evidence to find. I needed to protect you."

"You needed the money."

Hurt arced through his midsection.

"I trusted you." Her voice barely rose above a hoarse whisper, but it cut through him like a knife. "I thought maybe, just maybe, for the first time in my life I met a guy who wasn't total pond scum."

Fighting with her over this accomplished nothing. Words would never reach her. "You need to get out of here."

"I'm not going anywhere until I have Penny. Especially not because you say so."

"The kidnappers know Julius is dead. Who does that leave to pay the ransom?"

She frowned. "We caught one. Do you think the others will try to get the ransom anyway?"

"Maybe. They won't try to get it from Mrs. Caulfield. She's already announced her intentions."

"My aunt and uncle?"

"Likely choice, but there's a problem. Even if the kidnappers believed the cops weren't involved before, they have to know now, with the murder being investigated. This resort is hot. Too hot."

"Me?" She mouthed the word.

"Penny will tell them about you."

"She knows I don't have any money."

"She won't tell them that."

She shook her head. A single tear tracked silver down her pale cheek. He wanted to hold and comfort her so badly his arms ached. He suspected if he touched her she'd slug him. Or worse. She'd walk away and refuse to speak to him again.

"The whole world is hot," she said. "Penny is—is—she's a liability."

Perhaps quitting hadn't been such a good idea. Inside the Bannerman estate he had access to Caulfield's files and desk drawers. Like most egomaniacs Caulfield was addicted to recording his every action. He hoarded memos and other writings as if they were valuable antiquities. If he'd arranged the kidnapping he'd have records somewhere.

He'd have evidence. Evidence he meant to use against Frankie.

"We have an advantage."

She peered suspiciously from the corner of her eye. "What?"

"Risk factor."

She shook her head. "I have no idea what you're talking about."

"I'll make one assumption. We know whoever kidnapped Penny is an insider. But the fact that one of them got caught this morning means they aren't that well informed."

Her shoulders relaxed somewhat. "Okay."

"What that tells me is that an insider set this up, but the three people doing the dirty work are on their own. The ransom is their only payoff."

"I don't follow." She moved to the base of the stairs and sat on a step. After wrapping her arms around her legs, she rested her chin on her knee.

The urge to touch her grew so powerful he crammed his hands in his pockets. "Let's say I wanted to get rid of Julius. It has to look like an accident. Somebody else has to take the blame."

"So you set up a kidnapping and provide the murder weapon. Only you don't tell the hired hit man he is a hit man?"

"And I also make sure that the payoff cannot be traced to me. No matter how deeply anyone digs."

"So the only way the kidnappers get paid for murder is to return Penny."

"Exactly."

"Max is well acquainted with the kind of people who'd pull off a kidnapping." Her eyes acquired some shine, and color seeped back into her face. "He's been in the private security business for over twenty years. He must know every criminal in the state. That's where your risk factor comes in, doesn't it? He can't risk having witnesses who can name him or blackmail him or whatever."

"He would put the risk factor as close to zero as possible. Which means minimal contact. So I'm betting the kidnappers don't know who he is. Either he went through intermediaries or wore a disguise or made all the arrangements via secure communications. In any case, the kidnappers are left twisting in the wind. They took all the risks and have nothing to show for it. That's our advantage."

Her face expressed such hopefulness his belly ached. All attempts to shut out his emotions against her failed. He studied the toes of his boots. He wanted her friendship, high opinion of him and high regard. He wanted her trust. An image of himself on his knees, hands clasped, pleading for her forgiveness disgusted him. Yet, it held almost hypnotic appeal as well. He swiped a hand through his hair as if wiping away the thoughts.

"What can we do?" she asked hopefully.

"We have to get you out of here. No police involvement. No FBI. We can't involve your family, either."

"I don't understand."

"Two reasons. Caulfield ordered me to find evidence against you. It finally hit me this morning that he knows there is evidence to find."

Her gaze turned inward. Her brow twisted. "Do you think he's the man who called me? He got me out of the way so he could plant evidence in my apartment?"

"We better find out before the cops do."

She shook her head. "No, not possible. I moved, changed my phone number. Max doesn't know where I live."

He cringed inside. The list of his inadvertent crimes against her was growing long and damning. "He does. A couple months ago he had me find out where you're living and working."

She rose to her feet. Standing on a step, she looked down at him.

"Address, phone number, Martha's Pie House. Even where you bank."

"Give me one good reason why I should trust a single word you say."

He thought about last night. The sheer amount of emotion he'd felt troubled him then and troubled him now. She'd touched him. She'd roused long-dormant feelings. He'd go to the ends of the earth for her cause. If he could explain that to her maybe she would trust him. But he couldn't even explain it to himself.

Her chin quivered. "How do I know this isn't one of Max's tricks to set me up?"

He had no easy answer. None she would believe, anyway. "All I have is my word."

Eyes closed, she slumped. "Oh, who gives a damn. I don't care if Max sets me up to get the death penalty. All I want is Penny back."

"Then you have to get out of here."

"The man they caught could be telling the police everything he knows. He can tell me where Penny is."

"The other two won't sit around waiting to get caught."

"Do you really think they'll contact me? It makes more sense to extort money from my aunt and uncle. They look wealthy."

"I don't know anything for certain. I do know the game has started over. Everybody is back to square one. If the man the cops caught does talk, then we will make some progress. If he doesn't talk, who knows what can happen. I still think the kidnappers will attempt to contact you. You offer the lowest risk, since you have the most to lose."

Her expressive face told him she was hooked.

"We're running out of time," he said. "If Caulfield planted evidence in your apartment we have to find it before the cops do."

"They don't have probable cause to search my home."

"Mrs. Caulfield is putting on the heat. You refused to let the cops search your place before. It won't take much nudging from Caulfield for them to decide your refusal is their probable cause."

She let her head fall back, exposing the vulnerable line of her throat. She slammed a fist against the stairwell wall.

"If you're arrested we may never get Penny back."

A rumble of voices rose. He hurried to the corner and peered toward the private dining room. Two uniformed officers and an FBI agent argued with a group of people. Judging by the cameras and microphones the news media had discovered the connection between Julius Bannerman and Elk River Resort. The Colonel stepped into the hallway. His ringing voice demanded silence.

"Oh, no," Frankie whispered. "How did they find out?"

"Doesn't matter. We have to get out of here."

"I can't just disappear."

"It'll be easier if you do. Let's go."

Her head swiveled between him and the increasing noise down the hallway. "I don't trust you," she whispered. Her plaintive note hurt his heart.

He caught her shoulders and jerked her to him. He kissed her mouth, hard and hot, trying to tell her with his soul what his words failed to accomplish. She fought him, at first, then slightly, ever so slightly, she relaxed. He broke the kiss and stared into her eyes.

"We'll deal with your trust issues later."

"If you're lying to me," she whispered in reply, "I will kill you." She twisted out of his grasp. Her eyes blazed. "And keep your hands off me. Last night was a mistake, and I never make the same mistake twice." She pounded up the stairs.

It took J.T. only minutes to gather his belongings. Garbed in her ratty old parka, Frankie glowered at him from the doorway. He explained that he'd accompanied Julius and Penny to the resort in the limo, so they'd have to take her car. They slipped out the back way. Her car was covered in snow. They used their hands to clear the windshield and windows. He noticed she didn't have gloves so offered his. She ignored him.

"I'll drive," he said. "Get down in the back."

"Why?" she stammered, her teeth chattering. She fumbled a set of keys out of her pocket, but dropped them in the snow. Her hands were bright red except for painful looking white patches.

He scooped up the keys. "Because the cops might stop you from leaving." He hoped nobody inside the lodge spotted them. "Get in." He slid behind the wheel and waited. Seconds later she got in the back. "Cover yourself with those newspapers and stuff."

He could barely see out the windshield, but didn't want to waste time waiting for the defroster to kick in. He drove slowly around the lodge. News vans crowded the circular drive. Uniformed officers attempted to maintain order, but the reporters were like rowdy children trying for a shot at a piñata.

"What's happening?" Frankie asked, her voice muffled.

"You don't want to know." Avoiding making eye contact with any law officer, he maneuvered the car through the road jam of reporters. He made it all the way to the highway before a county sheriff's deputy flagged him down.

"Why are you stopping?" Frankie asked.

"Shut up and stay down." He pulled out his cellular phone and rolled down the window. Before the deputy could say a word, J.T. waggled the telephone. "Hey, I got a story to file and the damned mountains are blocking reception. Where's the nearest high spot—?"

"Get out of here!" the deputy yelled, waving him on.

J.T. gunned the engine and got out of there. He passed more news vans headed toward the resort. He pitied the Dukes.

"Can I get up now?"

He glanced at the rearview mirror. Her red curls bounced into view.

"I gotta clean out this car," she grumbled. She leaned an arm through the bucket seats. "If the reporters know about Elk River do they know about me, too?"

He met her eyes in the rearview mirror. He tried not to breathe too deeply. Her scent, heightened by the hot air blasting through the car heater, tortured him. He turned on the radio. He switched the radio to AM and fiddled with the dial until a station came in clearly.

"...live from Elk River Resort, scene of the heinous murder that took the life of the heir to the Bannerman jewelry fortune. Ellen, what have you got for our listeners?"

"Well, David, the rumors are true. Julius Bannerman was murdered in connection to a kidnapping. The FBI agent in charge refuses to confirm the identity of the kidnapping victim. The scene is tense. The sheriff's department, state police and FBI are involved."

In the background, people shouted questions, but due to the noise no replies were audible. Irritated, J.T. switched off the radio.

"Hey!" Frankie protested.

"Hold off until we get into town. Maybe we can find a station telling us something we don't know."

When they reached Manitou Springs he turned the radio back on. He found a station carrying the news about the murder and kidnapping. They were replaying Belinda's

press conference. A commentator named Penny as the kidnap victim. Frankie muttered from the back seat.

"You're going the wrong way," she said. "I'm up
north."

"We're switching cars."

"The police can't be looking for me. They think I'm still
at Elk River."

"We have reporters to worry about, too."

He pulled into the parking lot of the apartment complex
where he had an efficiency. He parked her car along the
curb. Alert for anything that looked, smelled or moved like
a cop he hustled Frankie to his car.

She wrinkled her nose. "This is a worse piece of crap
than mine."

"But it's paid for. Get in." He slung his duffel bag into
the back seat. From the back seat he retrieved a black knit
cap. He tossed it on Frankie's lap. "Put that on and tuck
in your hair."

Obeying him, she asked, "Have you got a plan?"

"I'm working on it."

Once on the road again, he handed over his telephone.
"Have you got a neighbor who can tell you if anything is
going on?"

"Sally might be home. She works nights." She punched
in the number. "Sally? Frankie. Yeah, yeah, it's true.
That's my sister. I'll explain it all later. I promise."

"Any cops?" he prompted.

"Hey, I'm in a real jam. Is there anybody hanging
around the apartments? Like a cop? No? Anyone asked you
any questions about me? Good. All right, I'll be home in
about fifteen minutes. What? Since when? Okay, see you
there." She slapped the phone shut. "She says my cat is
missing. She hasn't seen him in days, but I know he was
inside when I left."

Filled with a sense of impending doom he couldn't
shake, he grimly focused on traffic. The storm had swept
through the city and left behind six-foot-tall berms of fro-

zen snowplow tailings. The roads were rivers of slush, and he turned on the windshield wipers to clear goop off the glass. At the apartment complex where Frankie lived, he drove slowly through the parking lot. After two passes he figured it was safe.

He and Frankie hurried across the parking lot. She stopped abruptly.

He reached for her arm. She twisted out of reach. ''That's Cat,'' she said.

A big yellow cat lay in a small patch of sunshine on the asphalt. He had a huge round head and one ear had been torn in half. The tip of his tail twitched lazily. Scruffy and huge, he was the ugliest cat J.T. had ever seen.

She glanced at the second-floor windows. ''I know he was in when I left. I *know* it.'' Hand out, she approached the animal. He yawned, revealing rows of yellowed, needle-sharp teeth. ''C'mere, Cat.''

She scooped him up and slung him over her shoulder. Eyelids drooping at half-mast, he regarded J.T. He reached up a hand to rub the cat's ear and a half. Snake-swift, the animal hissed and swatted at him.

''He doesn't like strangers,'' Frankie said without much apology.

J.T. kept a safe distance as he followed Frankie up the stairs.

Chapter Eleven

The sight of her friend's face was so welcome Frankie nearly wept. "Sally!" she cried and held out an arm. Cat rumbled a warning against her shoulder. Frankie kept herself well between Sally and Cat.

"Keys," McKennon said.

"What the hell is going on?" Sally asked. Eyes narrowed, she looked McKennon up and down. She appeared to like what she saw. "Who's your friend?"

"Sally, this is J. T. McKennon." Half expecting to see a battalion of cops pounding up the stairs, she glanced nervously behind them. As soon as McKennon opened the door she rushed inside. Cat began fighting for release. She hustled him into the bedroom and tossed him inside before shutting the door. He yowled in protest.

"Now will you tell me what's going on?" Sally asked. She flashed a smile at McKennon. "I wanted to call when I couldn't find Cat, but didn't know how to reach you."

"Don't touch anything, okay?" Frankie prowled the tiny living room and galley-style kitchen. The place looked dusty, and Cat had shredded a newspaper into confetti, but it looked the same as when she'd torn out of here the other day. She explained to Sally, briefly, what had happened.

"Man alive," Sally breathed. "You don't have any idea where your sister is?"

The question struck Frankie square in the pit of her belly.

She caught the back of a chair and closed her eyes. Nausea churned her innards. At Elk River she'd felt helpless, but here she felt hopeless. The only person who seemed to have any idea about how to get Penny back was a man she should not trust. A touch on her shoulder made her jump. Seeing Sally's intention to soothe and comfort, Frankie thrust out a hand.

"I'm okay!" She didn't have time to fall apart.

"Check your messages," McKennon said. He pointed with his chin at her answering machine. The blinking red light indicated calls.

She pushed a button. Four messages had been recorded. Each was from Bob at the Pie House. He grew more angry with every call. The final message informed her that her services were no longer required.

"Bite me, Bob," she muttered.

"Record a new message on the machine," McKennon said. He wrote on a scrap of paper. "This is my cell number. Tell anyone with information about Penny to call."

She met his eyes. Ambiguity tore her apart. She didn't want to trust him. Experience said trusting him meant danger to herself and to Penny. Yet, his steady gaze and strength invited trust. His kisses, the way he'd held her, the passionate words he'd whispered in her ears gave her the only shred of hope she had to cling to. Her ridiculous heart said to trust him. "Do you really think they'll call me?"

"Yes."

His conviction almost made her forget she hated him. Almost. She recorded a new message. Her voice quavered so much she had to start over twice. McKennon prowled the room, poking and probing.

He opened the bedroom door.

"Don't—" Frankie warned, but too late. Cat shot out of the room and wrapped himself around McKennon's ankle. The big man grabbed the animal. Frankie rushed in to the rescue, but Cat bit McKennon's hand. Cat bounded away and jumped on top of the television set. There he sat, his yellow eyes narrowed in feline satisfaction. His scruffy tail slashed the air.

McKennon gawked at the cat. Blood dripped from his left hand.

Appalled and embarrassed, Frankie tugged McKennon toward the kitchen. She pushed his hand into the sink and turned on the water full blast. "I am so sorry."

"That animal needs an exorcist," Sally said. "He's a menace."

"I've never been attacked by a cat before." McKennon winced as Frankie applied a liberal squirt of dish-washing soap to the wound. "Did you train him to do that?"

"He came already trained." Two neat punctures went all the way through the web of flesh between his forefinger and thumb. Touching him tortured her. She wanted to kiss him and hold him and beg forgiveness for her nasty pet's actions. "Are you up on your tetanus shots? Scrub that, while I find the antibiotic." She searched through the cabinet next to the sink where she kept first aid supplies. She found a tube of antibiotic cream. As she moved to close the cabinet, she noticed an unusual shape amongst the aspirin bottles and sunscreen. She carefully moved a box of Band-Aid strips. "Uh-oh."

He looked where she pointed.

"That is not mine," she said.

Sally crowded in behind them. "What is it?"

McKennon tore a paper towel off a roll and used it to carefully grasp a squat glass vial with a metal seal outfitted with a rubber center. It was a quarter-full of clear liquid. He maneuvered the vial in his palm, atop the toweling, until the label was readable. "Butunal," he read.

"That isn't mine," Frankie repeated. "What is Butunal?"

"I'd guess some sort of barbiturate."

Openmouthed and incredulous, she stared at the vial. Her brain locked up. She knew Max was capable of planting evidence. She knew he had a damned good reason to finger

her for the murder. Even so, actually seeing with her own
eyes his perfidy took her aback. "Do you think it's the
murder weapon?"

Sally backed away, her hands raised. "This is way too
heavy for me."

"Are you absolutely sure you haven't seen anybody
hanging around the apartment?" Frankie asked her friend.

"I haven't seen a soul."

Frankie looked to Cat. He washed a paw, but his baleful
glare never left McKennon. Even though she'd had him
neutered and he had no reason to prowl, Cat liked to dart
outside whenever the opportunity presented itself. He could
have sneaked out the door when Sally came to feed him,
but she suspected somebody else had let him out. Somebody like Max. She wished the cat could talk.

Frankie made quick work of doctoring McKennon's
hand. Sally armed herself with a rolled newspaper to keep
Cat in line while Frankie and McKennon searched the
apartment. Frankie checked her closets and drawers with
extra care, rifling through all pockets, nooks, crannies and
even inside her shoes. The longer she searched the angrier
she grew. Even if she turned over the vial of Butunal, the
cops would never believe Max had planted it in her kitchen
cabinet.

"What's in these boxes?" McKennon asked.

Frankie rolled her eyes. Since moving in, she hadn't dec-
orated or unpacked anything she didn't use regularly. The
boxes he indicated contained books, papers and computer
disks. "Junk." She chuckled weakly. "Max's junk mostly.
Textbooks he paid for. Copies of work I brought home from
the office. I'm surprised he doesn't say I stole that stuff."

She turned to her desk. It looked exactly the way she'd
left it. She picked up shredded newspaper off the floor and
dumped it in a waste can. She'd turned away before it
struck her that there were wads of paper in the can. Since
acquiring Cat she'd gotten into the habit of emptying the

trash every day. Otherwise he partied hearty with anything made out of paper. Her mouth went dry.

Using her fingernails she fished a piece of paper out of the can. It was common, lined notebook paper. With great care she unfolded the crumpled ball, trying not to leave any fingerprints. "Look at this."

It was a pencil draft of a note. "Greetings, Julius Bannerman" had been crossed out, as had "Julius Bannerman: We are your worst nightmare come true."

"Frankie," Sally said. "Two police cars just pulled into the parking lot."

McKennon hurried to the window. "Time to go," he said. "Grab that trash can."

"There's only one way out of here," Frankie said. "Down the stairs. They'll see me." A sickening image flashed of herself wearing handcuffs and orange coveralls while trying to explain to a judge that she hadn't murdered Julius Bannerman and kidnapped her own sister.

"My place," Sally said. She rushed out of the apartment and opened the adjoining door. Waving an arm, she urged Frankie and McKennon inside.

McKennon had the Butunal vial, wrapped in paper towel, in his shirt pocket. Frankie held the trash can. She wondered what else Max had planted for the police to find.

Sally looked out the peephole in the door. "They're coming upstairs," she whispered. "They're at your place." Pounding emphasized her announcement.

A man called, "Police, open up!"

Frankie's hands shook so hard she had to put down the trash can. She stared at the balls of paper in sick horror. If the cops caught her with the evidence, Penny was going to die.

Sally kept watch through the peephole. Frankie and McKennon listened through the thin wall separating the apartments. Uniformed city police officers and plainclothes detectives pounded on Frankie's door, announcing their identity and possession of a warrant before breaking in the door. The trash can full of papers kept drawing Frankie's gaze. Deep, aching anger ignited in her chest, spreading until her blood felt hot as it pulsed through her veins. The only way Max could have acquired the vial of Butunal and the note drafts were if he had planned the murder and kidnapping from the beginning.

"The guys in suits are leaving," Sally whispered.

Frankie's breath caught in her throat. Now was McKennon's chance. If he still worked for Max all he had to do was open the door, speak a few words to the police and Max's problems were solved. McKennon could collect Belinda's bounty, too. A million bucks would go a long way toward his son's medical bills.

"Dang it," Sally muttered. "The cops aren't leaving."

McKennon watched the parking lot below. "Looks like they're waiting for you."

"Two of them are standing in the hallway," Sally said. She glanced at the trash can as if it contained a dead animal. "Talk to them, Frankie. Show them what you found. Anybody with any sense knows you wouldn't hurt anybody. Especially not your sister."

"Not until I get Penny back."

"We have to get out of here," McKennon said.

"I'll call my uncle. He can tell me if the kidnappers contacted—"

"No." He shook his head firmly. "Calls in and out of the resort are being monitored. They'll trace the call in seconds. You can't risk it."

"I have an idea," Sally said. She clapped her hands gleefully. "It's perfect!"

Twenty minutes later, transformed by Sally, Frankie emerged from the bedroom. She gazed down at herself in dismay. "Are you sure this will work?"

"The best way to hide is in plain sight. Now hold still." Sally adjusted the wig on Frankie's head, then stepped back to examine her handiwork. "You wreck my wig, and I'll kill you with your own cat. It cost me six hundred bucks. That's real human hair.''

Frankie tried to smile but failed miserably. The wig felt as if it weighed fifty pounds. Her temples throbbed. ''I can't believe you actually wear this thing.''

''You never know when I'll get lucky.'' Sally batted her eyelashes at McKennon. ''Big hair, big mouth, that's my trademark. What do you think?'' Sally was a bartender in a karoake club. She sang six or seven songs a night in the hopes that someday a talent scout would discover her.

McKennon swept his gaze slowly over Frankie. A faint smile tugged his lips. She almost groaned. She wore a honey-blond wig befitting Dolly Parton, a stretch-velvet sheath, clinging like a second skin, and a pair of high-heeled pumps.

''Interesting,'' McKennon said. ''I'll leave first. You wait five minutes than walk down to the bus stop. I'll pick you up.''

''What if the cops ask me for ID?''

''They're expecting a redhead to arrive, not a blonde to leave. Play it cool.''

''That's me,'' she said dryly. ''Cool-hand Frankie.'' She huffed a deep breath. ''Let's do it.''

Sally moved well out of view of anyone who might peek into the apartment. McKennon opened the door. He carried a shopping bag containing the evidence, covered by the Frankenstein coat. Frankie followed as if seeing a boyfriend out. He paused in the doorway.

''Sure you have to work, babe?'' he asked, loud enough for the cops to hear. ''Can't play hooky?''

The police officers eyed the exchange.

''Get out,'' she said. ''I'm going to be late as it is.'' She gave his shoulder a playful push. He caught her around the waist and pulled her to him.

Her body reacted with a shock of familiarity and longing, almost making her forget the seriousness of her situation. Almost making her forget the cops. Instinctively she wrapped her arms around his broad shoulders and met his kiss halfway. He kissed her quickly.

He grinned at the cops. He whistled as he walked down the stairs. Frankie turned a cool glare on the cops. She gave a little sniff as if they intruded. She closed the door.

Her knees buckled, and she rested against the wall. "They looked right at me," she whispered to Sally. Her heart pounded so hard her ribs ached. "What if they recognize me?"

"Do you hear anybody pounding on the door?" Sally hurried to the window. "Nobody is stopping him. He's getting in his car. Everything is cool. The cops aren't even looking at him. That's what you have to do. Just walk out like you don't have a care in the world."

"I don't know if I can. I'm so scared."

"You don't have a choice." She grinned. "So, uh, where did you find him? Hubba-hubba."

"I used to work with him." She hoped the heavy makeup job concealed the warming of her cheeks.

"I wish I worked with a guy who looked at me like that."

"Like what?"

Sally barked a laugh. "If you say you don't know, you're lying. That man has it bad for you. You make a cute couple."

"There is nothing going on between us."

"Yeah, right." She opened a closet door and pulled out a faux fur coat. Knee length, it looked like sable. Frankie slid her arms into the sleeves. It was as heavy as a real fur coat, and she was glad. It muffled the sound of her knocking knees. Sally's expression crumpled. "You going to be okay, kid?"

"As long as I make it past the cops."

The women embraced. Sally snuffled loudly. "You're my best friend. Stay safe, okay?"

"You got it." Afraid she was about to burst into tears Frankie pulled away. "Here goes nothing."

She opened the door and stepped into the hallway. She pulled the door shut and rattled the knob as if checking to make sure it was locked. Her insides clenched up so tightly she wanted to double over and vomit. She forced a snooty expression and looked at the police officers. Both of them were busy looking at her legs.

"You guys raiding a crack house or something?" she asked, grateful her voice didn't break. A search warrant had been stuck on her door. It took all her willpower not to stare at it. "What's going on?" She thrust her shaking hands into the deep, plush coat pockets.

"Have you seen your neighbor? Francine Forrest?" a police officer asked. He raised his gaze to her bust level.

She tugged the coat and revealed even more of her body. Anything to keep him from carefully looking at her face. Frankie shrugged. "She's stuck-up, doesn't talk to me. What did she do?"

The other officer cleared his throat and frowned at his partner.

The first officer said, "We just want to talk to her."

"She's probably at work." She shut up before she said too much. "I have to work myself. Have fun." She swished past, feeling their eyes tracking her legs. On the stairs, she gripped the railing tightly, certain the police officers were going to shout at her to stop. The high heels prevented her from giving in to instinct and running.

Once on the street level she strolled along the sidewalk as if she hadn't a care in the world. Cat, released by the invading police, had reclaimed his patch of sunshine. He watched her with cool insolence as if daring her to chase him.

Stay out then, she thought hard at him. He liked mice better than cat food, anyway.

Two men sat in an unmarked car. Only cops would sit in a car on a day this cold. Attempting an air of bored curiosity she glanced at them and kept walking. The bus stop on the corner looked a million miles away.

She reached the bus stop and caught the back of the bench with both hands. Her knees ached with the effort it took to remain upright. She wanted to look behind her to see if the police pursued, but didn't dare.

A man in a passing car slowed and honked.

"Hide in plain sight," she grumbled. She looked like a hooker. How very nondescript.

A sharp whistle behind her made her jump. She whipped her head about. A hank of thick blond hair fell over her eyes. She pushed the hair away and spotted McKennon in the parking lot of a fast-food joint. White exhaust puffed behind his car. She maneuvered between ice patches and puddles of slush. She all but fell into his car.

"I've never been so scared in my life." She hunkered down on the seat.

"You did good." His smile pierced her soul.

"What now? What's next?"

He pulled out of the parking lot and into the street. He turned south, away from her apartment. "I haven't the foggiest idea."

Whatever he came up with would beat getting arrested, she thought, and wearily closed her eyes.

"HE BROKE A WINDOW. Chuckie's gonna be so-o-o-o mad!" Paul's boots clopped on the wooden floor. He kept glancing at the window Bo had broken. The last time Paul broke a window Chuckie had yelled for about three days then made Paul mow Old Lady Broome's lawn and pull all her weeds. He hadn't broken this window, but if Bo fibbed and said Paul did it, Chuckie would blow his top.

"Shut up and sit down, you moron!" Bo yelled.

"Chuckie's gonna be real mad about the window. You shouldn't have broke it. You really shouldn't."

Bo stood on tiptoe. He slapped Paul upside the head. It didn't hurt, but it shocked him into silence. He slunk to the couch where Miss Penelope huddled like a mummy inside a wrapping of blankets.

"Give me one good reason why I shouldn't kill you right now."

Paul sniffed and swiped his nose with the back of a hand. "I didn't break the window."

Bo threw up his hands and stomped out of the room. Paul listened to the little man opening and shutting doors and cabinets. This was a pretty house even if it didn't have lights. The sun was going down and the house was almost as cold inside as it was outside. Paul didn't know who owned it, but he guessed they might get mad if Bo made a mess. They sure would get mad about the window.

Bo returned. His eyes looked like little fire lights sunk deep into his face. Paul fidgeted on the couch. Chuckie always said, "Don't make Bo mad." Bo looked plenty mad, and Paul was scared.

"No heat, no electricity, no food! What kind of vacation cabin is this, if they can't even keep it stocked?" He stalked out the front door, slamming it behind him.

"Paul?" Miss Penelope whispered.

"When Chuckie gets back, you gotta tell him I wasn't bouncing no balls or throwing rocks."

"What is Bo doing?"

"I dunno. He went outside. It's getting dark. Chuckie's awful late. He said he'd be back soon, but it's late."

"Listen, we have to get away from Bo."

Tears slipped down her cheeks. The bottom of the mask over her eyes was discolored by tears. She'd been crying all day. Even when he told her jokes, she cried. He patted her foot.

Her tears made his eyes moist and his throat choked up. "Don't cry, Miss Penelope."

"He's going to kill me. He killed my husband. Didn't you hear the radio? He murdered my husband and now he's going to kill me. You have to help me."

Paul cocked his head. Bo had been listening to the car radio all day while they'd driven around and around the mountains. Since it wasn't music, he hadn't paid any attention. Not even when Bo yelled back at the people talking on the radio.

"Bo didn't kill nobody. He's Chuckie's friend."

"He's nobody's friend. He murdered my husband. Julius. The man who was with me at Elk River. He's dead."

"Uh-uh! Bo gave him a shot. It was medicine." He began to worry. Sometimes medicine didn't work. That's what happened with Mama. The nurses at the hospital gave her lots and lots of medicine, but she went to Heaven, anyway.

"Listen to me," she said slowly. "He's a very bad man and he's done a very bad thing. Do you understand?"

Paul nodded before remembering she couldn't see him. "Uh-huh. He broke the window. Chuckie's gonna be real mad when he sees it. He don't like broke windows."

"You have to help me get away. He's going to kill me."

"Chuckie says to wait until he gets back."

"I don't think Chuck is coming back. The man on the radio said a suspect was taken into custody. That's Chuck. He's been arrested."

Arrested. Paul lifted a hand to his mouth, but caught himself before he sucked on his thumb. Only babies did that and he wasn't a baby anymore. He dashed at his tearful eyes. "Chuckie gets arrested all the time. I don't want to go to the Home. When he goes to jail I gotta go to the Home. I don't want to go there."

"Shh, shh, don't get all upset. Okay? I'm your friend, right? If Chuck can't help you, I'll help you. But you have to help me first. Then both of us can help Chuck. All right?"

"Chuck says I gotta do what Bo says."

"Chuck made a mistake. Bo is a bad, bad man. If you do what he says, then Chuck will go to jail and you'll have to go to that house you don't like."

She spoke aloud what he'd been worrying about all day. He didn't like Bo. The little man was mean and called him names. Worse than that he was mean to Miss Penelope.

"Go see what Bo is doing."

Paul left the couch and looked out a window. He could see the Bronco parked in the driveway. Deep snow buried the tires. "He's sitting in the truck."

Her head turned back and forth as if she tried to see beyond the mask. "Is there a telephone?"

"Uh-huh."

"Give it to me. Please?"

"It's hanging on the wall."

She struggled against the blanket swaddling. "Call 911, Paul. You can dial 911, right?"

"I sure can! That's for ambulances. And firemen."

"Right! Call them. Dial 911. You don't even have to say anything. Just call and let the phone off the hook. Okay? They'll find us. Do it fast before Bo comes back."

He wished Chuck were here as he looked between Bo and the telephone. Chuck always knew what to do. He was a straight-up kind of guy. Paul wanted to be straight up, too, but too many thoughts rolled around his head, and he couldn't grab one long enough to know what to do.

"Please, Paul, hurry."

"Dial 911," he muttered and went to the telephone. Maybe a fireman would come and start a fire in the fireplace. Then the house wouldn't be so cold. He lifted the handset. He knew his numbers, but sometimes he mixed them up. He stared hard at the number pad. The nine had the fishhook tail. He pushed the nine. He always remember the number one. Proud of himself, he pushed the one twice. "I did it!" he announced.

She slumped over so her head touched her knees. Her shoulders hitched. "Thank you, oh, thank you."

"Is a fireman gonna come now?"

"Listen to what the operator says, okay? Tell me what she says."

He pressed the telephone to his ear. "Nobody is saying nothing."

"Is it ringing?"

"Nope."

"Do you hear anything?"

"Nope."

"Hang up." She caught her lower lip in her teeth. "Now do you hear a dial tone? Does the phone work?"

He hung up the phone than lifted the handset again and listened. "Don't hear nothing, Miss Penelope. Think it's broken?"

A low wail broke from her lips. Alarmed, he hung up the telephone and rushed to her side. "It's okay, it's okay, don't cry now. Don't cry." Crouched next to the couch, he petted her hair. It wasn't so soft now, and tangles made it stick out. He felt bad about that. Ladies liked their hair looking nice, but his comb was in the Bronco and he didn't want to go there right now.

The front door slammed open. Bo stomped inside. Clots of snow dropped onto the rug and wooden floor. Paul cringed. Bo reminded him of a movie he saw once. A little kid in a wheelchair had to fight a werewolf. When the werewolf busted into the kid's house Paul had nearly wet his pants. He almost wet his pants now.

Bo was mad.

Chapter Twelve

Frankie stared out the window and studied the traffic on Platte Avenue. Mountains of snow reflected headlights, traffic lights and neon. The rumble of engines was accompanied by tires crunching through slush. Colorado Springs had dug out of the blizzard and now it was business as usual.

She paced the confines of the tiny motel room. The harvest-gold shag carpeting scratched her bare feet. The striped bedspread and matching draperies in muddy colors never seen in nature depressed her. Heat chugged from a vent set high in the wall, carrying musty old smells that enhanced the faint ammonia odor permeating the walls. She peeked out the window again. The little tourist motel, which also offered rooms with kitchenettes by the week, sat on a busy street corner. Platte Avenue used to be a main drag. Now it was a cheesy collection of 1950s buildings—kitschy bars and coffee shops, tourist motels and stark little strip malls— slowly being replaced by fast-food restaurants. She and McKennon hid in plain sight.

Sally's wig perched like an animal atop a lamp shade. Frankie tugged its strands and wished for a comb. No telling how long she'd need it for a disguise. The way her luck was running, it might be years.

She looked out the window again. She searched the traffic at the intersection for any sign of McKennon's car. He'd gone to purchase supplies, but doubts nagged her. Now was the perfect time for him to be the hero in Max Caulfield's eyes. He acted like her hero, but she didn't know how to tell if he acted for real or just plain acted.

Max had acted as if he loved her, but all he wanted was for her to pump his ego while he scouted around for the woman of his dreams. Penny had acted like a college student, but in reality sneaked around with a loser twice her age. McKennon had acted like her friend and lover, then betrayed her and now acted like a friend again. She no longer knew what was real.

Her belly growled. She hadn't eaten anything today. Hunger-weakness fueled her anxiety. A burger joint across the intersection from the motel tempted her, but that would mean leaving the relative safety of the room. Her height and curly red hair made her too easy to remember. The mere thought of pulling on that blasted blond wig made her head ache. She pawed through the purse she'd borrowed from Sally in the hopes of finding a stray mint or candy bar. Nothing.

She turned on the television set. Sitcoms played on every channel. She left it on for an illusion of company and to drown out some of the traffic noise.

Every instinct told her to leave. Chances were McKennon would return accompanied by Max or the cops, or both. She had nowhere to go, no money, no transportation and nobody safe who could take her in. She feared the telephone. By now every person in a position to help her had probably been contacted by the police and their phones were tapped.

Soft knocking startled her. Her heart leaped into her throat, and she couldn't breathe. She couldn't move at all.

"Frankie," McKennon called. "Open the door."

This was it, showdown time. Either he was alone or he wasn't. In either case she had no way to escape. She forced herself to open the door.

He hurried inside and kicked the door shut behind him.

He slung plastic shopping bags on the bed. No Max, no police, only McKennon who appeared happy to see her.

"I made a call," he said.

Braced for the worst, she sank onto the edge of the bed.

"There's a warrant out for your arrest. The police know you're with me."

She wasn't surprised, but was curious about what else the cops had found in her apartment. She sought any sign of deception, any sign of impending betrayal on his face. A heavy beard shadow gave him a scruffy, dangerous air—sexy, too, a wayward part of her mind chimed in. She frowned at herself and turned her gaze away. A soft spot ached below her heart. "Who did you call?"

"Ross."

The unexpected answer made her cock her head. "My cousin? Why?"

"He knows people. He has connections everywhere. And he's safe."

She agreed. "What exactly did he say?" Fear drained away, and her belly growled again. She glanced at the shopping bags. One of them must contain food.

"The man the police picked up is definitely one of the kidnappers. The car was stolen, he was carrying Julius's telephone, and he had a map indicating the same route the kidnappers demanded. It's not confirmed, but rumor says his shoes match prints found at the scene."

"Did he say where Penny is? Did he name Max?"

"He isn't talking. Or, if he is talking, the cops are keeping the information to themselves. Once they positively ID him, they may get some leads."

"What about me?"

He grinned, his gaze going far away. "That's *us,* baby. The cops have been calling my cell phone. I have Caller ID so I avoided speaking to them. I haven't checked my voice mail yet, but I imagine there are some interesting messages."

"I didn't mean to get you in trouble."

"I got myself into it." The full force of his disarming smile and bright eyes focused on her. Her joints threatened meltdown. "No question anymore about Caulfield trying to frame you. But he'll have to get through me first."

Her mood lifted. "What else did Ross say?"

"Your family is in an uproar. They're madder than hell about the arrest warrant. The Colonel is calling every congress person he knows. Ross is hiring an attorney for you. The attorney will advise you to turn yourself in."

"Not until we have Penny."

"With any luck the attorney can buy us some time." He produced a coffeemaker and a bag of coffee. Frankie's mouth watered at the sight. "I brought some rolls and sandwich fixings. Hungry?"

"Starving." She pounced on the nearest bag. It contained a dark blue sweat suit, heavy socks and toiletries. She clutched a plastic hairbrush in one hand and a sweatshirt in the other. He had thought about her. Not just food for her belly, but the other necessities of life: clean teeth, brushed hair and comfortable clothes. Wretched tears filled her eyes with grit.

Glad he was busy making coffee in the bathroom, she snuffled and scrubbed her eyes and swallowed until her throat loosened up. Don't be a dope, she chided herself. It's only a cheap sweat suit.

She set the bag of goodies aside and found the food. Within minutes she'd transformed the fixings into a picnic which she then attacked like a marauding bear. Bolstered by ham and cheese sandwiches, chips, cookies and coffee, some of her brain fuzz subsided.

She wiped crumbs off her mouth and gulped a slug of coffee. An ember of warmth kindled in her belly. For the first time today she didn't feel as if she were made of ice. "We need to turn in that vial of Butunal right away," she said.

McKennon regarded her. He sat on the opposite side of the bed. The room had a tiny desk but no chair. She won-

dered about the sleeping arrangements.... Now fed, other
hungers clambered to the fore. No matter how angry she
was, or had been, she desired him. She yearned for his skin
against hers. She craved the peace she'd found in his arms.

She roughly shoved such thoughts from her head. No
time for that right now.

"It has to be the murder weapon," she said. "The cops
can trace it. Maybe it was prescribed to Belinda."

He grabbed a handful of corn chips and held one up as
if it might contain answers. "It's dangerous."

"Tell me what isn't dangerous." She glanced at the bag
remaining on the bed. It contained the supplies she'd requested: a powerful lamp, magnifying glass, ruler and note
pad. "I have to keep the notes, but there isn't anything we
can do with the drug."

He chewed the remains of a sandwich, his expression
thoughtful. "You're right. I'll make arrangements with
Ross. He can handle the delivery. We'll write up affidavits
about finding the vial." His eyebrows rose. "Have you
been hospitalized at any time in the past six months?"

Bemused, she shook her head.

"Visited a doctor? An emergency room?"

"No. Why?"

"Is there the remotest possibility you had any opportunity to acquire the drug?"

She saw his point. She guessed the Butunal was kept
locked up in hospitals and pharmacies. If the slightest
chance existed she could have stolen it or been prescribed
the medication, giving the vial to the cops would drive a
nail into her coffin. "There's no way. I even skipped my
annual checkup this year."

They reached for the corn chips bag at the same time.
She bumped his hand. He jumped as if she'd burned him.
He shook his left hand hard and the bandaging gleamed in
the wan light.

"I forgot!" she exclaimed, embarrassed all over again
about her cat. "Did you get some more antibiotic cream?"

"It'll be all right. It's in a weird spot, that's all."

"Cat bites can be nasty." She scooted across the mattress and held out her hand in demand. "Let me see."

He obediently laid his left hand on her palm. She peeled the bandage strips away from one side of the wound. The bite marks were inflamed, but looked clean. "Wash this again and put a fresh strip on it. I'd hate for you to lose your thumb." She smoothed the Band-Aid strips back in place. She lightly kissed the wound.

Realizing what she'd done, she froze. McKennon grinned at her. "It'll be all right," he said, his voice gentle.

She wondered if he meant his wounded hand or her wounded heart.

"I'm going to shower and change," she said. She grabbed the bag containing the sweat suit and toiletries.

By the time she finished in the tiny bathroom, she felt a little bit better, but no less exhausted. She wanted to examine the ransom note drafts, but her eyes were so tired they burned and watered. She poured a fresh cup of coffee.

McKennon had stacked supplies on the tiny desk. He stretched out on the bed, his feet crossed. One hand was behind his head, and the other, his wounded hand, rested on his chest. On the television a late-night talk-show host made jokes about global warming.

"McKennon?" she whispered.

He didn't move. She noticed his telephone hooked up to a portable charging unit. Must have been a Boy Scout, she mused, always prepared. She looked between him and the cup of coffee she carried and the desk. A few hours sleep, that's all she needed. She dumped the coffee in the bathroom sink, turned off the pot, left on the television with the volume just high enough to offer a foil against the traffic noise, then slid under the covers. McKennon stirred, but didn't awaken. She wished he were holding her again, loving her, making everything all right.

She wished he could snap his fingers and make Penny safe. Grief rose and she jammed her fist against her mouth as a barrier against sobs. Tears soaked the thin pillow beneath her head.

She suffered ugly dreams of drowning and pitiful three-legged dogs she couldn't help because she was dying herself.

"It's okay, baby," a gentle voice soothed against her ear. "Just a nightmare. I'm here. It's okay."

She startled awake with a loud "Huh!" A heavy weight prevented her from bolting upright. It took several seconds for her groggy brain to realize McKennon held her. His warm breath caressed her neck. The nightmare imagery faded, and her heart slowed to its normal beat. Her eyes adjusted to the dimness. A news show played on the television. Sunshine highlighted the frayed edges of the shabby draperies.

"You were groaning," he said. "Bad dream?"

She rolled to her back. McKennon lay atop the covers, but had pulled some of the bedspread over himself. She felt squeezed in a sausage casing. "I hate waking up in strange places."

"What were you dreaming about?"

She no longer remembered anything except the sensation of dying. "Doesn't matter. Just a dream." She tried not to smell him. His scent intoxicated her and made her feel hot from the inside out. "What time is it?"

He left the bed and turned on a light. "Nearly seven-thirty."

Joints creaking, muscles thrumming as if she'd run a marathon in her sleep, Frankie extricated herself from the tangled covers. Seated on the edge of the bed, she bent over and rested her face on her hands. The bathroom door shut. The shower began to run.

"Bannerman" caught her attention and she sat up straight. On the television a reporter was saying, "Police sources have identified the alleged kidnapper of Mrs. Julius Bannerman." A mug shot of a round-faced man with light hair and nondescript features appeared on the screen.

"Charles Cashorali was released this morning from Memorial Hospital and is now in custody in the El Paso county jail."

An off-camera voice asked, "What is the link between Cashorali and the Bannermans?"

"Thus far—" the camera returned to the perky faced reporter "—no official sources are answering questions."

"And what about Mrs. Bannerman?"

"Well, Tom, she may prove to be the biggest mystery of this entire affair. Belinda Bannerman Caulfield denies a daughter-in-law even exists. Official sources have confirmed that Mrs. Bannerman married the murder victim only hours before the crime occurred. The FBI is currently investigating her disappearance, but will not confirm whether or not she's been kidnapped or if a ransom has been demanded."

The camera switched to a male reporter in a studio. "Thank you, Jane. We'll return to you as events unfold. Now let's go to the weather."

Why, she wondered, did television reporters even bother. They were talking heads broadcasting how much they didn't know about anything. She wished for a newspaper.

McKennon came out of the bathroom, clean, shaved and dressed in fresh clothing. She told him about Charles Cashorali.

He shook his head. "Never heard the name."

"Damn," she breathed. She'd hoped for a solid link between the kidnapper and Max. "They showed his picture, but I didn't recognize the face." Disheartened, she trudged into the bathroom. McKennon had started a fresh pot of coffee. For a long moment she stared at the gurgling pot. Steam curled from the edges of the filter basket. The aroma made her mouth water.

McKennon was so solid and dependable. He demonstrated his goodness in countless little ways. She crunched the sweatshirt in her fingers. The fleecy insides comforted her skin. A pair of socks tumbled to the floor, and the sight of them nearly reduced her to tears. She couldn't remember the last time anyone had taken care of her. Or when she'd allowed anyone to care for her. Troubled by her pathetic longings, she took a quick shower, brushed her teeth and worked her hair into a semblance of order.

McKennon had sandwiches ready and the desk set up for her to go to work on the ransom note drafts. He'd turned the sound off the television and had a radio playing.

"David Sams's morning show," he said.

While eating a sandwich, she listened to the radio talk-show host. His topic was police incompetence. The jumping off point appeared to be Julius Bannerman's murder. As she listened to him rant about the chief of police and the county sheriff, she decided he was a kook and completely uninformed. Callers who mimicked his sentiments were encouraged to ramble; callers who disagreed were called rude names then disconnected to the sound of a toilet flushing. She wondered what made him so appealing that he was on the radio five days a week.

"The kidnappers used his voice to make the tape. Do you think they're listening to him now?" she asked.

"You have something in mind?"

"Wouldn't Mr. Sams love the scoop of the century? If I call him maybe the kidnappers will hear. They'll know I'll do anything to get Penny back." She glanced at his telephone. "They can't trace our location. Can they?"

"If by 'they' you mean the radio station, I doubt it. It's worth a shot."

She'd finished a cup of coffee and was working on a second before the radio station gave out its number and invited listeners to call. McKennon handed her the telephone. She punched in the number. After three rings a woman answered and cheerfully asked if she wished to speak to David Sams.

"Yes, I do," she said. "I'm Frankie Forrest. The police think I murdered Julius Bannerman."

Silence filled the phone line. Frankie feared the woman

had hung up on her. She almost disconnected when the woman asked, "Is this a joke?"

Commercials played on the radio.

"I wish it were," Frankie said honestly. "I didn't kill Julius, but I'm being framed. Only that doesn't matter. What matters is my sister has been kidnapped and I need to get her back."

"Where are you?"

"I can't tell you that." Fear fluttered in her chest. McKennon placed a comforting hand on her shoulder. His long fingers squeezed. "Just put me on with Mr. Sams. I'll tell him everything I know."

"Can you hold?"

Frankie envisioned the screener calling the police and arranging for a signal search to trace the location of the cellular phone. "I'll hold."

Over the phone she could hear the radio show happening live. A delay caused a mismatch between what she heard on the phone and what came through the radio.

"How much should I tell him?" she asked.

"Tell him anything he wants to know."

Radio promos were playing when Frankie heard a click and David Sams said, "So you're Frankie Forrest. Give me a reason to believe."

His smug tone irritated her. "You can believe what you want, Mr. Sams. The fact is, I'm Frankie and my sister, Penelope Ann Forrest married Julius Bannerman. Whoever killed him also kidnapped her. Penny is still missing. I'm trying to find her."

"Is your radio on?"

She motioned for McKennon to turn down the radio. "Look, Mr. Sams, you don't know the whole story. Belinda Caulfield is making headlines, but it has nothing to do with police incompetence. She doesn't care what happens to my sister."

"How do you know Belinda Caulfield?"

"She's my sister's mother-in-law. I'm not a crackpot. I just want to get Penny back."

"What about the million-dollar reward Mrs. Caulfield is offering for the arrest of her son's killer? Does that interest you?"

"Only because it can get my sister killed. The police had a really good reason to keep the murder quiet. I don't even think it was a murder. It was an accident. The kidnappers wanted Julius to pay for Penny's return. Belinda refused to pay the ransom. I want the kidnappers to know that I'll pay. I'll do anything they want."

The talk show host chuckled. "You sound very convincing, Frankie. May I call you Frankie?"

His condescending tone triggered her temper. She felt the anger rising like a mushroom cloud. "I don't care."

"How about I call you a crank? Or a bonehead? Aren't you ashamed of yourself? This is a serious subject. The police in this town don't give a rat's behind about the citizens, and you're wasting my valuable time with your cockamamie story."

"This coming from a guy whose listeners are kidnappers? You're the bonehead, Mr. Sams. Do you know they used your voice to make their ransom demands?"

He barked laughter. Howling coyotes filled the earpiece.

"It's true," she insisted, trying to be heard over his sound effects. "They recorded your voice and spliced it into a tape. They used you and you want to make fun of me?"

McKennon waved both hands and shook his head violently. He had turned the radio low enough so it didn't distract her, but he heard both sides of the conversation.

David Sams launched into a rant about how the chief of police was nothing more than a pawn of the mayor and city council. Frankie kept trying to speak, but every time she got a word in, he activated another sound effect, accentuating her increasing frustration with firecrackers and gargling noises. Disgusted, she broke the connection and tossed the telephone on the bed.

"Can you believe people actually listen to his crap?" she asked. The final segment of her thwarted attempt played over the radio. McKennon turned it up. David Sams now warned other potential crackpots who were pretending knowledge of the Bannerman murder that they'd receive the same treatment.

McKennon turned off the radio. "If the kidnappers are listening, they'll know you're telling the truth."

"Right."

His telephone rang. Both of them froze, staring at the trilling instrument.

McKennon picked it up and frowned at the LCD readout. "The number is unavailable. Probably the police."

"Go for it," she said. She envisioned black vans topped with slowly turning antennaes prowling the neighborhood. She wondered how long it took to trace a mobile telephone to its location.

He answered with a crisp, "McKennon, here." He listened, nodding, then said, "I understand your position, sir, and will take it under advisement." He disconnected.

"Sergeant Norris," he said.

"From the state police? He's in charge of the murder investigation, right?" She remembered too well the interview with the investigator who had gone from solicitous to hostile in record time.

"Word travels fast. People heard you on the radio. He wants you to turn yourself in."

"Any news about Penny?"

"No mention."

"Then they can all go to hell." She plugged in the small, powerful lamp McKennon had purchased and set it up on the desk.

"I have to dump my car. They'll be looking for it now."

She cast him a frown. The dirty walls seemed to close

in on her. The stink she'd been ignoring now distressed her. "How are we supposed to get around? Roller skates?"

He chuckled. "Let me handle this problem. It's what I do best."

She sensed a deeper meaning behind his words. His eyes snared her.

"We'll work things out. Everything will be okay."

She nodded.

He smoothed a curl from her cheek. Sensations ruffled through her midsection, and her eyelids lowered of their own accord. "We will get Penny back."

"That, too," he said.

She forcibly turned away. How was she supposed to resist him when all he had to do was look her way and she turned into mush? She focused her attention on the ransom note drafts.

Max had planted seven sheets of crumpled notebook paper in Frankie's trash can. She picked one up as if it were a Fabergé egg encrusted with diamonds. She found a corner and tugged gently, careful not to tear the paper or smudge the penciled writing. She wished she'd remembered to ask for latex gloves. Her hands were sweating. She wiped them dry on her shirt.

With the paper as smoothed out as she could make it, she reached for the next. Behind her McKennon talked on the telephone. She tuned him out, paying him no more attention than she did to the television or the traffic noises. With painstaking care she restored the papers to as close to original condition as possible. No easy task since they'd been squashed. Sitting on the bed and stretching to reach the desk made her back ache. She had to pause every few minutes to knead out the kinks.

"Put your wig on and let's go," McKennon said.

She blinked in confusion. While she'd been working, he'd packed up everything in the room except for the papers and the blond wig. He dropped a plastic bag on the desk and rolled a hand, indicating she was to place the papers inside.

"I have work to do."

"Our ride is here. Ross is taking us to a safe house."

"You're kidding?" She gathered the papers into a pile and slid them into a plastic bag. "Ross is outside?"

He gathered all the bags and carried them outside. Frankie peeked out the window. He placed the bags in the trunk of a shiny black Lexus. The tinted windows prevented her from seeing the driver, but she recognized her cousin's car. Her lower lip began to tremble. Good old Ross. He never let her down. She vowed that from this day forward he'd be a bigger part of life—no matter how discouraging her situation.

She snatched the wig off the lamp shade and hurried into the bathroom. Sally had made it seem easy to put the heavy wig in place. Frankie fought the blasted thing as if it were a wild beast until she managed to get the majority of her hair underneath the netting. Now she looked like a hooker having a bad hair day. She shoved her arms into the Frankenstein coat and picked up the bag of papers.

McKennon gestured from the doorway. "You ride with Ross. I'm stashing my car."

She paused before stepping out of the cheesy motel room. Not a trace of clouds marred the pristine sky, and warmth barreled from the sun. Melting snow ran in rivers toward street drains.

"You can quit now," she told him. "You don't have to do this."

"Do what?" he asked. Dark sunglasses concealed his eyes.

"Turn the Butunal over to the cops and tell them where you found it. The cops don't want you. If you keep helping me you'll end up in serious trouble."

"This is personal. I'm sticking with you."

She shook her head. "I don't believe you. You don't care that much about getting even with Max."

He touched a finger to her chin. "I'm not talking about Max." Before she could respond, he had her by the arm. He opened the passenger door of the Lexus and all but shoved her inside.

"Hey, Cuz." Ross's merry gray eyes took in the blond wig and sweat suit. "Nice look." He looked past her and said to McKennon, "Ten minutes."

McKennon shut the door, and Ross drove out of the parking lot.

"How are you doing?" Ross asked.

She fingered the plastic bag, which contained her only hope of proving she hadn't engineered the murder and kidnapping. "Been better. Does Dawn know what you're doing?"

"She and I are joined at the hip. All of us Dukes stick together." He tossed her his version of an admonishing frown. "You shouldn't have skipped out on us. Mom and Dad are worried."

"I know, but I had to move fast. Good thing I did, too. The cops almost caught me at my place. What's going on at Elk River?"

"Everyone is looking for Penny. The Feds set up roadblocks, but I don't think it'll do any good. Too many roads and back trails. Agent Patrick isn't happy about potential black marks on her record. She likes being assigned to Colorado. Have to warn you. You are on her permanent list. If she can't find Penny, she'll look straight at you for a scapegoat."

"She'll have to stand in line." She held up the bag. "These are drafts of the ransom note. Max Caulfield planted them in my apartment. I need enough time to prove he wrote them."

Ross whistled in appreciation. He drove toward the neighborhood where he and Dawn lived. "How are you going to prove Caulfield planted the papers and the drug?"

"I haven't thought that far ahead." The truth was, if she

couldn't find Penny, then none of the rest mattered. She closed her eyes and leaned back on the butter-soft leather seat. The cops and Max weren't giving her time to think at all.

Chapter Thirteen

"Okay, Cuz, this place is about as safe as any in Colorado." Ross Duke handed Frankie a set of keys. "There's a Caddy in the garage and plenty of food. If you need anything else I'm only a phone call away."

Frankie pulled the wig off her head and scratched furiously at her itching scalp. She walked through the condo. Though small, it was luxuriously furnished with white leather sofas, flokati rugs, a gas fireplace with a marble mantelpiece and expensively framed prints on the walls. Heavy silk draperies shut out the world. It appeared immaculate, but smelled dusty. "Is this yours?"

"It's Connie Haxman's. She keeps it for her ex-husbands. She doesn't mind them visiting, but she doesn't want them staying at her place." He shrugged as if the socialite's quirks were of no concern to him. He jerked a thumb at a spiral staircase. "The bedroom is upstairs. There shouldn't be any reason for anybody to come to the door." He turned to McKennon.

The big man set his duffel on the floor. "I owe you, Ross."

Ross chuckled. "Keep my cousin here out of trouble and we'll be square." The chuckle turned into a laugh. He pointed at Frankie. "Little Miss Goody Two-shoes. I always knew you had a troublesome streak in you somewhere."

"Ha-ha," she said dryly.

Ross sobered. "The attorney will contact you. Cooperate with him."

"I'll cooperate with everybody. As soon as Penny is safe."

After Ross had left them, Frankie moved the graphology supplies to a breakfast counter. A decent work space and good overhead lighting would make the job of studying the ransom notes much easier than it would have been back in the motel room. She pulled the seven sheets of crinkled notebook paper out of the bag.

It occurred to her that even if she proved Max had written these notes, Penny could still die. A wave of fearful melancholy stripped the strength from her body and left her slumped over the counter. Who was she trying to kid?

McKennon rubbed her back in slow, comforting circles. "What is it?"

Plagued by images of Penny's elfin face dead-white and forever still, perhaps lost for all time in the lonely mountains, she lifted her gaze to him. "Why don't they call? You said they would call. I am so scared."

His hand stilled on her back, the pressure light but firm. She could read his expression easily now. He was worried.

"All my life I've taken care of her. After my dad walked out Mom didn't handle things so well. I know she wanted to take care of us, but it was hard for her. When Penny was a baby I'd hurry home from school to change her diaper and make sure she got fed. Mom forgot sometimes. She was depressed. Then she got really sick and I had to take care of her, too. I wanted to be a doctor so I could find a cure for her."

Memories rushed in, filling her, distancing her. If one word could describe her life it would be *fear*. Fear of not doing enough, of not being enough, of not being in the right place at the right time. Fear of doing something wrong. Now sickening dread coupled with helplessness created a fear such as she'd never known before.

"What about you?" he asked. "Who took care of you?"

"I took care of myself."

Then he was holding her, and she hadn't the strength to do anything except rest limply in his arms. "You're a good woman. You've got a big heart and a lot of guts."

If only he knew the truth. Good intentions didn't count when everything fell apart. "I'm scared."

"I know. But I'm here. I'll take care of you."

She lifted her gaze to his face. His dear face, so handsome and strong. Her desperate yearning to believe, to trust, to let him care for her, troubled her. "Okay," she whispered, but didn't mean it. She could not mean it. She did not know how.

His telephone rang. The peculiar birdlike trilling made both of them stiffen. He pulled the unit out of the holster and frowned at the readout.

"The kidnappers?" she whispered.

He shook his head and turned away from her. He walked away and spoke in such low tones she could not hear what he was saying. Sensing his need for privacy, she turned to her work. Fear or no fear, she had a killer to discover.

J.T. glanced across the room at Frankie. She lined up the papers then plugged in the little lamp. The determination on her face looked all the more fierce because of her wan complexion and dark bruiselike circles under her eyes. His heart ached for her.

"What does that mean?" he asked the caller.

From Carson Springs Dr. Trafoya said, "I'm not certain exactly, Mr. McKennon. As I've explained before, we don't understand fully what is happening inside a comatose brain."

Clamping down on his excitement—he'd had too many hopes dashed before—J.T. asked, "Does this mean he's waking up? He's never had a pain response before."

The doctor spoke in his usual noncommittal manner. "The pain response could be caused by some chemical or electrical discharge in his brain. It could be seizures. It could be allergies. It might be a random reflex. I'd like to run a few tests to see if I can duplicate the response.''

''Do whatever you think is necessary.''

''I'm keeping you apprised,'' the doctor said. ''The probability is that this was a fluke and will not be repeated. The tests probably won't show anything. Jamie's prognosis hasn't changed.''

''I understand.'' He finished the conversation and hung up. A pain response. As he did every day when he checked Jamie's status, the doctor had poked the soles of the boy's feet with a pin. For the first time in four years Jamie's foot had twitched. For his own sake, J.T. didn't want to read any more into the doctor's words than the doctor had been willing to express. Still, the hopefulness he so carefully controlled leaped wildly in his heart.

''McKennon?''

He opened his duffel to retrieve the phone charger. ''Nothing to do with you,'' he said.

''You have the funniest look on your face. What is it?''

''It was the hospital. Jamie reacted to pain stimulus this morning.''

Her eyes widened and she shoved wayward curls off her face. ''That's good news?''

He plugged the charger into a nearby outlet and hooked up the phone. He pondered ''good news.'' In the days and weeks following the accident that had killed his wife and damaged his son, he'd considered every sunrise Jamie survived as good news. When the doctors pronounced Jamie in a coma, he'd considered every twitch and sigh from the boy as good news. When Jamie breathed on his own, that was good news. Every ounce of weight he gained was good news. Then the weeks turned into months and the months into years, and McKennon stopped thinking in terms of good and bad. Jamie survived. Jamie would someday wake up. What happened until he did awaken meant very little.

''It's different,'' he said. ''The doctor doesn't know why

it happened. He's going to run some tests. He says it could be a seizure.''

"Oh." Her eyes dimmed. "Sorry. Are you going to go see him?''

He wanted to. He missed Jamie. Usually he visited every morning around 3:30 a.m. In the quiet, before rounds began and visitors who kept normal hours arrived, he talked to his son and read him stories and bathed him.

"I'll be okay alone," Frankie said. She slid off the stool and padded across the room. "You should be there if something happens.''

He touched her face, exploring with his thumb the strong planes of her square cheekbones. He wanted to make love to her. Muffle some of their mutual pain through mutual pleasure. He eased a corkscrew curl off her cheek and tucked it behind her ear.

She caught his hand. Her skin looked milky-white against his darker, coarser skin. Vivid memories of the long, lean length of her fitted so perfectly against his body tormented him. She pushed his hand away from her face and averted her gaze. Color bloomed on her pale cheeks.

"Go see your son.''

He caught her shoulder as she turned away. She stiffened.

"Are you still angry with me?" he asked.

The color deepened on her cheeks. Her lips thinned. Under his hand her muscles tensed. "It doesn't matter.''

"It matters to me. I care about you.''

"The only thing that matters is getting Penny back. What you do to me after that doesn't matter one little bit.''

He dropped his hand. "Do to you?''

She backed a step and raised a hand protectively to her throat. Her eyes were wild and wounded. "You lied to me about Max. For all I know you're lying now. I don't know what your agenda is. I want to trust you, but…I…it's hard.''

He started to protest that he hadn't lied, except, technically, he had. Lies of omission were lies nonetheless. Desire faded, replaced by shame and anger. He shoved his hands in his pockets. He called himself an idiot for lacking the words to ease her mind and allow her to forgive him.

He'd never been one for talking about what he felt. Nina had talked enough for two people, and he'd always been content to listen. She'd always seemed to know what was in his heart.

"I don't have an agenda. I'm through with Caulfield."

"That's what you said before."

"That's what *you* said. I was wrong to give you the impression he fired me. I'm sorry."

She fiddled with the neck of the sweatshirt and shifted her weight from foot to foot. "Walk out now, McKennon. Go see your son. I can take care of myself."

"No."

"Then tell me why you're helping me."

She needed an answer. A good answer to restore her faith in him and restore her trust. He did have an answer, except it had to do with the way she'd touched his heart and breathed life into his soul. Being with her made him feel alive again, as if he had more than a dreary past. Around her he sensed a future. Helping her gave him a reason to live beyond his wounded son's bedside.

He was falling in love.

Telling her that would fly like a box of rocks.

Finally he said, "You're good in bed."

She startled. Her hand fluttered aimlessly, a slim white bird. "What?"

"No, you're better than good, you're great. The other night was the best sex ever." He grinned, ashamed of causing her shock, but enjoying it anyway. "You're fire and ice all rolled up into one spectacular package. Your body is incredible. I'd swim through piranha-infested water just to look at your breasts. Just thinking about you naked makes me hard. On the off chance that I can get you in bed again I'd hitchhike to the moon."

The tip of her tongue darted between her lips.

"Didn't you think it was great sex?"

Her face and throat flushed. "It wasn't bad," she muttered and stalked to the breakfast counter. As she slid onto the stool she cast him a wary glance.

He pursed his lips and blew her a kiss. She snatched up the magnifying glass and focused on a sheet of paper.

He'd spoken the truth, albeit not the entire truth, nor was it the truth she'd expected. Hell, he hadn't expected it. She wasn't trying to chase him off, though, so he considered his ploy a success. Succeeded too well. He wanted to lift her hair and kiss her neck. Run his hands up under the baggy sweatshirt and cup her breasts. Dizzy with growing arousal he jerked his attention off her. It didn't help. The white leather couches looked soft and inviting. The furry flokati rugs invited him to tear off his clothes.

Needing something to do he entered the kitchen. Being separated from her by the counter was sweet torture. He found coffee beans in the freezer and a grinder in a cupboard. He made a fresh pot of coffee. The scent of brewing coffee reminded him of her.

A quick search showed the pantry stocked with staples and boxed mixes. The freezer was full of instant meals, steaks and frozen desserts. He selected steaks, frozen twice-baked potatoes, mixed vegetables and a blueberry muffin mix. After a day of eating sandwiches he was ready for a hearty meal. The stove had a built-in grill. He puzzled over the controls until he figured out how to make it work.

"Max did not write these." Frankie sounded disgusted.

"How do you know?" he asked.

"I've seen Max's handwriting. This isn't it."

He glanced at the sheet she examined. "Block printing. That makes a difference."

"Surprisingly enough, no." She rested her chin on a fist. She appeared much calmer than before.

Beautiful. He could spend the rest of his life exploring the texture of her full lips.

She bristled. "What are you staring at?"

Your mouth, your eyes, the perfection of your skin....
"I'm not staring. I'm listening." He turned his attention to preparing a meal. "Why doesn't printing make a difference?"

"I use the Gestalt method. I look at the big picture, the overall effect of how the writer fills the page. Here, look at this." She turned the page. Using a pencil, she pointed to the left-hand margin. "Look at how the writing avoids the left-hand side of the page. It swoops in and out, almost as if afraid to get too close to the edge." She shifted the pencil to the right margin. Letters crowded the pale blue margin line printed on the paper.

"Okay," he said. "What does it mean?"

"In Western civilization to cling to the right is to cling to the past. Aiming for the left is risk-taking. This writer is basically insecure and afraid of taking risks. He clings to the past. He likes routine. Change upsets him."

"You're right. That doesn't sound like Caulfield."

"And look at the size of the printing. Max has large handwriting, very thick and extravagant. He's sensual. Indulgent. He fills up a page, and his words run into each other on the tops and bottoms. This writing is small, almost hesitant. It wavers all over the place. That tells me this person is disorganized. Near the right margin, the pencil pressure is heavy and certain, but it loses force the closer it gets to the left side of the page. That's a sign of anxiety and uncertainty."

"You can see all that?"

"Can't you?"

Mulling over her observations he returned to cooking. "Can you tell if a man or a woman wrote it?"

"Unfortunately, no. But in context with what I see, I'll guess it's a man."

She was acting like the Frankie he knew from the office. Confident, assured and a tad condescending. Sexy. "Explain."

"Human nature. The writer is deeply conflicted. He shows signs of being an extrovert, but is also extremely selfish. That he'd mastermind a kidnapping, and possibly a murder, shows a degree of confidence. But it's fake confidence. An act. It's difficult to imagine an insecure woman going through with this. Much less, convincing two other people to help her."

"I disagree," he said. He used a spoon to beat muffin mix and water into a batter. "I know a lot of women who put on pretty good acts."

"In general, female phonies tend to be pleasers. The worse they feel, the nicer they act." A smile broke through like sunshine through a storm cloud.

The spoon slipped from his suddenly numb fingers and fell into the batter. He grumbled at his clumsiness.

"We'll see who's right when we catch him. In any case this is definitely not Max's handwriting."

"That makes sense. He wouldn't turn over anything that could incriminate him." He spooned batter into muffin cups. "What about age?"

"No telling. Ideally, I should know the age and sex of the writer before I begin analysis." She pulled a notepad in front of her. She began to write. "Here's what we're looking for. A friend and or an acquaintance of Max's. Are you sure you've never heard of Charles Cashorali?"

"I'm good with names. I don't remember any Cashorali."

"If Cashorali wrote these then we're wasting time." She shook her head firmly. "No. Max got his hands on this stuff. That doesn't mesh with the risk factor. You know if Max doesn't trust the kidnappers then they probably don't trust him. He sure wouldn't let Cashorali see his face."

"There are ways around it," McKennon commented. "Caulfield could know more about Cashorali than Cashorali knows about him."

She wrote rapidly. "And don't forget the Butunal. This

person had access to the drug somehow. Would a doctor prescribe a barbiturate in injectable form?"

"Unlikely. Drugs like that are hot on the black market. It could have been picked up on the street."

Frankie's nose wrinkled. "How many drug dealers do you think Max knows? When I first started working for him he was managing a lawsuit against a drug dealer. Some rich guy's kid overdosed on heroin. Max built a civil case for wrongful death against the dealer. He had me doing research on all kinds of creepy people. I know he personally conducted dozens of interviews. I typed them up myself."

He mulled over Caulfield's connections. Before marrying Belinda much of Caulfield's business involved finding missing persons, including runaway teenagers. Drug connections were valuable resources in the runaway underground.

"We also know the writer is highly disorganized."

"Not much of a description," he said with a grin.

"Actually that isn't true. Highly disorganized people tend to have highly disorganized lives. We're looking for a person with a spotty work history, poor personal relationships and financial trouble. Perhaps even legal problems." Good humor softened her face, and a trace of a smile curved her lips. "Kind of like me lately."

He appreciated her ability to maintain her sense of humor. He slid the muffin tin into the oven, then set to work on the steaks and potatoes. "That eliminates Mrs. Caulfield's employees. Her people are well organized. She insists on it."

"But it doesn't eliminate Julius's friends. Losers have loser friends." She frowned at her list.

He racked his brain for the names and faces of Julius's friends. Mrs. Caulfield hadn't liked any of her son's friends and didn't encourage their attendance at her social functions. Caulfield and Julius had shared the house grudgingly and maintained distinctly separate lives. If they had conflicts they kept them well buried.

"The author being a woman is beginning to make sense."

She snorted softly. "Why is that?"

"Julius had many female acquaintances. Caulfield likes women." Concentrating on remembering, he slid the frozen potatoes into the microwave oven. "Soon after Caulfield moved into the Bannerman estate one of Julius's exes showed up. I don't know if she was an ex-wife or an ex-girlfriend, but she was upset. She caused a scene in her attempt to speak to Mrs. Caulfield."

"What did she want?"

"Money. She was in financial trouble."

"What's her name?"

He thought for a moment. "We weren't introduced. She never did speak to Mrs. Caulfield. Nor Julius for that matter. Caulfield handled it." Eyebrow quirked, he grinned at her. "I don't know how he handled it. He spoke to her privately. She went away."

"How come she didn't speak to Julius?"

"I got the impression that she'd tried, but failed. Mrs Caulfield was her last resort."

Excitement made her eyes sparkle. "That's it! You know how Max uses people. He must have recognized the ex would be useful someday. So he paid her off, but stayed in touch. He convinced her the kidnapping would be the perfect revenge against Julius. And against Belinda, too. Did you tell the cops about the incident?"

"I'd forgotten all about her. Until now."

"I bet Max *forgot,* too." She scanned the papers. "This writer is definitely disorganized and insecure. But if somebody is directing him, or her, that changes everything."

"There's one little problem with this scenario." He adjusted the flames on the grill and slapped on the steaks. Ice crystals snapped and crackled. The meat sizzled, and a plume of beef-scented smoke rose to the overhead vent.

"What might that be?"

"Caulfield wouldn't put himself in that position. If this

woman gets caught, she wouldn't protect Caulfield. Even without evidence that could lead to an indictment there is always Mrs. Caulfield to consider.''

''What if she's in love with him?'' She lifted her chin in challenge. ''You said yourself he's cheating on Belinda. Maybe she's his mistress. Women in love are stupid.''

He suspected she spoke of herself. Suddenly he wanted to argue with her. Lust could make a man act stupidly. Infatuation could make a woman act stupidly. But love? True love wasn't blind and it didn't wear blinkers. True love saw clearly every fault, wrinkle and foible, but accepted the loved one, anyway. True love was strength in its purest form.

''You know I'm right,'' she insisted.

He poked the steaks with a fork. He shook his head. ''He wouldn't risk it.''

''I think it's worth a shot. Can you find her?''

''With enough time, maybe. And if I didn't have to worry about getting arrested as soon as I stepped outside.''

She resumed studying the papers.

He left her to her thinking while he finished putting the meal together. The savory scent of grilled meat mingled with the sweet aroma of hot muffins. He told Frankie to take a break. She left her work reluctantly. When she laid eyes on the table, her expression turned hungry and appreciative.

''You're tidy and you can cook,'' she said. She slid a potato onto her plate. ''You must have been the perfect husband.''

''Nina found plenty of areas where I needed improvement.''

She chewed a piece of steak and declared it perfect. ''What was Nina like?''

She sounded so normal, even friendly, he was grateful. He gave the question consideration. ''She was an optimist.''

''What do you mean?''

"She always looked on the bright side. Things always worked out." He glanced at his silent telephone. "Usually she was right."

"Were you high school sweethearts?"

He grinned in remembrance. "We met in a bar. I'd just gotten out of the Marine Corps and I took a temporary job as a bouncer. She was a bartender. The first night we met she told me we were perfect for each other."

"How did she know?"

He lifted a shoulder. "She was right, as usual. We got married a week later."

Frankie's mouth fell open.

He laughed. "Sounds crazy, but we had a good marriage. Her philosophy was, if you want something, you can make it work. She never worried about the little stuff. She saw the big picture and went for it."

"I bet you miss her."

"I do." It struck him as odd that he was having trouble rousing an image of Nina's face. She'd been small and blond and lively, but details eluded him. "We were good together." He bit back the urge to add, *You and I are good together, too.*

"I'll never get married." Her stiff posture and tone offered a challenge.

"Hmm. Funny how *never* works out. I thought I'd never be interested in another woman." Grinning, he ate a big bite of potato.

"Because of…great sex?"

"That, too."

She swiped a napkin across her mouth. "You cooked, I'll clean up. Thanks for the meal." She left the table and carried her plate into the kitchen.

Her sudden departure bothered him. His appetite diminished, but he finished eating. He carried his plate into the kitchen. She scrubbed the grill. He sensed by the tension in her shoulders that she knew he was standing behind her.

"Am I saying the wrong things? Or does it matter?

You'll get upset about anything that comes out of my mouth.''

She hung her head. ''Maybe you're saying the right things,'' she said quietly.

Her reply pleased him. ''I'll shut up, then.'' He found a plastic garbage bag and scraped the plates.

She turned around and bumped into him. She jumped back as if burned and flung out her arm. The dishrag she held snapped like a flag in the wind, struck papers on the counter and sent them floating to the floor.

''You're too damned big, McKennon.''

''For what?'' To his way of thinking they were the perfect size for each other. Her eyes enchanted him, flashing with passionate emotion, concealing none of her inner turmoil. Meaning only to calm and soothe, he reached for her.

She cringed into a corner between the counter and the stove. ''I'm not having sex in a kitchen!''

''Who said anything about sex? But as long as you're bringing it up, why not?''

She surprised him with a laugh. ''Bringing it up? I'm not bringing anything up. Get out of here. Let me finish cleaning.''

Hopeful about possibly salvaging their relationship, he did as she ordered. He went around the counter and retrieved the papers.

''Were these in order?'' he asked.

''Not really.''

''What about the words themselves? Do they mean anything?''

''I don't know. The only thing I noticed was that the writer had some trouble figuring out how much ransom to ask for. He, or she, asked for half a million in one draft and five million in another.''

He sorted through the papers. A shadow caught his eye. Curious, he slid the paper underneath the brightest spot of the lamp. Someone writing on another sheet of paper had created an imprint on this sheet. It looked like numbers. He shifted the paper first one way than the other.

"What do you see?" Frankie asked.

"Digits." Hating to tamper with the evidence, but needing to confirm his suspicion he picked up a pencil. Using the side of the lead he lightly rubbed the impression. "It's a phone number."

She leaned over the counter to see. "This is great! It's an honest to goodness lead. We can use Cole's directory to find out who it belongs to."

He shook his head. Excitement built in his chest. "It won't be listed. This has a cell phone prefix."

Chapter Fourteen

"What if nobody answers?" Frankie asked. She held McKennon's cell phone. The thing felt as if it weighed five hundred pounds. Her sweaty hand was clammy against the plastic housing. Her heart pounded so hard her eardrums throbbed. She turned wide eyes to McKennon. "What if he does answer?"

"Identify yourself. Tell whoever answers you're looking for Penny." He nudged the paper closer to her. The smudged number seemed to jump off the page.

She punched in the numbers. Holding her breath, she listened for the ring. One ring, two rings, three. "Nobody is answer—"

A cautious voice said, "Hello?"

Frankie nearly fell off the stool. For a terrifying moment her tongue refused to work.

"Who's there?" a man demanded.

"Frankie Forrest," she said in a rush. "I'm Penny Forrest's, uh, Penny Bannerman's sister. I'm looking for her."

A long silence followed.

Growing panicky, she blurted out, "Look, I'll do anything to get her back. She's my sister and I love her, and I don't care how I get her back just as long as I do. Please, do you know Penny? Can you help me?"

"How did you get this number?" His voice was high, almost girlish, but with a distinctly masculine rough edge.

"It doesn't matter, does it? Look, I don't care about the cops or the FBI. I didn't want them involved in the first place. Do you know where Penny is? Is she okay?"

"Gimme a number."

Startled by the harsh command, she blinked, uncomprehending.

"Gimme a phone number!"

"Oh, the telephone number." She rolled a hand at McKennon. "You want a phone number."

McKennon wrote rapidly. He shoved the telephone number before her and she repeated it, slowly, making sure each number was spoken clearly. The man disconnected, leaving her with a dead phone and an aching numbness in her belly.

"He hung up on me."

"But he asked for the number. He'll call back." His eyes gleamed with green fire. Muscles leaped in his jaw. He looked dangerous. "If he says he has Penny make him prove it. Demand to speak to her."

"And if he won't do it?"

"Then the number is useless."

She curled her lips against her teeth, fighting the impulse to blurt out, *She's dead.* She refused to entertain that thought. Refused to let the idea take hold in her brain. Never taking her eyes off the silent telephone, she paced in an aimless circle. Memories rose of teaching Penny to swim. Penny had disguised her terror of unknown waters behind high-pitched giggles. "I won't let anything happen to you," Frankie had assured her. "Nothing can happen to you as long as I'm here."

"I'm here, Penny," she mouthed, willing her thoughts to cross the universe and find her sister safe.

The seconds crawled, the minutes crept past with such excruciating slowness, Frankie thought she might go mad. She glared at the digital clock display on the oven. The numbers appeared frozen in time.

McKennon picked up the condo telephone.

"What are you doing?" she demanded.

"If it's the kidnappers, Ross needs to know. He has the money."

She groaned and dropped her face on a hand. She'd forgotten about the money. She didn't see how they were supposed to smuggle four heavy suitcases out of Elk River Resort without the cops or FBI finding out. This wasn't a kidnapping, it was a Quentin Tarantino movie. All they lacked was John Travolta shooting up the condo.

She silently beseeched the telephone to ring. She caught a glimpse of herself in a wall mirror. Her hair sprung from her head in clownish corkscrew curls and her eyes were demented. She looked nuts out of her mind.

"You're strong, baby," her mother used to tell her. "You were born strong."

Frankie stared at her reflection. The wild woman staring back didn't look strong. She looked as if the slightest touch might shatter her into a million pieces.

Furious at herself, furious at the kidnappers, she raked both hands through her hair. She jerked at tangles, taking dark satisfaction from the pain she inflicted on her scalp.

I am strong, she thought. *I was born strong.* She jerked and pulled at her hair with her fingers until her hair looked almost normal.

Until she felt almost normal.

Feeling eyes, she turned about slowly. Head cocked, McKennon peered at her, his expression puzzled. She supposed she acted rather strangely.

"What did Ross say?"

"He's on his way to Elk River. He'll work with Mrs. Haxman to come up with a plausible reason why she needs the money back right now."

"How many FBI agents will accompany the money to the Springs?"

"Ross is resourceful. Trust him."

A sigh slipped past her teeth. If worse came to worst she'd rob a bank to get the money. Let the cops pop her for a crime she actually committed.

McKennon's telephone trilled. Frankie jumped, and her heart thundered in her breast. He glanced at the Caller ID readout and his face turned to stone. Thrusting the telephone at her, he said, "It's for you."

She answered with a crisp, "Frankie Forrest here." The connection was harsh with static. She wondered if he were still in the mountains.

"I want my money," he said.

His squeaky voice roused an image of a rat in human form. A narrow, buck-toothed face. A scrawny body. A demon's red eyes. Pure evil in human form.

"I want my sister. Do you have her?"

"It'll cost you to know."

"You get nothing until I know she's alive." In the background she heard a rushing sound and a faint mechanical roar. She listened closely and decided he was in a vehicle with the heater blowing. "Let me talk to her."

"How about I send you her foot in a box?" His voice lowered.

Short hairs raised on Frankie's nape. Creepy claws skittered along her spine. Her stomach ached and the large meal she'd eaten threatened a return appearance.

"Listen to me," she growled. "Every cop in the state is breathing down my neck. They aren't looking for you, they're looking for me! But you trust this, bubba, as soon as they catch me they will be after you. We're both running out of time. Now, I want Penny and you want cash. Simple. We make a trade. We don't have time for games. Got it?"

He actually laughed, the noise tinny through the static.

"You let me talk to her right now or the conversation ends. You get squat."

"Fine," he whispered.

"Frankie!"

The sound of Penny's scream sent arrows of ice through Frankie's heart. "Penny? Oh, sweetie, are you all right?"

"Julius is dead!" she wailed. "He's going to kill—"

"Shut up!" Flesh smacked loudly against flesh.

Frankie bit back her cries of protest. Penny was alive.

"Hey! Don't you be hurting her!" another person yelled.

"I'll hurt you both, moron. Shut up. And shut her the hell up, too!"

"Stop it," Frankie said, as calmly as she could. Her insides fluttered and jumped. The rat-man sounded dangerous and mean. "Nobody needs to get hurt. Are you listening? Where do you want the money? But no games, just you and me. You give me Penny, I give you the money. A straight-up trade."

"You are in no position to bargain."

"Neither are you. Let's just do this short and sweet."

"Uh-uh, the ante is up. Let's call it payment for my pain and suffering."

Frankie staggered backward. McKennon caught her shoulders in both hands, preventing her fall. On watery knees, she stared blindly into the distance. Three million had been a nearly impossible sum to raise and he wanted *more?*

"I want an extra ten g's. You hear me? Fifty grand in cash— small bills."

"Fifty…thousand?" she said stupidly. What happened to the three-million-dollar demand?

"You heard me! Fifty grand and not a penny less." He barked a wicked laugh. "Or you'll be Penny-less, got it?"

"I got it," she said. Fifty thousand? Either this man had the world's worst memory or else this kidnapping was even more bizarre than it appeared. "Where and when?" She snatched up a pencil.

"You better understand something. I got me a nice little Glock 9mm. Fully loaded, that's thirteen rounds. If I spot one cop, or even anything that looks like a cop, I'll pump all thirteen into your sister. You get her back in a garbage bag."

Frankie smacked her gummy lips. "No cops."

"You go south through Fountain and pick up Squirrel Creek Road. Head east. About a mile past Peyton Highway there's a dirt trail. We trade off there. No tricks, no tracking devices, no cops flying planes overhead. I will know.''

"No problem," she said through her teeth. She'd accompanied Max to the firing range before. He favored 9mm semiautomatic pistols. She'd seen firsthand what a 9mm round did to a paper target. She didn't want to even imagine what it would do to a young girl.

"You come alone.''

"No problem. What time?''

"Sunset.'' The kidnapper killed the connection.

Her shaky knees failed her. McKennon guided her to a stool, and she slumped over, exhausted. She recounted the kidnapper's end of the conversation. "Call Ross,'' she said. "We've got until sunset to come up with fifty thousand dollars.''

Easier said than done. According to her cousin, Agent Patrick wanted to negotiate with the kidnappers via a press conference. She'd arranged for the conference to happen tomorrow morning. The Colonel and Elise Duke would make their pleas for Penny's safe return. Frankie watched the clock in the oven with horror. Where previously time had crawled, now the numbers seem to flip through the minutes like an old-movie, transition trick. If they didn't get the money, Penny was going to die.

"Maybe we should let Ms. Patrick in on what we know,'' McKennon said.

"Absolutely not! She had her chance and she blew it. I'm not taking any chances with Penny's life, just so that woman can keep her cushy job in Colorado.'' She slammed a fist against her palm.

Ross called again. Agent Patrick wasn't budging. Connie Haxman had asked for the money returned, but the FBI agent cajoled her to wait until they reestablished communications. The only way Connie could have reasonably demanded her money would be to tell the FBI that communication had already been established. Connie offered twelve thousand dollars, the most cash she could quickly gather on such short notice. Ross claimed he and Dawn could put up another thirty. Frankie nearly wept at their generosity.

And she nearly wept because it wasn't enough.

McKennon tossed her the wig. "Get dressed, baby. We're going to the bank."

"What?"

"I have some money set aside."

It took a few seconds for her to understand why he had money set aside. His son was severely injured, and the cost of his medical care must be astronomical. After seeing his car and where he lived, she knew he granted himself no indulgences or luxuries. She shook her head. "Is it Jamie's money?"

He lowered his gaze to the floor. "His college fund."

An ache formed below her breastbone. He loved his son more than life itself—she saw it every time he mentioned the boy. All he had to go on was hope for a recovery, hope that the child would someday grow into a man and need a college fund. She touched his hand, lightly, with only her little finger against his. He didn't merely offer money, he admitted to himself that his son might never awaken.

"I'll pay you back," she said. "Every dime, with interest. I promise. Jamie won't miss out on college because of me."

He smiled wanly. "We'll discuss the terms later."

"I always keep my promises." She stared until he finally met her gaze. "Always."

"So do I. Let's move."

FRANKIE AND MCKENNON met Ross south of Fountain. On a deserted farm road she searched the gray landscape. Another storm rolled across the sky. The clouds hung heavy and featureless like a sheet of hammered lead. Clouds blotted out the mountains. Only the barest hint of Pikes Peak was visible, misty and undefined. The rocky, snow-covered peak seemed to hang in midair.

Icy wind bit Frankie's cheeks. A few stray flakes of snow swirled around her face. She shivered inside the Frankenstein coat.

"Here." Ross handed over a blue nylon gym bag. "Small bills. You've got the rest?"

"Yes. We'll get her back."

"You sure I can't go along?" Ross smoothed a hand over his greatcoat, revealing the bulge of a firearm strapped to his hip. "I'll be good backup. You're going to need it."

Frankie had refused to tell even her beloved cousin where exactly she was to meet with the kidnapper. She was taking no chances. "You wait right here. We'll holler if we need you."

He looked around at the bleak landscape. The country east of the interstate looked so different from the mountains to the west that it could as well have been in another state. Here the land rolled in a treeless plain, scoured by nearly constant wind, stretching forever, broken only by the dark ribbon of foliage growing along Fountain Creek.

"I'll be right here." Ross gave Frankie a quick assuring hug.

McKennon tested the remote trunk opener on Connie Haxman's Cadillac. The trunk opened with a soft click and a sigh. He pulled off his coat, folded it and laid it inside the trunk. He slipped his handgun out of the holster and with a press of his thumb released the clip. He checked the rounds before slapping the clip back into the gun.

Frankie's belly hurt. Rat-man had sounded exactly as she imagined a vicious killer would. If he harmed Penny, McKennon would kill him. Of that she didn't harbor the slightest doubt.

"Stay out of potholes, okay?" He climbed into the trunk. It was roomy, but he was big, and he curled up awkwardly with his coat under his head. "Shut the lid and let's move."

As she pulled the lid closed, he said, "As soon as this is over, you and I have some things to discuss."

"Hope we can discuss it through a glass partition," she wisecracked. "I'll probably end up in prison."

"I'm serious."

She searched his solemn but beautiful green eyes. Wordlessly, she pushed the trunk closed. Her cousin gave her a thumbs-up. She flashed him a wan smile and slid behind the wheel.

I'm coming, Penny, she thought and put the big car in Drive.

Past Fountain Creek the landscape seemed even more featureless and forlorn. Mile after mile of snow-covered fields were broken only by an occasional farmhouse and barbwire fences. She played in her head McKennon's instructions: "Keep your head up and maintain eye contact. Keep your hands in view at all times. All he wants is the money. Just hand it over and don't get into arguments with him."

She reached Peyton Highway. She kept an eye on the odometer as it clicked through tenths of a mile. When she'd driven a mile, she slowed the car to a crawl. So little daylight remained that she could see nothing. "He isn't here," she called. She tried to keep the panic out of her voice. "Can you hear me? I can't see a dirt road."

"I hear you. Keep going."

With the high beams on she searched the road ahead for any sign of a vehicle. She spotted a Bronco. Her heart leaped into her throat. She called a warning to McKennon. The big vehicle was parked off the road, facing south. The headlights were on and exhaust belched from the tailpipe. Praying it was the kidnapper and not a rancher checking cows or fences she pulled off the road.

"Keep the engine running," McKennon called. "Be cool, baby. I won't let anything happen to you."

She exited the car. "Hello? It's me, Frankie Forrest." She swung the nylon gym bag in a slow arc and rested it atop the Cadillac's roof.

Two people emerged from the Bronco. In the poor light

Frankie had trouble making out who—or what—they might be. One looked like a kid dressed up in army clothes. The other appeared deformed and possibly drunk.

''Come here.''

Frankie recognized rat-man's voice. Her mouth went dry. She slid the bag off the roof and forced her legs to move.

''Frankie?'' Penny's voice was hoarse and raw.

''I'm here, sweetie.'' She walked steadily and held the gym bag at arm's length, an offering to evil. She noticed no one else was inside the Bronco and wondered what had happened to the other kidnapper. She imagined he was waiting out of sight, perhaps armed with a rifle and scope. Her shoulder blades itched.

Penny wore a black mask, a man's bulky sweater and had a blanket wrapped togalike around her body. No wonder she looked deformed. The hem of her nightgown fluttered in the wind. Rat-man shoved a pistol against her throat.

She stopped in front of rat-man. The name fit. He couldn't have been more than five feet two inches and even wearing bulky camouflaged clothing he looked scrawny. His eyes were big and rather buggy, surrounded by dark, bruised-looking flesh. She glanced at his feet. In spite of army boots they appeared as dainty as a girl's.

Penny wore a mask, and judging by the condition of her hair, she'd been wearing it throughout her entire ordeal. If rat-man didn't want Penny to see his face, why show himself to Frankie? An ice lump filled her belly. He was going to kill her. And why not? It made no sense to leave witnesses. She prayed McKennon shot and killed him before he got away.

Frankie dropped the bag at her feet. It struck the frozen snow with a thud. ''Here's the money. Want me to count it for you?''

His buggy eyes darted, settling for a moment on the Cadillac before returning to her. ''Open the bag.''

Shutting her ears to Penny's distressed gasps, Frankie

crouched and unzipped the bag. She pulled the opening wide to reveal the jumble of rubber-band-bound currency. ''Turn her loose and take—''

A noise rose. Moaning, animal-like, it quavered in misery and rage. Frankie and rat-man startled and swung toward the source.

''Paul!'' Penny screeched. ''Stay down, Paul!''

A dark mountain seemed to rise from the snow. Uncertain what it was she saw in the tricky dusk light, she watched a man-shape unfurl. He was huge.

He was hurt. Arms outstretched like a movie monster he staggered toward rat-man. Rat-man aimed the pistol at the lurching giant.

As a gawky, too-tall, skinny, carrot-topped teenager, Frankie had needed some defense against the merciless teasing and tormenting from her peers. Other awkward girls developed social graces or found a way to hide. Frankie had developed a right hook. She didn't hesitate.

She decked rat-man. Pain flared all the way to her shoulder, but she didn't care if she broke every bone in her hand as long as she hurt him. His pistol flew through the air, turning in silvery circles, catching glints from the headlights until it disappeared into a snow bank.

Rat-man fell and took Penny down with him. She screeched and kicked and flailed her bound hands. Screaming at him to let Penny go, Frankie lunged for her sister. Steel flashed. Pressure arced across her belly. Frankie stumbled backward. Icy air stung her belly and she stared at the horizontal opening in the Frankenstein coat. He'd sliced a gash from the side seam to the zipper. She struck the gym bag, fought for balance and went down hard.

Penny screeched again. Rat-man had her by the hair. The quickness with which he sprang to his feet stunned Frankie.

''You are dead,'' he snarled. He flicked the knife at Penny's throat. She screamed.

''No-o-o-o-o!'' the giant roared and lurched atop rat-man.

Frankie scrambled to her feet.

Rat-man, the giant and Penny went down in a heap. Penny's screams were muffled by the struggling men. The giant garbled his speech, incoherent, but very, very angry. Rat-man drove the knife into the giant's shoulder. The blade buried itself to the hilt. The giant screamed and launched himself sideways, hauling rat-man over his body and flinging him through the air like a toy. Frankie dived for Penny.

She hauled the terrified girl to her feet. Penny flopped like a doll with cloth limbs. Frankie fought for balance on the frozen snow.

A shot cracked the air. The shock wave thrummed against her eardrums. She pushed Penny to the ground and dropped atop her, shielding her with her body.

Silence. Deafening silence as if a thick blanket had dropped over the world. Slowly Frankie grew aware of the engines idling and Penny's birdlike gasping and her own heart pounding. She lifted her head.

McKennon, his gun drawn, stood over rat-man and the giant. Both men sprawled in the snow. Blood seeped from the two like a spreading shadow.

"Frankie?" He never took his attention off the fallen men.

She disentangled herself from Penny and sat upright. She felt the cut in her parka. Downy feathers floated from the gash. Rat-man's knife had sliced through the coat and her sweatshirt, but all she'd suffered was a thin, stinging scratch. "I'm okay."

She pulled the mask off Penny's face. The girl's eyes were round and shocked. Frankie felt anxiously around Penny's throat and face, but found no blood.

"You're safe, sweetie. It's all over." She helped Penny to her feet. The girl swayed and blinked as if she couldn't believe she was still alive. Her teeth began to chatter.

"I have to get her to the car," Frankie called.

"Paul." Penny shook her head. "Paul!"

"Wait—"

Penny broke from her sister and ran clumsily across the snow. She wore socks on her feet. The toes flapped. Stumbling and slipping, she reached the giant's side. She dropped to her knees and lifted his head, cradling him to her breast.

Frankie's mouth dropped open.

"Paul, can you hear me? It's Miss Penelope. You're going to be all right. It's okay, everything is okay. You'll be all right." She lifted her tearful gaze to Frankie and screamed, "Get an ambulance! Bo shot him. He's dying!"

JAIL SUCKED, Frankie decided. The indignities of being strip-searched, fingerprinted, photographed and deprived of her shoelaces had been awful, but bearable. She coped okay with the constant noise—including a cell mate who'd wept piteously throughout the night. She'd even managed to choke down baloney-on-white-bread sandwiches. Despite the lights that never dimmed, she'd slept, too. Not knowing her sister's condition, however, was driving her mad. Nobody would tell her anything. Nobody would speak to her at all.

She missed McKennon. One glimpse of his face would sustain her, but she didn't know what had happened to him, either.

Jangling keys and heavy footfalls on the linoleum floor announced a deputy walking down the aisle. He stopped in front of the cell. Frankie rose from the hard bench that served as a cot.

"Step back and put out your hands." She obeyed and he handcuffed her. "Your attorney is here. Come with me." He led her through the maze of cells and hallways in the El Paso county jailhouse. She wondered where they were keeping McKennon, but didn't bother to ask. Nobody answered her questions in this place.

The deputy deposited her in a windowless room. He made her sit down, and he handcuffed her to a ring welded atop a metal table. The table was bolted to the floor. She imagined prison was going to be a lot worse than this.

But Penny was safe.

The room was hot and stuffy and stank of sweat. Her own perspiration made the scratch on her belly itch. She longed for a shower.

The door opened. A slightly built man with a round, good-humored face entered. He set a briefcase on the table. "Stephen Oswald," he said. "Your aunt and uncle hired me to represent you."

"What are they charging me with?"

"Kidnapping, murder and conspiracy." He waggled his eyebrows. He took a seat. The scraping of the metal chair legs against the floor made her wince. "How are they treating you?"

She lifted her shoulders in a quick shrug. "Okay. Do you know how my sister is?"

"She's fine. They kept her in the hospital overnight. She's dehydrated, but otherwise healthy. She's with your family right now."

"What about the kidnappers? Dead?"

He opened the briefcase. "Let's worry about you."

She shook her head. The strange sight of Penny mourning over the giant named Paul haunted her. She didn't know if he'd been a kidnapper, or some poor heroic schnook in the wrong place at the wrong time. "I need to know."

He regarded her for a few seconds while he fussed inside the briefcase. "Beauregard Moran is dead. J.T. McKennon shot and killed him. The other man on the scene, Paul Cash-orali, had been shot, as well, and stabbed. His condition is stable, but he'll be in the hospital awhile. Paul is mentally handicapped. The police tried to get a statement from him, but all they found out was that he's worried about his brother and your sister, and that he didn't break the window. I somehow doubt if he'll be found competent to stand trial."

"He saved Penny's life. Rat-man was going to kill her."

If she lived a thousand years she'd never forget the sight of the giant lurching wounded across the snow. "Wait a minute... Did you say his name was Beauregard Moran?"

"Do you know him?"

The name struck familiar chords. She rubbed her aching temple with the pads of her fingers.

"Charles Cashorali has been released from the hospital and is currently in jail. He has a long record. Property crimes mostly. He's a car thief. According to him Moran planned everything. He hasn't named you, but then again the district attorney hasn't gotten to him yet." He shuffled some papers. "Now, as for you—"

"How is McKennon? Where is he?"

The attorney rolled his eyes. "Your friend is fine. He made bail and was released."

"What did they charge him with?"

"Aiding and abetting a fugitive. I'm afraid your cousin, Ross Duke, faces the same charge. This is a real mess, Miss Forrest, and it's bound to get messier. The FBI and the state police are fighting over jurisdiction. Quite frankly if the Feds get you, your chances of making bail are zilch."

"Joy," she muttered. "Answer me one thing. Tell me exactly how Julius died. What killed him?"

His brow twisted and he pursed his lips as if to whistle. "That's a weird one. The cops are extremely interested in your take on it. That vial of Butunal you turned in? It wasn't Butunal, it was Valium. Julius Bannerman had a prescription for Butunal, and the cops are checking the vial to see if it was prescribed to him."

Uncomprehending, she shook her head. "I don't understand. It was clearly labeled."

"*Mis*labeled. Butunal is a mild sedative. It's useful for anxiety, and it has few side effects. An overdose will put a person to sleep and give them a headache, but it won't kill them. It also doesn't interact with MAO inhibitors the way a barbiturate does."

"I still don't get it."

"Julius Bannerman was being treated for clinical depression. He took MAO inhibitors. The combination of those, Valium and alcohol is deadly. Actually he was playing with fire with the booze, but you know how hard-core alcoholics are. Their systems get hardened. The Valium proved to be too much for him. He died of cardiac arrest and respiratory failure. How did you get the vial, Miss Forrest?"

She stared wide-eyed at the attorney. Thoughts clicked into place. Everything that hadn't made sense before now opened her mind's eye with perfect clarity. "You better get those cops in here. I know who killed Julius and I know how he did it. And I think I know why."

Chapter Fifteen

Frankie felt surprisingly calm in light of what was at stake this morning. She sat next to her attorney in the district attorney's conference room. A court stenographer was seated at a small table, her machine ready to record the proceedings. If this meeting went the way Frankie hoped, then she would walk out the door a free woman. If not...well, Penny was safe and she'd have to satisfy herself with that when she went to prison.

The door opened and a secretary ushered Max and Belinda into the room. The assistant district attorney greeted them and held a chair for Belinda.

Frankie met Max's gaze. His eyes were black mirrors, reflecting her disgust with him. *I know the truth,* she thought at him. A muscle twitched in his jaw.

After the Caulfields were seated, the door opened again. Agent Patrick, Sheriff Eldon Pitts, Sergeant Norris of the state police, and another gentleman Frankie didn't recognize entered the room. Frankie searched their faces, too, but none would meet her gaze. She shifted uneasily on the chair.

McKennon entered the room. Frankie's breath caught. Emotion choked up her throat, adding its ache to the fear clenching her chest. He'd saved her life—saved Penny's life.

He removed his sunglasses and tucked them into the

breast pocket of his suit jacket. His black hair gleamed under the fluorescent lights. He wore his goon face and looked neither right nor left as he took a seat at the table.

"Well, everybody is present. Thank you for coming," the ADA said. "Before we begin, Mr. Caulfield, Mrs. Caulfield, Mr. McKennon, would any of you care for legal representation at this time?"

Belinda bristled like an offended bird. The black, netted hat perched upon her hair bobbed. "There is no need." She turned her steely gaze on her husband. He arched an eyebrow and shook his head.

"No, thank you," McKennon said.

The ADA cleared his throat. He nodded at Sergeant Norris. "Very well. As you all know we have not yet formally charged Miss Forrest with the murder of Julius Bannerman and the kidnapping of Penelope Ann Bannerman. We have some questions that must be answered first."

Sergeant Norris had opened a large briefcase and from it he pulled items to place on the table. Seven clear envelopes, each containing a draft of the ransom note; a smaller envelope containing the vial marked Butunal; an envelope containing a computer disk; a fan-folded computer printout; and an envelope containing the ransom note.

"What exactly is going on here?" Max demanded.

"We have questions, sir. Are you certain you don't wish legal representation at this time?"

"Of course he doesn't!" Belinda exclaimed. She pointed a jeweled finger at Frankie. "She's the criminal."

The ADA cleared his throat again. He mumbled an apology about getting over a cold. "All right, Miss Forrest. You may begin."

Max jumped to his feet and slapped his hands on the tabletop. "I haven't the slightest interest in anything this woman has to say. I don't have time for a dog-and-pony show. Belinda, let's go."

Belinda remained seated. As fiercely as an eagle she glared at Frankie. She appeared extremely interested in everything Frankie had to say. Making noises of disapproval, Max settled on the chair. He clamped his arms over his chest.

Frankie hesitated. She'd made only one request of the district attorney and now it appeared he had denied it. "Mr. Wiley? I thought we had an agreement, sir."

"Regarding?" the ADA asked.

"Mr. McKennon. What is he doing here? You said if I cooperated, he wouldn't be charged with conspiracy."

"He's a material witness, Miss Forrest."

Hoping that didn't mean he was also considered a conspirator, Frankie drew a deep breath and began. "When I contacted Bo Moran he demanded an extra ten thousand dollars in ransom for my sister. He wanted fifty thousand dollars. The original ransom was for three million, but Moran didn't know that. The three million dollars wasn't a ransom. It was extortion. I'm sorry about Julius, Mrs. Caulfield. I truly am. He didn't mean to kill himself. All he wanted was the money."

"What?" Now Belinda slapped the table. "Kill himself? I'm not going to sit—"

"Ma'am," the ADA interrupted. "Please hear Miss Forrest out."

Frankie noted the slight widening of Max's eyes. He was finally getting it. This meeting wasn't for his benefit, but for Belinda's. "Julius set up the kidnapping. He wrote the ransom note. He hired the men who kidnapped Penny. He prepared the syringes with a drug he considered perfectly safe."

"This is ludicrous. Maxie, let's go."

"We have testimony," the ADA said, "from Charles and Paul Cashorali that Penny was already drugged when they arrived at the honeymoon cabin. Bo Moran injected Julius with a syringe that Julius provided."

Grateful for his interruption, Frankie continued. "Julius knew if he and Penny stayed in your home you'd run her off the way you've run off all his other wives. If he simply walked away you'd have cut him off, but he needed money. So he set up a fake kidnapping. He had to make it real. He knows you're no pushover, Mrs. Caulfield. You wouldn't fall for a trick. He risked Penny's life in order to fool you."

"I don't believe a word of this."

Agent Patrick leaned forward. "We've collected handwriting samples from Julius's condo. We've compared the writing and concluded Julius wrote the drafts and the note. We also found a notepad in the condo which contained impressions that match writings found on the drafts. We also found tape recordings of David Sams's radio show. I believe we'll be able to prove conclusively that Julius made the tape the kidnappers used."

Frankie did not quite dare to believe she'd been vindicated yet.

"I don't believe a word of this," Belinda repeated, but softly. Color had drained from her sallow face.

Frankie went on, "We all know Julius wasn't bright enough to have pulled this off alone. So he enlisted the one person who not only had the brains, but the desire. Right, Max?"

"I'm leaving." Max rose. The tips of his ears had turned red.

"There was a problem wasn't there, Max? You knew Julius stood a good chance of getting caught. You knew he'd eventually confess everything to his mother, including your role. So two things had to happen. Julius had to die, and somebody had to take the blame. That's what you set up."

Max looked around the room as if aghast that anyone would allow Frankie to spout such nonsense. "You can't prove any of this! It's absurd." He settled a hand on his wife's shoulder. She swatted it away.

Frankie looked to Sergeant Norris. "Was I right, sir? About the phone call and the computer disk?"

The state investigator nodded.

"You called my apartment, Max. You tipped me off

about the wedding. You wanted me out of the way so you could plant the evidence in my apartment.''

"I don't even know where you live.''

McKennon made a soft noise. He placed a small black notebook on the table. ''My field notes.'' He slid the notebook toward the ADA. ''You'll find notes concerning the period when Mr. Caulfield requested I find out where Miss Forrest currently lives and where she works. You already have my deposition concerning Mr. Caulfield's request that I collect evidence against Miss Forrest.''

Max backed a step away from the table. Arrogance left his face. ''You can't take his word over mine. He's sleeping with her. They're conspiring against me.''

Sergeant Norris placed a finger on the computer printout. ''We took the liberty of checking your phone records, Mr. Caulfield. A call was placed from your private line to Miss Forrest's telephone on the date in question.''

In all her vengeful fantasies about Max, Frankie had imagined revenge would taste sweet. It did not. There were no winners here, and it saddened her. ''You're the one who replaced the Butunal with Valium. Julius believed the Butunal was perfectly safe. You knew the Valium would kill him.''

"This is outrageous!'' Max glared at Frankie, but she didn't flinch. ''You murdered Julius. You and your sister. Why isn't Penny here? She's the person with the opportunity and the motive to replace the Butunal with Valium. Not me.''

"Valium?'' Belinda whispered. ''You gave Valium to Julius?''

''What about Bo Moran, Max? You introduced him to Julius.''

"I didn't know Bo Moran existed.'' He leveled a hateful stare on McKennon. ''Until you conveniently killed him so he couldn't testify against your girlfriend.''

The ADA called for order and asked Max to hold his

comments until Frankie finished. Belinda scooted her chair a few inches away from her husband.

"You were so pleased with what a hard worker I was, Max. I wanted to please you. I took work home every night. Put in countless hours of unbilled overtime. I typed up hundreds of reports for you on my home computer. I saved them all to disk, too. I'm careful that way."

On cue Sergeant Norris picked up the bag containing the computer disk. "One of the reports contained on this disk concerns Beauregard Moran. You interviewed him regarding a civil suit you were investigating, Mr. Caulfield. It's a Q&A report."

"The only thing *that* proves is that she knew Bo Moran! You'll find nothing about him in my files. It's her word against mine."

Sergeant Norris shook his head. "Excerpts from this report are on public record in the court transcripts."

Max pointed an accusing finger at Frankie. "You hated Julius and you wanted him dead. Everyone knows it. A dozen witnesses can testify to how you punched him in the nose. They can testify to your threats against his life."

Belinda gazed up at her husband. Slowly, as if rusty gears instead of muscle turned her neck, she faced the ADA. "Six weeks ago I asked my husband to fetch a vial of Valium for me. I was having trouble sleeping and he has grown adept at administering my medications. He claims he dropped the vial. He claims it broke." Her voice dropped to a horrified whisper. "He stole the Valium and used it to murder my son."

Max crossed his arms and glared at a spot high on a wall. "I believe I should like to contact my attorney now."

FRANKIE SHOOK HANDS with her attorney. "Thank you, Mr. Oswald. You must be pretty persuasive in order to get the district attorney on my side." She covered a yawn with her hand, then flashed him an apologetic smile. Half expecting the cops to claim they'd released her by mistake, she glanced at the elevator they'd ridden to this level of the parking garage. "I can't believe they let me go. I'm really free."

"Justice prevails. But I can't take the credit." He looked beyond her and smiled. "Mr. McKennon mounted the campaign. He convinced the ADA to look into the phone records and your back-up disks."

Frankie turned around. McKennon walked toward her. His footsteps barely made any noise despite the tendency of concrete walls to magnify every sound. Garbed in black, broad-shouldered and impressive, he was to her the most beautiful man ever to walk the earth. He shook hands with the attorney, who then made his farewells.

"How are you doing?" McKennon asked.

She hunched inside the Frankenstein coat. The sun shone today, but inside the garage the temperature was icy. For the first time in days she felt warm on the inside. "Jail sucked. Being out is great. What about you?"

"Hungry as a bear. Can I buy you dinner?"

She'd eaten only oatmeal and baloney sandwiches while in jail. Her belly growled. She lowered her gaze. "I should buy you dinner. I owe you."

He removed his sunglasses. His eyes were bright and warm. "No debt. Call it a labor of love."

Surprised and wary, she peered at him from the corner of her eye. Somehow, someway, in the midst of all the fear, anger, despair, guilt and excitement, another emotion had sneaked its way into her heart. She didn't dare call it love. Not yet, anyway.

Or did she? J. T. McKennon was everything a man was supposed to be. Loyal, strong, responsible and determined—not to mention those gorgeous green eyes and soul-searing, heart-melting kisses. She couldn't discount the fact that he'd seen her at her very worst and he still cared. She suddenly wanted him to see her at her very best, as well.

Car tires squeaked on the concrete. A sleek, black Lexus drove into view. As it drew near she recognized Ross behind the wheel. He lowered the window and flashed a sunny grin. "Hey, Cuz. How's the jailbird?"

She leaned over to kiss him and saw Penny in the car. Subdued, the girl fiddled with a sparkling diamond ring. Her soft blond hair fell over her face. Frankie's belly constricted. They hadn't talked since that awful night on the plains.

She gestured for Ross to roll down the passenger's side window, and she walked around the car. Penny refused to look her way. "How are you doing, sweetie?"

"Okay."

"I hear you're going to be a mommy. Did the doctors—"

"I'm not pregnant." She turned her head enough for Frankie to see one baleful blue eye. "I—I lied."

Anger crept over Frankie's scalp. She glanced at McKennon. Arms crossed, sunglasses in place, he leaned his back against a post. "Do you want to go somewhere and talk?" she asked her sister.

"We have nothing to talk about." Penny resumed fiddling with the gaudy wedding ring. It was much too large for her slim hand.

Frankie bit her inner cheek to keep from snapping out a retort. Penny is an adult, she reminded herself. She's in shock, grieving and needs some space. She noticed Ross lift an eyebrow. He must be expecting a major explosion. She drew in a deep breath. "Okay."

Penny's eyes widened. A rush of color pinked her cheeks. "I want you to leave me alone! I didn't want to go to that stupid college. I loved Julius, but you hated him because you can't stand anyone else loving me! You were just plain jealous because he paid attention to me. Now he's dead!" Fat tears rolled down her cheeks.

Ross placed a hand on Penny's shoulder, but she shrugged away.

"You know it's true, Ross! She's a bully. She smothers me to death, and she pushes me around and she treats me like a little kid. Not everybody is perfect like you, Frankie!''

Anger encircled Frankie's throat. She wanted nothing more than to drag the little ingrate out of the car and shake her. Except...maybe she'd spent so long being the perfect mother substitute for Penny that she'd lost sight of Penny as a person.

"You hang on to everything," Penny continued, her voice ragged with tears. "That stupid old coat and those ugly boots you've had since high school. *Me!* You never let anything go! Well, I'm going, and you can't stop me."

Frankie stepped away from the car. She looked again to McKennon. His impassive face revealed nothing of what he felt. Because of him she could be strong right now. She shoved down fearful reactions and forcibly remembered how great a love she felt for her sister.

"I'm sorry," she said quietly. "You're right. I'm too controlling and I treat you like a kid instead of an adult. I don't listen too well either. I am so very sorry."

Penny's mouth compressed into a suspicious frown.

Ross leaned over. "She'll be staying with Mom and Dad for a while. She'll be fine at the resort."

"Of course she'll be fine. You'll be okay, Penny. I have faith in you." She stopped before assuring Penny she'd call or visit. Her baby sister wanted space, and Frankie intended to respect her wish—even if it killed her. "I'll see you guys later."

Hands in her pockets, head down, she waited until Ross drove away.

"She'll come around," McKennon said.

"Maybe." She managed a weak smile. "It's hard letting go. But she's safe. That's all that matters, right?"

"Right. So how about dinner? You promised me a date."

She glanced down at her shabby self. What she really wanted was about three hours in a blistering-hot shower to wash away the jail stink. "Can we make it later? I want to go home."

McKennon drove her home. Her heart throbbed in silent agony. If Penny decided to sever their relationship completely and forever, could Frankie live with it? She didn' see where she had a choice. At her apartment complex she opened the car door then paused. Without looking at him she asked, "What you said about a labor of love. Do you say that to all the girls?"

"Only to you."

She smiled. "You really do know the right things to say Call me. I know you have my number."

She spent the next few days cooped up inside her apartment. Gray weather matched her gray mood. She slumped around in sweatpants and ate cereal straight from the box and refused to pick up her mail. The only bright spots were when McKennon called. He didn't pressure her, and she was appreciative. He seemed to understand she needed time to reassess her life. She missed him horribly. She woke up one morning missing him so much she hurt inside. She glowered at her gloomy apartment and glared at her gloomy reflection in a mirror, and felt not self-pity, but self-disgust

She called Ross and asked him if he had any job leads He worked as a consultant for dozens of corporations and knew everybody who was anybody in the corporate world He called her back within an hour to tell her he'd set up an interview for her. She should have called him months ago.

She tackled the mess in her apartment. The cops had trashed the place. She spent hours putting everything back in order. She hung pictures on the walls and unpacked knickknacks to arrange on shelves. It was too cold to open windows and air out the place. She mixed up a batch of brownies so their aroma would drive away the staleness.

She found thread and a needle to repair the damage Bo Moran had done to the Frankenstein coat. As she held the faded, much-mended parka on her lap she paused. Penny was right. She held on to things long past the point when holding on made sense.

She stuffed the coat in a garbage bag, then tossed in her rotten old boots for good measure. They had holes in the soles and were splitting at the seams. She marched downstairs to the trash container and tossed the bag inside. A twinge of genuine pain distressed her, but she made herself run back to her apartment before she could change her mind.

McKennon called. "I have good news."

"Save it," she replied. "I made a batch of triple-fudge brownies. And if I don't say so myself, they're to die for. Come on over. I'll put on some coffee for you."

Excited by the prospect of seeing him again, she primped and preened. She sorted through every piece of clothing she owned before deciding on a royal-blue cotton sweater with a scooped neckline. She smoothed her hair into a sexy twist and darkened her lashes with mascara.

She met him at the door. For a long moment she filled her soul with the sight of his dark good looks and incredible body. No matter what happened between them, she would never stop thinking he was the sexiest man alive.

"May I come in?" he asked.

She stepped aside. He looked around at her apartment and made an approving noise. "I've missed you," she said.

"Good." He stopped in the middle of the room and cocked his head as if listening. "Where's your cat?"

"He deserted me, too." She harrumphed. "An old guy who lives downstairs let Cat move in. Cat likes it better down there. Darned animal pretends he's never seen me before."

"Sorry."

"It's okay." She shrugged. "You never really own a cat, anyway. They're just roommates who don't pay rent." The scent of hot brownies did a great job of making the apartment smell good. She imagined she could smell McKennon, too. A stirring deep in her midsection caused weakness to flicker through her knees. "So what's your good news?"

He leaned his forearms on the counter. "I got a job."

"That's wonderful. Another security job?"

"Better. A guy is opening two martial arts studios. H hired me to manage them. His name is Daniel Tucke Sense of humor, easy-going. Not overly concerned wit cash flow. Should be interesting to work for."

She set a cup of coffee and a plate of brownies in from of him. "Good money?"

"Good enough. Plus I can pick up extra cash teachin classes. He's looking for an office administrator. You' good with details. Interested?"

"Maybe. Could you stand working with me again?"

He smiled. He had a gorgeous smile. "On one conditio You date me instead of the boss."

She arched her eyebrows flirtatiously. "Depends. Ho good-looking is he?"

His mouth dropped open. She laughed. A good laug straight from the heart. Chuckling, he picked up a browni and sank his teeth into it.

"Actually, I have a job interview on Monday. A nation headhunting firm is looking for a handwriting analyst. I' let you know how it works out."

"Okay. But now that I know you can bake, you defi nitely aren't dating anyone except me."

Her good humor faded. She picked at crumbs on th counter. "I'm pretty unstable right now. I'm lost witho Penny to take care of. That's all I know how to do. Yo deserve better than a flake like me."

He shook his head in firm denial. "You're not a flak You're a wild thing, and that's what I like best about you. An intense expression darkened his eyes. "That's what love about you."

Her throat threatened to close. What did she know abo love?

His telephone rang. Saved by the bell, she thought. Cow ard.

McKennon scowled at the Caller ID readout. "Excus

me.'' He opened the phone and put it to his ear. ''Mc-
Kennon here.'' He listened, nodding. His frown deepened.
Finally he said, ''Are you certain? No mistake?'' He looked
as if someone had punched him in the belly and he couldn't
breathe. He snapped the phone shut. ''I have to go to the
hospital.''

''Your son?'' Alarm jangled in her skull.

He nodded. ''Dr. Trafoya said he's showing signs of
waking up.''

''That's wonderful!'' In the face of his utter stillness her
elation faded. Then it occurred to her; he was afraid. For
four years his son had been lost. God only knew how many
times his hopes had been dashed and his faith sorely tested.
She gathered his hands in hers. He was cold.

''I saw him this morning. He looked the same.''

''Do you want me to go with you?''

His brow twisted and he appeared suddenly young and
uncertain. ''I'd like that.''

McKennon said little on the drive to Carson Springs Hospital. Frankie respected his need for silence. She imagined
he steeled himself for heartbreak if the doctor was wrong.
As he parked the car she felt strange about accompanying
him. His relationship with his son was intensely private. At
the same time she felt humble and grateful he wanted her
company. She offered her hand, and he grasped it like a
drowning man.

Carson Springs looked more like a college campus than
a hospital. Airy rooms, brightly colored walls and people
talking and laughing. The presence of patients in wheel-
chairs revealed it for what it was.

In Jamie's room Frankie hung back by the door. The
room smelled of medications and disinfectants. It reminded
her of her mother's lingering death. In spite of her discomfort, the child on the bed compelled her attention. He was
so tiny. A tow-headed waif with arms so thin they looked
like sticks.

McKennon loomed over the bed. He stroked the boy's cheek with a touch so gentle it made Frankie want to cry.

"Jamie? It's Daddy, sweetheart. Can you hear me? Are you awake?"

A doctor in a white coat entered the room and Frankie moved out of his way. He flashed her an absent smile in passing. "Good afternoon, Mr. McKennon. Looks like we have a medical phenomenon in progress."

"He isn't awake." His tone was accusatory.

"He's sleeping. Just plain old sleeping." The doctor pulled the covers away from Jamie's legs. He picked up a tiny foot and tweaked the toes. Jamie's foot flexed, and his head turned. "Wake up, kiddo. Don't make your dad think I'm a liar." He pinched the ball of Jamie's foot then slapped it. "Do what you did before. Show your daddy what you can do."

The boy turned his head from side to side. He made a raspy noise.

"Oh, my God," McKennon breathed. Tears glimmered on his lower lids. He patted Jamie's cheek and shook his shoulder. "It's Daddy. I'm here. Do you hear me? Wake up now. Wake up."

Drawn by the quiet drama, Frankie crept to McKennon's side. The little boy opened hazel green eyes as bright as a bird's. His mouth opened and closed, opened and closed.

"I know you can see me, boy. Are you Daddy's good boy? Jamie, can you understand me? Jamie, are you awake? Jamie."

Knowing she witnessed a miracle, Frankie slipped an arm around McKennon's waist. She stared at his face, and joy filled her to know a man so true and loving. A man who understood the power of love and the power of hope. A ray of sunshine broke through the clouds and sparkled against the window. Golden light banded the boy's face. He squinted and averted his face.

"Jamie," McKennon breathed. Unabashed tears slipped down his cheeks. "Oh, sweetheart, I love you so much."

And I love you, Frankie thought.

Little Jamie McKennon smiled.

"STOP THE WEDDING!"

Frankie gasped and her heart leaped into her throat. Her fingers tightened, and petals drifted from her bouquet to the floor. J.T. slipped a protective arm around her shoulders.

"Hold on a sec, okay?" Frankie said to the minister. Almost afraid she hallucinated, she turned around slowly.

Penny stood in the doorway to Sweet Pines Chapel. A breeze fluttered through her pale hair. Her blue eyes shimmered with tears. One by one members of the Duke family and Frankie's and J.T.'s friends shifted on the pews to look at the girl.

Emotion filled Frankie's throat, and she couldn't speak. She didn't know what to say. In the eight months since the kidnapping and the awful scene in the parking garage, not a single word had passed between her and Penny. Frankie knew Penny lived near downtown Colorado Springs where she shared a duplex with two other girls. She worked in a boutique. Every week Frankie mailed a chatty note to which Penny never replied. She'd sent a wedding invitation. She'd told no one, not even J.T., how much Penny's refusal to acknowledge her marriage wounded her.

Penny blushed cherry-red.

From the pew where he sat upon Elise's lap, Jamie hooted and waved an arm. He bounced impatiently. He couldn't talk yet, but he knew how to break an awkward silence. Elise petted his hair and shushed him.

"I'm sorry, so sorry," Penny said. She crept forward with her arms extended. "I blamed you and thought I hated you, but it wasn't your fault. It's all me. I've been such a brat. And I miss you so much. I don't know if you can ever forgive me. I—I—please don't get married without me, okay?"

Frankie gazed up at her handsome husband-to-be. By his side she'd found true love and purpose. Each moment she spent with him and Jamie was a glorious challenge and an opportunity for joy. His green eyes glowed with loving encouragement. He nodded every so slightly.

Elise nudged the Colonel and made him scoot over. She patted the bench beside her. "Come sit with me, dear." Jamie bounced on her lap and waved frantically at a speaker mounted on the wall. He wanted music. Penny slipped into the pew.

Frankie found her voice. "No! Don't sit down."

Penny gasped and her hand flew to her mouth. Tears spilled in a torrent. A murmur of surprise rippled through the room.

Frankie indicated the spot next to her. "Stand here with me. I want you to be my maid of honor." She shifted her smile to J.T. "Is that okay with you?"

"I'd be honored."

Penny joined her before the minister. Frankie handed her the bouquet to hold. "I love you, sweetie. I'm so glad you're here." She faced the minister, and J.T. squeezed her hand. Her heart was full. "Now where were we? Something about how J.T. has to obey my every command, right?"

"Something like that," J.T. said, and squeezed her hand again.

Elk River, Colorado
Where men still stand tall—
and know how to treat a woman.
Next month meet Daniel Tucker and join
the rest of the Duke family
for a thrilling tale of romantic suspense
by Sheryl Lynn.

#518 UNDERCOVER FIANCÉ

only from Harlequin Intrigue
June 1999

Concentrate, focus… Daniel Tucker envisioned concentric circles of red, yellow and black narrowing into a bright red bull's eye. Easy now, picture the dart sailing in a perfect arc. Two thoughts intruded: This was stupid. He was bored.

Scowling, he fingered the dart, testing the point against the ball of his thumb. A potential client should be arriving anytime now, his only client in over a month. Antistalking laws were growing teeth. He felt like a soldier in the final days of a war. The more battles his side won, the more he grew obsolete.

He craved a useful purpose—he wanted something else, too. He hadn't figured out yet what that something else might be.

Shaking off the gloomy musings, he sank back into the inner landscape of his mind and mustered the image of the bull's eye. He drew back his arm, joints loose, wrist relaxed, the crimson sweet spot glowing like a beacon. He tossed the dart.

A high-pitched squeal shattered the silence. Daniel tore off the blindfold.

There she stood, the most beautiful woman he'd ever seen. The yellow fletch on the dart quivered in the door-jamb scant inches from her face.

The face of an angel with wide blue eyes and a full, soft mouth. Luxurious chestnut curls fell in soft waves to her shoulders. A wine-red jacket hugged her lush bosom and narrow waist and flared over graceful hips. Visions of dart-boards winked away, replaced by an image of this goddess rising naked from the sea, riding a seashell while cherubs—

"Are you nuts?" She looked between him and the dart. "You almost put out my eye."

Her dulcet contralto vibrated within his heart. Daniel snapped his mouth shut. He tossed the blindfold on the desk and straightened the knot of his tie with a jerk. A glance at his watch showed four o'clock on the dot. The goddess must have accepted the "Please Come In" invitation posted on the office door.

"Some people think so," he said and rose. "You must be Janine." She was so stunning to behold he had to keep checking to make sure her perfection wasn't an illusion.

A thin line deepened between her eyebrows. "Yes, I'm *Ms.* Duke." She clutched a large paper shopping bag— Nieman-Marcus, he noticed—before her like a shield.

He rolled a hand, gesturing for her to enter. Reality seemed to shift. Women who looked like this only existed on a movie screen or on the airbrushed, expertly lit, artfully arranged pages of glamour magazines. He swept darts off the desk and into a drawer. The clattering assured him he was awake and she was for real.

"I'm Daniel Tucker."

She eyed the dart warily.

He moved around the desk and held a chair for her. "Man, J.T. said you were a knockout, but as usual he understated."

"Pardon?" She clutched the bag to her chest.

Those fabulous eyes glared up at him as if he were a bug in need of exterminating. He caught a whiff of light floral perfume with a note of vanilla. He wanted to bury his nose in her hair and snuffle like a horse.

"J.T. said you're beautiful. I bet you hear that all the time." He closed the office door and offered coffee.

She lifted that perfect chin. "I did not come here to be judged like a show dog, Mr. Tucker." She frowned at the dartboard hanging on the back of the door. "Or to have my eyeballs skewered."

"Sorry about that, ma'am. I'm learning how to throw blindfolded."

"Whatever for?"

Because the living was so damned easy he wondered why he even bothered getting out of bed in the morning. He lifted his shoulders. "New Year's resolution. Sure you don't want some coffee? Special blend, made fresh. Tea? Soda?" *My heart, bank accounts and car?*

"No, thank you." She set the shopping bag on the floor at her feet. "I'd like to discuss business. Did J.T. tell you about my...problem?"

"Only that you have one."

"I need confidentiality. This is a personal problem. I want it solved without involving my family."

"Confidentiality is my specialty." He leaned back on the chair, but stopped himself before throwing his feet up on the desk. Her posture would make a finishing-school teacher proud; his should at least rise above slovenly. He opened a drawer and swept beanbag animals, puzzles and a miniature croquet set off the desk and out of sight. "What exactly is your problem?"

"I seem to have acquired a stalker."

That dampened his good humor. He leaned forward and rested his forearms on the desk. "Go on."

She looked around the office. The room was spacious, but cluttered with a jungle of plants and two computers. The screen savers on both computers had words scrolling across the monitors. One said, "Vote for Dan Tucker, Emperor of the Universe." The other said, "Smile, you're gonna die anyway."

The frown line appeared between her eyebrows again.

Daniel tried to guess her age. Her complexion was as smooth as polished marble. From what he could see, she didn't sag or bag anywhere. Late twenties, he guessed. No wedding ring.

"What exactly do you do, Mr. Tucker?" She peered at his duck decoy telephone as if it might offer information. "J.T. didn't elaborate. Are you a private investigator? A security specialist?"

Lately he hadn't been doing much of anything. "You might say I'm a professional problem solver."

"And your credentials? References?"

"Confidential. My specialty is helping abused women escape their abusers. My clients come by referral only, and I don't keep their names on file. Not even the CIA could trace anyone through me."

"I see."

"I also own some martial arts studios. J.T. runs them for me. His wife, Frankie, is your cousin, right?"

"Yes." The frown line deepened. "I haven't been in an abusive relationship. A man insists we're in love, but we don't have a relationship, and he won't leave me alone. I don't know if you can help me."

Janine lowered her gaze to the bag at her feet. She twisted a hank of hair around her fingers. "He insists what we have is true love." Her slender throat worked and the hair-twisting increased. He recognized fear. Perfect hair, makeup and clothing aside, this woman suffered, and his heart went out to her.

"Before we continue with your problem, I want you to understand something about me. I fight dirty."

She stopped twisting her hair and raised her eyebrows. He could spend a lifetime studying her incredible face. He'd give his left leg to see her smile.

"People who stalk are not reasonable. Some of them have serious personality disorders. Some are mentally ill. All of them are obsessed. Colorado had an antistalking statute. It's fairly new, though, and not always well implemented. Unless violence is involved, the courts tend to give stalkers probation with a stipulation of counseling. Repeated arrests often do more harm than good. The stalker goes through the court system and comes out feeling stronger for the experience. So I fight dirty.''

''You use violence?''

''On occasion. Most of the stalkers I deal with are angry men. Bullies who beat up women and children. I'm a tenth-degree black belt and I'm qualified with weapons you've probably never heard of.'' He waggled his eyebrows. ''Bullies don't like the taste of their own medicine.''

''My stalker isn't violent.''

''Stalking *is* violence. You must realize that on some level.''

Her slender throat worked with a hard swallow.

''Being nice does not work. Being polite, but firm does not work. I have discovered, in many cases, that the judicious use of mayhem, does work.''

''I see.'' The softly hesitant words held volumes of skepticism.

''Have you gone to the police?''

''No.''

''Have you confronted your stalker?''

''I haven't a clue as to who he is.''

He straightened on the chair and the wheels squeaked. He'd wanted a challenge, and a doozy landed in his lap. He'd never dealt with an anonymous stalker before. They usually targeted celebrities or politicians.

''I don't want anybody killed, Mr. Tucker.''

''I haven't killed anybody.'' He curled the corners of his mouth in a tight smile. ''Yet.''

She lowered her gaze to the shopping bag, as if it contained the secrets of the universe. Perhaps it did. ''He's threatened my family,'' she said quietly. ''I want him stopped.'' She stroked the bag. Her hands were slim with long fingers. Clear polish on her nails had been buffed to a high shine.

Her vanity intrigued him. She knew damned well how

gorgeous she was. He felt a connection. He was vain as hell, too.

"I'm at a loss. If I knew who he was, I'd talk to him. But he could walk in this room right now and I wouldn't have a clue as to his identity."

"Anonymous stalkers need to control as much as they need love. Anonymity helps maintain the control. You can't reject him if you don't know who he is. How has he threatened your family?"

She reached into the bag and rustled amongst papers. She brought out a pink envelope and placed it on the desk. "This came in the mail the day before yesterday. It's why I called J.T. I didn't know what else to do."

"You did right to call him. Stalkers don't go away by themselves." He shook a folded sheet of paper from the envelope. He noticed the envelope bore no postmark. A bad sign. It could mean the envelope missed the marking machine in the postal service, or it could mean the envelope had been personally delivered. The letter consisted of three short paragraphs. The first two paragraphs extolled Janine's virtue. The third paragraph chilled his blood.

> It isn't fair for him to keep us apart. He works you to death, taking up all your time, and now he is ruining the most romantic day of the year! Valentine's Day is our day! I'll help you, love. Your father is a tyrant. Death to all tyrants! I will make him go away. Then you and I can live together in the mountains forever, happily ever after.
>
> 　　　　　Love you gobs and gobs and gobs, Pinky.

"Am I paranoid?" she asked. "Or is he threatening my father?"

"Sounds like a threat to me. I always take threats seriously."

Color drained from her cheeks.

"What's the deal with Valentine's Day?"

"It's my parents' wedding anniversary. Did J.T. tell you about Elk River Resort?"

"He said you're the general manager. I looked it up on the Internet. Nice web site. Did you create it?"

A trace of pride shone in her eyes. "Actually my sister does our on-line advertising. She's very artistic. Elk River is a family operation. I cannot leave my job. My family depends on me. Not to mention, I'm hosting a party for my parents. We'll have guests from all over the world. It's their fortieth anniversary."

"When did the stalking start?"

She lifted the shopping bag onto the desk and gestured for him to look inside. "A year ago. I was having lunch with a friend here in Colorado Springs. Pinky stole my Day-Timer."

He peeked inside the bag. It contained envelopes, most of them pink, plus cassette tapes and bundles of cards in all shapes and sizes. An impressive collection for only a year's time. "I take it you're the type of lady who carries her life in a book?"

Her eyes narrowed and her full lips thinned. Her expressiveness startled him, enchanted him. No glamour magazine cutout she, but a living, breathing mortal.

"No offense intended. But some people are organizers and some aren't. What was in the Day-Timer?"

"Everything." A faint blush blossomed on her cheeks.

Daniel repressed a sigh.

"Names, addresses, my schedule. It was right before Christmas, so it contained information about my entire year. The first letter arrived a week later. He sent a box of chocolates, too. I threw them away. The letters and gifts kept coming. When I realized he wouldn't stop, I began saving them. I keep looking for clues. He knows all about me, but I know nothing about him."

"What about the cassette tapes? You're taping phone calls?"

She twisted a hank of hair around her fingers. "He's never called me. The tapes are recordings of love songs, religious sermons and radio commercials. It's a jumble of nonsense. I don't know why he sends them."

"Maybe he's hearing messages from you. He's letting you know he's receiving them."

"Please…"

"I'm serious."

"That's insane."

"That's delusion at work."

She rolled her eyes. "At first I was angry because I was certain he stole my Day-Timer. Then I thought he would grow bored and give up. But the letters have grown increasingly personal. It's as if he knows everything about my life. He knows everything I do." She closed her eyes for a moment and sat perfectly still. When she looked at him, her expression held a tremulous plea that touched him deeply. "Very little frightens me, but Pinky scares me to death. I don't like it. I won't tolerate it. Can you help me, Mr. Tucker?"

"I'll do my best." He began emptying the bag, sorting the contents into stacks of letters, cards and cassette tapes. "You haven't told anybody about Pinky? Your parents? Friends?"

"No, and I have no intention of doing so. My father is seventy-seven years old. He doesn't need the stress. I want this problem solved with the least amount of fuss possible."

He suspected her need for privacy went much deeper than concern about her father's age. He'd talk with her about it later.

"The party I'm giving for my parents is very important. We're hosting a family reunion, plus, friends we haven't seen in years will be attending. I can't cancel the party just to make Pinky happy."

"You're right about that. It would only encourage him. Let me sort through this mess. I'll see what I can pick up, maybe come up with a profile about his character. Then we'll discuss strategy.''

A trace of a smile curved her luscious mouth. She opened her slim handbag and withdrew a leather-bound checkbook. "About your fee—''

"I don't have a fee.''

"Pardon?''

He adored the way she said that. All snooty and refined, like a princess momentarily ruffled by the riffraff. "I have more money than I know what to do with.''

"I pay for whatever services I receive.''

"I don't take cash from stalking victims.'' He cocked his head, studying the gentle contours of her oval face and the sculpted lines of her cheekbones. He resisted examining her shoulders and breasts, but awareness of her alluring body heated his blood. He'd like to have her in his debt.

He'd really like to have her in his bed. Thaw the ice, rev her engine, goad her into calling him *darling*—and mean it. He pushed his tongue against his palate and kept his mouth shut. Now would definitely be a bad time to let her know what he was thinking. Especially since the frigid glare she gave him said she suspected exactly what he was thinking.

"How about a trade?''

She drew her head aside. "A trade?''

"I get rid of Pinky, you give me a honeymoon.''

"Pardon?'' Her voice had risen slightly, and the corners of her mouth twitched.

Seeing her fight a smile convinced him that heat pulsed beneath her icy veneer. "You've got the Honeymoon Hideaway, right? Fancy cabin, room service, moonlight and romance. I could really go for that. Can you set up a honeymoon for me?''

"I could…'' She relaxed—Daniel nearly melted into a puddle beneath the desk. "Are you engaged to be married?''

I'm going to marry you.

The thought shocked him. Still, the sheer rightness glowed in his being like a bright, white light. The last time intuition had struck so hard he'd impulsively purchased a lottery ticket and changed his life forever.

"Not yet. We'll just keep it open-ended."

She lowered her gaze to the checkbook. "I'm going to have to think about this. Perhaps I haven't explored all my options."

He touched the stacks of pink envelopes and fancy cards. He knew he could help her. He needed to help her. One way or another, he had to see her again. "If you give me twenty-four hours to study Pinky, I can outline a plan of attack. Then you can decide if you want my help."

"I'd be more comfortable if this were strictly business."

"Barter is as good as cash. So what do you say?" He extended a hand over the desk.

"Well…J.T. does recommend you highly." She shook hands with him. Her skin was cool and silky. Luckily for Daniel the desk was between them, or he'd have drawn her hand to place over his heart.

"I'll buy you dinner, then. Tomorrow, seven o'clock."

She cast him a cutting glance that might have cowed a lesser man. Daniel was enchanted. Finding the key to unlock her icy heart might prove to be the most enjoyable challenge of his life.

"I doubt your girlfriend would approve."

"Business, Ms. Duke, to discuss Pinky. How about we meet halfway, in Woodland Park? The Alpine, seven o'clock."

Her eyes acquired a gleam as she gave him a long, considering look. With absent grace she slid one hand along the edge of her lapel. Those elegant fingers trailed tantalizingly over the rise of her bosom. Daniel's heartbeat thudded heavily in his ears.

"Do you really think you can help me?"

"Yes, ma'am."

"Very well," she said. "Seven o'clock, the Alpine.

Don't be late.'' She glanced at the dart stuck in the door frame. A half smile appeared and stole the remainder of his heart. "Do leave your toys at home.'' She strolled out the door. .

Daniel stared at the tantalizing sway of her hips.

Pumped up by the prospect of becoming a hero in the enchanting Ms. Duke's eyes, he tackled the contents of the Nieman-Marcus bag. He didn't know squat about anonymous stalkers, but he was a quick study.

He'd find a way to get rid of Pinky or die trying.

Looking For More Romance?

Visit Romance.net

Check in daily for these and other exciting features:

Hot off the press

View all current titles, and purchase them on-line.

What do the stars have in store for you?

Horoscope

Hot deals

Exclusive offers available only at Romance.net

Plus, don't miss our interactive quizzes, contests and bonus gifts.

PWEB

HARLEQUIN®

I N T R I G U E®

COMING NEXT MONTH

#517 HER BABY, HIS SECRET by Gayle Wilson
Men of Mystery
Previously thought dead, ex-CIA agent Griff Cabot reemerges to save his baby daughter from kidnappers. But the ransom demanded is an assassination. Can Griff get to his child in time—and forgive the only woman he's ever loved for not telling him he was a father?

#518 UNDERCOVER FIANCÉ by Sheryl Lynn
Elk River, Colorado
Daniel Tucker is the only man for the job, an expert determined to flush out Janine Duke's deranged pursuer—and hell-bent on shaking her up in the process. Posing as her overly demonstrative "fiancé," Daniel seems to be taking his role all too seriously. Leaving Janine to wonder if she's in more danger of losing her heart to Daniel than her life to a madman....

#519 THE STRONG, SILENT TYPE by Jule McBride
Years ago, moments before her wedding, Claire Buchanon's bridesmaid was killed and her fiancé Dylan Nolan disappeared and became a suspect. Now, Claire's about to marry another man when a mysterious stranger begins to stalk her. But he is hit by a car and left with no knowledge of who he is. Claire finds his eyes eerily familiar... Is it Dylan—and what is he doing back in her life?

#520 SECRET LOVER by Shawna Delacorte
There's nothing more alluring than a mysterious stranger with sinfully sexy lips. Mystery writer Andrea Sinclair found herself inexplicably drawn to Jim Richards—mind and body. It was like she already knew him. But Jim, who was instantly attracted to Andi the woman, needed to keep away from Andi the investigator, the only person alive who could expose his carefully hidden identity.

Look us up on-line at: http://www.romance.net